BALANCING GAME

An Award Winning Story Made into a Movie

Novel by:
Joseph Eliashvili M.D.
Mark Ellis

outskirtspress
DENVER, COLORADO

This is a work of fiction. The events and characters described herein are imaginary and are not intended to refer to specific places or living persons. The opinions expressed in this manuscript are solely the opinions of the author and do not represent the opinions or thoughts of the publisher. The author has represented and warranted full ownership and/or legal right to publish all the materials in this book.

The Balancing Game
An Award Winning Story Turned into a Movie
All Rights Reserved.
Copyright © 2014 Joseph Eliashvili M.D. and Mark Ellis
v1.0

Cover Photo © 2014 thinkstockphotos.com. All rights reserved - used with permission.

This book may not be reproduced, transmitted, or stored in whole or in part by any means, including graphic, electronic, or mechanical without the express written consent of the publisher except in the case of brief quotations embodied in critical articles and reviews.

Outskirts Press, Inc.
http://www.outskirtspress.com

ISBN: 978-1-4787-2706-4

Outskirts Press and the "OP" logo are trademarks belonging to Outskirts Press, Inc.

PRINTED IN THE UNITED STATES OF AMERICA

"Madness in great ones must not unwatched go."

— William Shakespeare
Hamlet

Part 1

Prologue

A man dressed like a judge walked down the corridor and saw a haggard younger man with long hair and a heavy beard standing against the wall. The bizarre individual held a ruler in his hands, measuring something invisible in the air. His "honor" approached the strange man and asked:

"Sir, would you mind telling me what you're doing?"

"Watch me," the weirdo commanded without interrupting his activities. "I am in the process of measuring the height of my future unhappiness. You see, today I am a thirty-three-year-old problem free happy man. I figure if I somehow measure the height of my happiness today, then I will know the height of my unhappiness tomorrow."

After finishing his statement explaining his strange behavior, the odd fellow straightened his posture, lifted his head, spread his arms towards the ceiling, and screamed shamelessly:

"Everything in life is balanced! Happiness and unhappiness! This is terrifying! Today I am an extremely happy man and I'm scared, for I know the amount of sadness that awaits me tomorrow."

The shouting calmed the man down. A second later, he sat comfortably on the clean hospital floor and whispered loudly: "I wish I wasn't so damned happy today."

The robed judge soon realized with whom he is dealing:

"Are you really crazy?" He asked.

"Yes, I am," replied the man obediently.

"Are you stupid too?" the judge continued to inquire.

The strange man appeared insulted at the judge's question. His eyebrows furrowed and his anger became readily apparent as he raised his voice.

"Am I? Answer me! Am I stupid? You are the judge. You tell me! Am I?"

The judge recoiled uncomfortably because he did not expect the question.

"I don't know if you're stupid. I just don't know this yet."

At this time, the door at the end of corridor opened and an elderly lady with a trustworthy face wearing a nurse's uniform appeared. "Medication time," she announced with authority.

Rules and regulations required that the two men follow the nurse's orders. The power of her authority seemed unchallengeable, and indeed neither of the two men dared to provoke her. A conscious effort was being made to restrain the two men and their respective will powers. But no regulations and no rules could restrain them from their most powerful desires, their favorite things in life. While they quietly disappeared behind a big door, both were determined to follow their calls of duty. The strange man had strange things to do; the judge had his own strange things to judge.

Chapter 1

1

It was a dark and cold January night. I did not have to stand in the middle of an empty street to appreciate the magnitude and severity of winter's uncomfortable insult. Sitting in front of the widely open window in a small dark room provided me with more information than I could handle.

The small room was very empty or at least, so it seemed to me; even though there were two people occupying much of the space. The moment was marked by senselessness, most likely caused by an ingestion of excessive amounts of alcohol. The darkness and cold, both easily correctable for some unidentified reason remained steadfast. The light remained switched off and the window stayed wide open. But both people seemed satisfied or at least accepting of the harsh conditions of that room.

I have never been sure which part of my brain is influenced by alcohol, particularly strong Russian vodka, but I guess the part of the brain that becomes inhibited is the part that had some vital function, or something to do with logic.

Logic was not with me at that moment. I was sitting on a comfortable chair fully clothed wearing a heavy warm coat. And still, I was not dressed warmly enough. I knew that although my faculties were not entirely functional, I could still sense my own shivering and quaking.

Even though the room was remarkably uncomfortable, I was able to handle the inconvenience surprisingly well- maybe because there was something magical that reigned over the room or maybe because there was something peaceful about that space. I have known this startling powerful peace before- a striking peace that paralyzes me, stunts my reactions, and makes me complacent in a pleasant suffering. Inactivity, or maybe laziness, coupled with a strong desire to enjoy the moment's only seemingly uncomfortable trance, kept me lightheaded, with semi-closed eyes in dead tranquility.

I could not say for sure how long all of this continued. Such rare combinations of static events surprisingly give me unexplainable pleasure. It's a pleasure that comes to me from conveniently depriving myself of the real world and all of the responsibility, the pain, and the guilt that comes with that real world.

But even within no logic, there is logic enough. Whatever begins should have an end. And the end does come to this nothingness.

The other person in the room, whose silhouette I could see on the wall in the shape of a crippled man in a wheelchair, shifted. I could hear the ruffling sound that his movement created.

And suddenly the silhouette emerged from the shadows, from a shapeless non-entity developing into a full-bodied character; and as he developed into a solid structure rather than the fluid reflection he had been, he began to speak.

"Al, I want you to do me a favor." Then a pause followed; the extended pause gave me some degree of reassurance, rather it was actually more of a false hope. There was the possibility that my brain, which was swirling in flammable fluids, may have altered my perception of the pause. But the pause seemed like more of a reflective moment, rather than what it really was, the pause that is given when one man is trying to find the most appropriate way to give another man bad news.

Yet again, the man repeated.

"Al, I want you to do me a favor. I know today is your birthday. That means you wouldn't have a problem with doing me a favor. Am I right, Al?"

I remained silent in anticipation of something big coming my way.

"I want you to kill somebody for me."

And suddenly my trance was disrupted, and the alcohol started to lose its power over me and set me free. Reality struck me like a thick darkness and the cold rapidly saturated my bones all the way through my soul.

All of a sudden there were people in this room.

2

I vividly remember that day- The Day of my life. I remember every little detail that took place on that day. I recall the biggest event of my life, the one that was played out before me that day, two years ago, as one of those Greek tragedies those ancient Greek writers are famous for. I remember all the above because I was there. I was the main character in this ultimate play. And as a conscientious actor, I still remember my part by heart, long after the curtain of the last show came down.

I remember when I got up on that day and what time of the morning it was. I remember how long it took me to shower, what I ate, and what I wore. I remember with whom I talked. I remember the names of every patient that I came in contact with. I also remember every minute in detail of what happened at my place that night; the night that changed the whole world for me, the night that would change me for the whole world, and the night that I stopped being me.

Somewhere in our brain, we store our memorable years, days, hours, minutes, or seconds. While Pandora's box may have taught the lesson to be wary of the unknown, sometimes our greatest fears and pains are the known... the known, but long forgotten. That is the problem with selecting to relive certain memories.

3

The Day was exactly two years ago. It was also my thirty-first birthday. At this age of my life, having a birthday didn't put me in a festive mood. The only thing it did bring me was an ability to find time that I could spend with myself. It would enable me to realize how fast time flies and how many things in our lives remain unachieved.

I got up at 7:20 am; took a shower for eleven minutes, ate Kellogg's Raisin Bran and left my apartment at 7:50. It was quite cold on that January day. So I was dressed accordingly. I had on an extra black sweater under a heavy long oversized coat.

As a fellow in my final year of advanced psychiatry, I had to spend some hours in a psychiatry outpatient clinic. There, I would see patients with the medical students and residents assigned to me, as a part of their medical rotation. While I do remember the names of the patients I saw that day in the clinic, there is no need to name those names. I could go on with detail after irrelevant mundane detail of that day, the same way a master criminal can account for every step he took on the day he committed his crime. But I will not, because they have no relevance to what took place later the same day.

I would rather concentrate on the important things that shaped the day, the way I remember it today.

While in the clinic seeing patients, I received a few telephone calls reminding me about the party that I was to hold in my place that night.

The department of advanced psychiatry had an unwritten rule: all fellows had to have social gatherings on birthdays, at their homes. Apparently, this was a part of the teaching program. By implementing this rule, the department hoped to develop a sense of camaraderie among the fellows, who otherwise were virtual enemies of each other because of severe competition and every day fellowship pressure.

THE BALANCING GAME

Everybody felt both of the above in great quantities, and this in turn made us all very tense.

While I strongly resented the idea of having a party, or any kind of gathering in my place, I understood clearly that there was no escaping it. Throwing a party would cause me less stress than getting the grief of not throwing it, so I had to arrange some kind of event at my tiny place.

There was much legitimate reluctance on my part to go through this unpleasant event. I strongly believed this was a waste of time and money; neither of which I possessed in excess. Besides, I wasn't what people would call a party animal. On top of everything else, during my residency and fellowship years, I really didn't acquire too many acquaintances that I could call friends.

So, for obvious reasons, I was totally unenthusiastic about the upcoming party.

Too often we are required to do things in our lives that we don't like. This wasn't the first time that I came across this well-known lesson of life. But this was my last year of the psychiatry fellowship in The Methodist Medical School, so it was unwise for me to fight the ingrained system. These were the days when the fates of our professional futures were decided on the desks of our teachers' offices in the forms of letters of recommendations. Those letters held the secrets to the degree of our future successes.

So, I cleaned up my small one bed room apartment and invited the people I had to invite: some that I somewhat liked, some that I had no established opinions of, and some that I hated.

While a few people avoided my social gathering, to my surprise, most people did show up.

The number of people that attended was definitely more than the fire marshal would allow in my small apartment. Because of the size of the room and the number of people present, there was a definite accentuation of the smell of Chinese food and hard alcohol marinating in the air. I could have cut that odor in half, if I wisely obeyed my stiff budget and spent half of the amount I actually did.

The party started slowly. As a host, I did not demonstrate any ability to enhance its excitement. I clearly lacked this skill and never boasted that it was my forte in life. But whatever I could not do, whatever I did not do, was accomplished anyway quietly by my friend, Russian vodka. This mind altering liquid easily penetrated my guests' vulnerable states and intoxicated them with remarkable ease. This penetration soon transformed the party into a cheerful, good, and careless place and changed me from a worried host to a casual observer.

As long as the people around me continued to pleasurably intoxicate themselves, I had plenty of time and space to observe these young people transform from smart to dumb, from caring to apathetic, from "I'll do it" to "someone'll do it" people. Under the spell of the hard drink and soft music, they were relaxed and drunk with merriment. They did not look like they were in tight possession of the seriousness and control that were trademarks of each of these fellows from the famously competitive medical school.

Their minds were occupied with a strong desire to enhance the degree of detachment from reality, and they were achieving this sinister desire by continuing to indulge themselves. It was interesting to see the way they were affected, the very minds that were so intensively and expensively trained to deal with other disturbed minds. It did not take long before I could see, hear, and feel the euphoria around me- it was so profusely exuded and even exhaled by the pleasantly intoxicated.

While watching them, it struck me alarmingly, that these very people, soon could and would influence and dominate the thoughts and behavior of the world for it was they, indeed all of us, that represented one of the nation's best medical schools. This realization scared me for a while, but just for a short while. I had more important things to concentrate on in those days than worry about the gloomy future of mankind, having to deal with these pompous young characters as their mental masters of tomorrow.

My eyes narrowed significantly from the excessive intake of alcohol, and I could no longer see that far into the future. My vision could see only the people in my immediate vicinity and my intoxicated mind preserved enough sobriety to desire for these young geniuses to leave my place already, so that I could finish my reading and complete a paper that I should have finished that day.

By ten past ten everybody felt and even looked worn down from too much of everything, including the amount of hours spent and the amount of alcohol consumed. It was also a harsh January night with a biting wind to complement its cold and darkness. I could not really pinpoint, which of the above reasons determined the ending outcome of the party. Most likely the cocktail of all the above scored in my favor. But it did not really matter what exactly helped liberate me from the occupants of my territory.

What really mattered was that at long last, I walked out what looked like my last guest. Then, I was alone. The unpleasant feeling of being forced into throwing the party was gone, and all that remained was a weighty relief; and it was a great feeling.

I looked around. The post-party condition of the living room was indescribably disgusting. I needed a break from the thick funky stench and decided to get some fresh air.

4

Soon I found myself in the streets of a cold New York.

When passing the coffee shop around the corner, I noticed David Axel and Shirley McKeen sitting inside. I tried to avoid their field of vision by deliberately hastening my walk. I could not make it, and I was soon beckoned to their table. Within a minute, I was sitting next to them, drinking a cup of coffee- very sweet and very light.

David and Shirley were both fellows just like me in the same department. David was very talkative. Shirley was the silent type. Usually I prefer to sit next to people who do not talk much, but in this case, David's constant jabbering did not irritate me. On the contrary, Shirley's silence bothered me.

In a matter of a few minutes, David would fill you with all kinds of information; politics or sports, music or gossip. In contrast, Shirley had nothing to offer.

I devoted to David only minutes of my attention. My cup emptied quickly and soon I assumed the vertical position, clearly delivering the impression to my company that I was about to leave.

"Not so fast Al Letne," David reached into his inside pocket and produced something meticulously wrapped. "I almost forgot. This is for you. Open it."

In a second, I was holding in my hands a tie with a five-dollar price tag still on it.

"Wow, five dollars worth of a birthday gift. I didn't know I was worth this much to you. You are too kind." I said semi-jokingly.

"Don't flatter yourself Al. This is from all of us." Shirley finally interjected. "Like they say, Al- it's the thought that counts. You're missing the whole point of the symbolic gesture. This tie could mean friendship, if that word is in your vocabulary." David tried to say something, but Shirley continued, "There is a birthday note for you. Maybe you want to read it."

The small note was handed to me. I read it without interest. In the note, standard birthday wishes were expressed and fulfilling my dreams were strongly emphasized. At the end, the whole staff of the advanced psychiatry department signed their names.

I looked at the list and whistled in surprise. At the top of the names of well-wishers, Greg Entel led the way.

"Well, well. Look who's number one on this team?" I said without hiding my amazement.

THE BALANCING GAME

"That's creepy Al, really creepy." David was now examining the note. In disbelief, he shook his head a few times. "Everybody knows how the son of a bitch hates you more than anything on earth. He never hides it. He bosses you around, humiliates you, and laughs at you. I remember after one of your patients committed suicide, he even suggested that you be tried for homicide. I never understood what he has against you."

I said nothing. David was right.

"I know why you guys don't like him," Shirley suddenly came around. "Greg Entel is your chief fellow. He tells things the way nobody else tells it. He says it straight the way he sees it. It's his responsibility to do that. In fact, that's his job. Of course, you hate him. You're jealous of him. He's rich, smart, and good looking... and confident. He is what you always dreamed you'd be, and how about his girlfriend; did you see her? You have a good reason to be jealous. Of course you don't like him."

"Shut up Shirley," David implored. "Just because you love to kiss his ass, doesn't mean we have to do the same. But about his girlfriend, did you see her?"

I had not seen see her. In fact, I had not seen Greg's face either.

"I hate that son of a bitch, how about you Al? I know you don't love the guy." David expected me to back up his statements. I could have, but I opted against it. I do not usually say bad things about people I do not like, or at least not behind their backs. I did not raise myself that way.

I said nothing. Already on my feet for a while now, I gave both of them a good-bye nod and hurried out the door. I had a lot of old things to finish up before I could begin anew tomorrow.

I left them inside and came out in the street. The night was cold, windy, dark, and threatening. "Just like my life," I muttered to myself and smiled.

Chapter 2

1

When I walked into my apartment, it was exactly twenty minutes to eleven. I obtained this knowledge by looking up at my absurdly bright wall clock with neon hands. After closing the door behind me, I switched off every electrical device I could find-the light, the radio before I collapsed, literally, collapsed on the chair nearest to me. I wanted to relax for a few minutes before I would take on the books. Although the vodka was still doing some mingling in my brain cells, I was able to perceive adequately the high degree of relief brought to me by the mere fact of being left alone. I truly believe that at that time, I needed a break.

But just as I thought that I was safely alone and raised my face and both arms to thank god or somebody up there, I started to hear some noise, or to be exact, voices coming out of my bedroom. For the average layman, a person hearing voices can be interpreted differently depending on what those voices are saying. Sometimes because of the substance expressed, the voices could be quite pleasurable. But for a trained psychiatrist like myself any kind of voice, that is heard without seeing the person owning the voice is bad news.

I did not expect anybody in my apartment, so I rushed to my tiny bedroom to evaluate my sanity.

It did not take too long for me to find out that nothing was wrong with my head. In fact, at that particular time, I no longer felt any significant affect of the alcohol that still continued to occupy the vitally important areas of my body. For a moment, I had to endure a pleasant double pleasurable surprise. On my emotional side, comfort came pretty quick. I did not lose my mind. My brain with all its faults, continued to operate under my control. This realization came to me when I was challenged to deal with a more physically based pleasure... though some parts were affected more than others.

Only the city lights provided some means to observe the nakedness of a woman's silhouette. As soon as I entered the room, the shadow jumped out off my bed and now she was standing in front of me, about five feet away.

A few ridiculous rationalizations as to why this shapely woman was in my bed popped into my mind. The first one was that I charmed this beautiful vulnerable creature to a degree of insanity; perhaps my charisma charmed her out of her sane mind and now she was impatiently waiting to have her way with me.

The second theory was that because of my birthday, somebody decided that this female shadow was a better present than a cheap tie for a hard studying fellow who did not have much time or financial resources for romance. In fact, it would serve both as a birthday gift for me and a gift for everyone else if I was distracted by her lovely charms.

But maybe I was too slow in thinking. Maybe I was not quick enough to thank god or whoever governs over... everything. First, my wish came true when I was granted the solitude I so desired. Second, I was sent a beautiful woman directly into my bed, something that I welcomed any time of day. Maybe that's why the almighty whoever or whatever, known to have a high degree of intolerance towards the slow thinkers, or the ungrateful, decided to punish me in a hurry. Soon I was clearly hearing noises that only a man could issue and saw in the bed another shadow that could only belong to a man. I quickly realized that there was a third person in the room, a person of the masculine persuasion, who was without a doubt an unwelcome visitor.

Who was I kidding? This extra person was already in my bed

and he was enjoying her undivided attention and affection regardless of how quickly I reacted or the appropriateness of my gratitude. Overwhelming evidence and common sense made things clear for me quite easily now; my wishful dreams had to wait a while- a long while.

When I returned to earth, a trip that did not take much time, I backed off, slammed the bedroom door as I marched to the living room exasperated. I walked to a window and just stood there watching nothing, looking at nothing, and trying desperately to think of nothing. But, the powerful sexual arousal, triggered by the curvaceous female shadow was doing all my thinking for me. And it did more than that; the palpitations of my heart, sweating of my skin, and tremors of my hands could be easily attributed to the shadow as well.

2

A few minutes of solitude and emptiness were soon substituted with scenes from my memory. The face and body of my last girlfriend visited me with a remarkable clarity. She was attractive; she was intelligent, articulate, imaginative, and very sexy. I knew all this. She was also bored and annoyed. She told me so. On one rainy Sunday she called me up and in a very cheerful fashion announced her decision to dump me.

"Why?" I asked.

"No particular reason," she said. After she told me "No particular reason," she disappeared from my life entirely. I was left with personal speculations and theories. But there was one hypothesis that I settled upon as if it was truth.

I believe she dumped me because of my inability to seduce her every time she expected seduction. This theory might sound funny to some people, but for me it was no joking matter. Every time I saw her, she expected me to design and plan elaborate scenes tailored for her specific sexual fantasy needs. In those scenarios, she would play an innocent and naive woman trapped in a powerful and inescapable sexual circumstance. Each time, she would invariably present herself as a victim who felt compelled to give up her most valuable possession- her virginity. She loved that final act of the play the most.

In practical terms, this meant that twice a week I had to take her out for romantic and often expensive nights. After a few drinks, she would plea for me not to take advantage of her euphoric mind and weakened body. "I know I can trust you," she would tell me playfully before every single drink. She repeated her entreaties not to be treated like an immoral woman, touting her virtues, one more time before she would succumb to my requests.

The play would continue in my place. Her coat would depart from her body, as would her sweater. She would make sure I would take a look, a good long look, at her breasts that incidentally would somehow be uncovered for a few moments during her slow methodical dance. She would continue to flirt and tease. Then she would become lightheaded; her favorite excuse to secure herself a spot in my bed. Next, there would be her inability to take a deep breath, and her need for more air. There would be a need for her to expose the upper part of her body. There would be a lot of comforting, touching, kissing, sweating, and wetting. Finally there would be a big finale, the climax itself of the act of seduction. She would offer no resistance physically but would scream a few times mentioning something about me breaking a gentleman's word.

After these acts took place a few times; I probably showed some disinterest in my seducer's role. I had my reasons. My part of the play was too expensive for my resident's wallet. I was also beginning to be uncomfortable with the oddity of the whole situation, and the reasons for her needing the production before the climax. It cost me a lot of money to produce these shows. And the time it took for me to get to my goal was too valuable to me; the theatrics made me impatient and irritable. Eventually the lack of money and time, luxuries that I did not have in excess, decided the fate of our relationship.

So, when she did finally dump me, I was kind of relieved. The strange things we did together had to be stopped. This breakup was actually a big break for my time and budget. On a sadder note, there was a departure for me from a kinky, sexually preoccupied and overcharged young woman with a great sexual imagination and an even greater body. Sex with her always was full of immeasurable pleasure, only slightly tainted with tantalizing sinister thoughts. The thoughts that are always present when we commit something forbidden, something naughty. I was standing by the window, remembering Lisa's, shall we say, tastes. I missed her so much at this moment that I lost track of space and time. When a female voice tried to communicate with me, I had to be awoken from a world wrought with my own nostalgia, a world that no longer existed.

"Al Letne, are you okay?" The voice was distant, hardly audible, yet sensual at the same time. My awakening from nowhere, did not take long. With a voice like that and a shapely body, it did not take me long to reanimate and to find myself once again in the dark room at this late hour. The body of a shadow and a voice wrapped up in a sexy tone was something I had to deal with immediately.

"Of course I'm okay!" I could hear my voice rise in anger. At this time I still continued to stand by the window observing the nothingness beyond my windowsill.

"You sound angry," her voice was now soft, causing my anger to diminish rapidly. "Life is too tough on you Al?" she asked disarmingly.

I turned around. Two feet separated me from this beautiful shadow. Now I was glad the light was not on. The darkness gave my imagination a lucky chance, an opportunity, to really create her face in my mind. I felt the same feeling of power that only comes to writers and artists in the process of creation. I could give her any color hair, eyes, or skin. With the unlimited power I possessed, this woman with a great shadow's body and seductive sexy voice literally was under the mercy of my imagination. While creating, I had to be clear about one thing. Whatever beauty I created, would not belong to me.

"I'm not angry" and I was not, "I'm just inconveniently... disturbed. I was just hoping to have complete control over my place right now." I made my complaint with all the sincerity I could muster.

"I understand," she said, without displaying any hint of understanding.

A few moments of silence were accompanied by a growing curiosity on my part. I wanted to know who she was and what she was doing in my bed.

"I'm Mary, your best friend's girlfriend and I just had sex in your bed. What else do you want to know Al?"

She did answer my questions quite satisfactorily. But, I still wanted to know who the hell was my best friend. Who was the lucky son of a bitch who was using my bed to satisfy his sexual needs?

"You can ask me any question you want Al. Owning this place gives you a lot of authority around here. Besides, today is your birthday, isn't it?"

Mary sounded sweet and relaxing. She also had clothes on her body. This combination of things added up to my realization that nothing life threatening or even nerve-wrecking was taking place; so I relaxed.

"Okay, Mary, you really look... umm, sound like a nice girl. We could have tried some small talk, but you see, I'm really tired. I'm not really on my A game. You wouldn't mind if I keep the lights off, so when your male friend shows up, he would get the hint; you both should be leaving really soon."

I still did not know who danced in my bed with Mary. She said he was my best friend. But what best friend? I didn't have a best friend. There were a few people I hang out with on my free time, of which I did not have much. They were friends, but not exactly close friends. Certainly none of them would classify as my best friend.

"Mary, since you didn't give me enough information about your sexual partner, I'm having a problem figuring out who exactly my best friend is. Let me think; Patrick was too drunk. Willie- I saw him leaving, unless he came back through the window. Could be David, that guy is really slick. But, he has a good alibi. I just left him in the coffee shop."

Cheerful giggling interrupted my loud thoughts. Mary appeared amused. I could tell the way her shadow was jerking in the dark. "Guess again, guess again. You must have more friends."

I needed help. No more names were summoned by my brain and not because it was late, or because I was too tired or because I was drunk, but because I simply didn't have many friends. Period. It was actually disheartening.

And then I got help. I got the answer to the puzzle.

"You should be ashamed of yourself Al." A cocky voice of a confident male emerged from my bedroom. "I'm kind of disappointed in you Al, I thought I was your best friend. You didn't even mention me among your friends."

I couldn't see his face. The darkness was coloring it in the same shade as the surrounding chairs, shelves, table... That moment, the color of his face was the same as any inanimate object in the room. The power of the darkness blended Greg Entel's form with my apartment on that memorable night; the night that aged us both prematurely.

He was right. I did not mention him as a friend in my list of friends. Greg Entel was no friend of mine. In fact, if asked whom I hated the most; my answer wouldn't be the guy who stole my wallet leaving me literally starving for five days, nor would it be the girl that rejected me as her prom date, leaving me with a rejection phobia, that I still struggled with.

Out of everyone I have ever met, I would have to say I hated him most. Greg Entel was a nightmare to a person like me. Being the senior fellow with unlimited power and being the vindictive person that he was, Dr. Greg Entel was capable of significantly decreasing the quality of my life with remarkable consistency. Armed with abilities that were hard to match, like a mesmerizing ability to articulate his thoughts, phenomenal mannerisms, the grace of an aristocrat, and financial stability that was hard not to envy, Dr. Entel was out of my league. And I had to tolerate his understandable superiority, his condescension, and his cruel nature. He also had twenty-one publications in major medical journals and magazines. I had only four.

The great qualities Greg possessed would not have bothered me, if I did not know his vicious determination to humiliate, belittle, persecute, and prosecute me. He believed for whatever reason that I lacked the ability to be a leader, create anything new, stand up for my beliefs, and take responsibility for my actions.

He would make me repeat word for word the cases he would present, accusing me of not paying enough attention to his presentations. When I would succeed in repeating what I was asked to repeat, the way I was asked to repeat it; he would say nothing. He would turn his back towards me, completely ignoring me by not commenting on my presentation.

It was sickening the way he would single me out to pick on among the other fellows on the faculty. While the others were subjected to numerous insults from him deserved or undeserved, it was me who was the target of his vicious and unexplainable attacks.

3

All of my life, I was desperately striving for a better future in spite of my limited talent, looks, and financial resources. Hard work and sheer desire were my virtues to help me become somebody, after so many years of being nobody. My father used to tell me time and time again, "Some things aren't meant to be Al. Don't kid yourself. All the nice places under the sun are already taken." My father, the alcoholic, was trying to let me down easy about the difficulties of the world, and although the comments may seem discouraging, as they naturally are, he meant to prepare me for my life's inevitable failures. This was his unorthodox way of protecting his son from the emotional instability that I might acquire from my future failures.

I would argue with him. I would tell him that he was wrong. I would tell him that while he is drowning himself in the alcoholic ocean, a lot of people made contact with the sun. And I would tell him that these people were in no way any more special than I was. Hard work was the way to get a "piece of sunlight." As I got older, I would have repeated this more, much more, but I noticed his attention was not available to me anymore. He would be in a different world, a world of no sun, no warmth, but a cold that came with its own peace. Seeing him depart towards that place while I was still here would anger me. The anger would be strong enough to make me scream; "there must be one more sunny spot left for me!"

My poor father. He proved his point in rather dramatic fashion. At the age of forty-nine on a sunny day, he just dropped dead. Just like that. With his constant companion, the bottle, in his hand, he collapsed in the middle of an empty street. The day was hot. The month was July. The sun was beating. He was alone in the middle of an empty street, lying and dying there. The cruel sun was shining now only on him.

I was told his last words were blabbering about how this was the only way he could gain a spot in the sun. The police interpreted this as a drunk man's ranting. For me, this was my father's message that only dying on a sunny day in the middle of an empty street of a big city would grant people like us, a place under the sun.

4

Very recently, I was advised by our chief of psychiatry Dr. Fisher, that I had a chance to get an assistant professor's job in our medical school. Knowing that the obvious candidate Dr. Greg Entel was about to sign a contract for a very prestigious government job in Washington D.C., I was starting to feel my karmic hard work paying off in what would be the biggest personal achievement of my life. Dr. Fisher was pressing me to finish a scientific paper I started, which would make me published five times in major medical periodicals. This paper was the one I was expected to finish today, which was part of the reason I wanted so desperately to be alone.

But instead, my number one enemy was in my space near midnight, acting like it was his place. I continued to stand by the window that remained ajar. The element of surprise was really significant- so were the elements of anger and probably hate. All my anger and all my vitriol was directed at the person standing in my bedroom... on my turf.

"Sorry Al, I had to use your bed. You know- one of those emergency situations. I kind of figured you had no use for it. I hope you understand." I could not see his face. All I was able to perceive was that a very tall, very lean shadow was talking to me in this disrespectful manner.

I said nothing. I did not want to give him any extra excuse for lengthening his stay by maintaining the conversation. By remaining silent, I was hoping he would remove himself and his gorgeous girlfriend from my premises quickly.

"By the way Al, talking about emergencies. Can I use your bathroom? I want to get lighter before we take off. That is what you want us to do Al?" His voice had a highly charged sarcasm to it. I tried not to get irritated. The idea of him going away soon was more important to me than defending my pride. I had priorities. But, sticking to the priorities was not easy.

"Sure Greg, of course you can use my bathroom. You used everything else. What the hell, why not the bathroom?" On his way to his destination, while seeing what I figured out was his back, I could not stop myself from saying something to him. This something would sound innocent, but coming from me and addressed to him in a situation like this, probably disclosed my animosity to him; "whatever you have to do, just do it quick. So you can leave and I can finally get on with my life."

Was that the mistake? Did this really contribute to what took place later? I guess I will never know.

I saw his shadow stop moving. I could see him turn around. He seemed to stand facing me.

"Thank you Al. It will be a really quick one," he said. It is not what he said, but the way he said it. The way he took his time, the way he lowered his voice. I knew there was something else coming, something more sinister in nature. Even back then, I felt something big coming, but there was no way I could have understood just how life-altering the event would be.

"Al, a thought, a strange one, a really strange one just occurred to me. I can't see it. But I can clearly hear it. You know what it tells me? Ask me Al, ask me what this strange thought tells me. It concerns you; it very much concerns you."

I had to ask. I had no choice. I wanted him out. I also wanted to know, what he was about to say.

"What does it tell you?"

"You really want to know?"

"What is it? I really want to know." I insisted.

"This thought is crazy, really crazy. It tells me to forget the job I'm offered in D.C. It tells me to take the job you covet so dearly. It's less prestigious, but it has its pluses; it is in New York, it is closer to Mary. The best part is I'll be doing you a favor. I'll be taking the job away from a loser like you, a job that you are not capable of handling. You know what? That's what I'm going to do. Al, you can relax now. You can have as much time, as you like. You don't have to pressure yourself. Aren't you happy having a best friend like me?"

THE BALANCING GAME

He said this and then started to laugh. Twenty seconds later he was still chuckling. I could hear his obnoxious laugh even from the bathroom. He clearly made sure, I would hear this manifestation of pleasure from a man that achieved his euphoria at the expense of the misery of another human being; in this case, as usual, it was me at the end of the wrong end of the laugh.

A few seconds of disbelief were quickly replaced by my calm and calculating mind. Once again, like during many of my previous great losses, I found out how my mind was programmed. Obviously, you worry when you have a chance to succeed. You do not worry when that hope dies. Then you just grieve. Hopes are direct causes of anxiety. If there is no hope, then there is no anxiety. My grief is cool, calm, and subdued.

I took this heavy punch rather well, as I did after every heavy punch that life landed on me. Being a very amateur boxer for a short time, during my restless teenage years, built not only the chin on my face, but it also gave me perspective. It developed the chin of my mind. My mind had a good chin. My recovery time was short. I was in my full processing mode somewhere on the count of five or six. I never went down too hard. Now I didn't just look like a boxer that wanted revenge. Now I was the boxer who wanted revenge.

I looked at Mary who continued to stand in the corner of the room. Motionless and probably tired, but she would not sit. Maybe she had a problem seeing the chair or maybe she thought her odds of leaving this place were much higher if she was standing.

I couldn't see her face, but I genuinely felt sorry for her. I stood up and took a few careful steps towards her. In the darkness, I was successful in avoiding the table and chairs.

"And you love this person?" I asked her, when I positioned myself next to her.

"Of course I do." She sounded feisty standing by her man. "You people don't like winners because they beat you all the time. Besides people like him need love just like anybody else; and of course he is not getting love from the people he beats on his way up. He doesn't treat me like he treats his competitors."

Of course she was right. Everybody needs at least some kind of love and he was not getting any from people like me. I had no problem understanding this. I just felt sorry for her that it had to be she who fulfilled his love.

But it wasn't her that I had to worry about. There were my needs that had to be cared for. A need to hurt Greg leapt to the forefront of my mind. I felt some powerful unexplainable urge inside of me to react to the insult that I was so cruelly subjected to. My primitive instincts called for some kind of satisfaction- any kind. The urge to retaliate was pretty much the same; experienced by me in those confused younger years; when searching for my identity, guided by my inexperience. When a neighboring bully would pick on me, I did not need much time to make a decision. Then it was easy. I did not have to take too many things into consideration. All I had to do was to overcome the fear of a getting hurt. Getting angry was enough for me to make a fist and swing it.

The need for retaliation continued to grow. But as a grown man, I had to understand the days of fistfights were long gone. Changed times and circumstances required a more intellectual approach now. I spent a few futile seconds by the window standing motionlessly. Then I realized that it served no purpose for me to stand closer to the outside world, when there were things to be done in this room.

Soon I was walking around the room like a mad man in a desperate attempt to come up with a plan to hurt Greg, of course I preferred to hurt him badly. Hurting him was the only way my injured pride would regain its damaged emotional health. I did not have much time. I had to think of something immediately. I could not afford to let Greg leave the place without beating him in something. Whatever it was did not have to be that big. It did not have to be a physical beating; it did not have to be stealing his gorgeous girlfriend. Something symbolic, even a spitting contest, might satisfy my instinctive demands. I just wanted him to lose to me in something. His loss would deeply wound his pride.

I spent a minute or so walking and thinking. Many discomforting thoughts emerged quickly in my head but were dismissed at just the same speed. I put all my psychiatric experience at work and summoned all the ability that I had to think and remember. Analyzing weak sides of Greg was nearly impossible, but I did not get discouraged. I knew he could not be perfect. Nobody is. Now I started to look for his weaknesses even within his strengths. In a matter of seconds, I went through numerous strong qualities he possessed. I ignored all of them except his confidence. He was overconfident.

I thought about his overconfidence, and explored everything I knew about him from his demeanor to his retorts. Yes, he was definitely overconfident. But in and of itself, overconfidence is not valuable unless I could find something I could use to exploit his haughty nature. I had to exploit his perceived strength as his main weakness. But, when I thought about this weakness of Greg's, he suddenly no longer seemed unbeatable. Obviously, the image of the mighty Achilles was discarded, and all I could see was this fault. Now all I had to do to come up with a small idea that would expose his heal, but, this task no longer seemed as difficult as it had only seconds before.

I simply had to rummage through my weaknesses and strengths. This task was much easier. I knew myself better than I knew Greg. Very soon, I remembered something that could help me beat the son of a bitch.

Ever since I was a kid I had a fear of alcohol. I feared it because I knew it was a big part of my life and would always remain so. I was exposed to it every single day during my most vulnerable years. I had a father to watch, and copy. I had first-hand experience to see how powerful alcohol could be over a person. How a person addicted to it, could literally lose everything and almost everybody. I had a father that knew best.

With his longtime flirtation with alcohol, he set a powerful example for me, of what not to do and what not to become. It was not easy. I could not understand what I was seeing. I could not stay away from alcohol, when I was in constant contact with it every single day. My father, my closest ally in this world, was in love with it.

But I knew I had to find a way to survive. "This is not the way, this is not going be me," I said to my father when he was flat, pinned to the floor, on his back, unconscious with a toxic level of alcohol in his blood.

I was ten years old then. I remember what I did. I had a clear understanding of what my enemy was by that time. I also knew I could not run away from it. I had to coexist and I had to deal with it. So rather than avoid the confrontation, I went straight for it. From the shelf filled with bottles of vodka, I took out the bottle that looked the most menacing. I held it in my hands and looked at it. I even talked to it. I told it, how much I feared it- how much I hated it. Because of the fear and because of the hate, I wanted to taste it. I always thought the best way to defeat your enemy was to know it, to see what it was made of. So, I sipped a few drops of it.

The head to head confrontation took place. Nothing really happened. The little bitterness that my mouth experienced did not last long. But what did stay with me long was the feeling that I could handle it. At the tender age of ten, I already accomplished something in my life. While I could not get rid of the fear, I certainly damaged the image of invincibility that it projected. I also established contact with the enemy. Now I could watch it. Now I knew it would not surprise me. So, I lessened my degree of fear. By doing so, I might have saved my own life. What kind life would I have had if an unknown enemy haunted me and I would not even know what it looked like. I took away from my enemy its capability to take me by surprise. By doing so, I castrated my enemy.

From that day on I would pay a visit to vodka every day. This visit would be like paying respect to an adversary. I would sip a few drops from the bottle. I would tease it. I would let my enemy know that I knew it was there. I was letting it know I was here too. My education in drinking went on to an advanced stage after receiving a few educational sessions from a Russian drunkard who lived next door in the scary building, my own private Boo Radley. It was interesting that my advanced education in drinking did not come from my alcoholic father who certainly had plenty of experience to share. Rather it emerged from this man with no memorable name or face. He taught me how to hold the glass, how to have respect for what was inside. He also had his own way to drink this colorless liquid; a way that would preserve his sobriety long after ingesting a large amount of the drink. He would use this to his advantage when he wanted to scam money from other casual drinkers who had a few too many. After listening, hearing, and seeing a few of his highly demonstrative lessons and successfully using the knowledge I received, I certainly felt confident with vodka; confident enough to challenge anybody.

I sighed with relief. An idea came to my head; the formula for success. My confidence in my idea grew significantly, after I convinced myself I really did not have many options at my disposal. It seemed like this was the only way I could get my satisfaction. I stopped my pacing near Mary, very close to her, and proceeded with my plan.

"Mary," I said, as she continued to be silent. She could not be sleeping standing up. I noticed those perfect features react to my voice.

"Mary, I want you to listen carefully to what I have to say." She did not say anything, so I went on completing my thought. "A few minutes ago, you said you love Greg. Did you really mean it or did you just say it?"

"I meant it Al." I could clearly hear her firm retort as if she was losing her patience.

"What would you do for him Mary? What would you do to prove your love for him? What would you do for love?"

"A lot," she replied quickly although she seemed perplexed.

"You said a lot, but didn't say, I would do anything for him. You just said a lot. You don't know exactly how much your "a lot" would cover? How far it would carry you?" I continued to inquire.

"Far enough Al. Wait a minute here. Why are you asking me all these questions?" She questioned me back. "I don't like where this is going."

"Because, I want to know if Greg asks you'd sleep with me, would you do that for him? Would you?"

"What?!?" She screamed. "Al you're crazy, or you're crazy drunk. I'll pretend I didn't hear that."

"But you did hear it, and I want you to hear this again. If Greg, for whatever reason, asks you to go to bed with me, would your 'far enough' cover that?"

"You are dreaming Al. We are not into this kind of kinky stuff. Just forget it." And, then she paused for a few seconds and asked me with overtones of sarcasm, but some degree of curiosity. "Why the hell would Greg ask me to sleep with you? Is it because the two of you are such good friends?" The second question was clearly meant to demean my line of questioning.

"Because, I'm going to make him ask you exactly that. So, when he does ask you, would you do it?"

"I don't need this. I don't have to listen to this. I want to go home. Where is Greg?"

"You didn't answer my question."

"You're crazy. You really must be out of your mind. Now I understand why he treats you the way he does."

"Mary, listen to me. A few minutes ago your boyfriend gave me the most damaging information I could imagine. It's not even what he said, but the way he said it. The way he seems to enjoy when bad things happen to me. You say you love him. That's fine. That's your problem. My question to you is very simple. Are you just saying it, or would you really do anything for him. I think you don't give a damn about him. That's my diagnosis, and you know I'm right." I attacked this poor girl to make her give me the answer I needed to hear, to proceed with my long shot scheme.

A little dose of many ingredients: alcohol, time, tiredness, intimidation, cunning, produced my desired answer. I could see she was losing her composure. Her shaky hands were making aimless movements.

"You are an asshole. Greg would never put me in that position, but if he did, I would have to think about it." That was the best I could have hoped for under the circumstances, but it gave me the fuel I needed to make my next move.

I looked at the wall clock. The neon lit hands were telling me the time. It was passed eleven ten. It was still my birthday. I was going for a victory and I was in a hurry. I had to have it within fifty minutes, if I wanted to reward myself with a special present. By now part of my plan was unfolding properly. Now, there was an increase in the degree of not only my confidence, but also my optimism.

I was ready for Greg. When he showed up, his shadow continued to look confident, very confident. When I noticed this, my heart rate jumped significantly. I smelled an anticipated victory. I knew I could trick him in my trap by exploiting his liability.

"Okay, Mary. We're done here. I promised the birthday boy I'd leave him alone. Classy people always keep their promises. Besides, Al had a rough day and has bad news to digest." The way he was walking in this minimally lit room, his shadow looked sober and his speech was not slurred in the slightest.

He said something to Mary about leaving as he approached the door. Simultaneously, he opened the door and waited for Mary to join him. And Mary did join him in a hurry, disappearing quickly behind the open door.

I became little nervous of course, seeing the door widely open, Mary out of the room, and him one step away from leaving, which would mean my plan was foiled. Still a remarkable confidence remained in me. I knew, he would not leave the room without delivering some kind of victory speech, or at least giving me some "friendly" advice. I was putting myself in his head as much, as I possibly could. My psychiatric training was finely tuned and anticipating his narcissism clearly.

I watched him carefully. His head turned. He looked down at me. That could only mean, I read him right.

"Al, birthday boy, it's eleven twenty now. You still have some time, forty minutes to be exact to enjoy the privileges that this day brings to you. I know you are a good student. Maybe you want to learn something tonight. Maybe I'll give you a little lesson. It will be free, a gift from me to you, from one friend to another."

So, he did want to deliver a victory speech after all and of course, it came in the guise of "friendly" advice. The actual advice was immaterial. He was in the process of making a major mistake, the one that was still very correctable. But what was really disastrous for him was that he did not know he was making a mistake. This realization was very encouraging to me. He continued to be negligently relaxed and still saturated completely with self-absorption.

"Al, I really don't hate you. I just feel sorry for you. I'm trying to give you a very important lesson. Know your place in this world. Evaluate yourself. Be careful when choosing your goals in life; make sure you have what it takes to tackle those goals. You cannot be a prince, if you are not born to a king or queen. If you don't realize this, you'll be following the stars and some men are not meant to touch those stars. That'll also make you crawl even lower than those who know their place. Think about if that's what you really want for your future."

He paused for a few seconds, but was not finished just yet. He wanted to make sure his student was absorbing the material that he was imparting. I continued to face him. The teacher, adviser, lecturer; whoever he appeared to be tonight, was satisfied. Now he could finish his monologue.

"There is nothing more disheartening, than when you find out that you're cheating yourself."

I listened to all this nonsense, not as a good student, but as a smart student. I heard what I needed to hear. I saw what I needed to see. Now I was ready to play my part. Maybe he was a good teacher. But he was too relaxed.

"I think I understand what you are telling me Greg. I really appreciate this. At least you're telling me this straight and I know you mean what you're saying. I know you mean well too."

That is what I said as I amazed myself by overcoming a gigantic hate towards this person and disguising myself as a weak defeated creature. My tone reflected a sincere acknowledgment of inferiority. I listened and heard enough. From now on, I had to talk more and he had to listen more, if my plan were to be successful.

"Of course I mean well. Why wouldn't I mean well at a time like this, you being a birthday boy for another thirty-five minutes? As long as you understand your status I have no problem with you." His voice was sincere, but almost boisterous. Now I really felt my plan would succeed. He was hooked, and the worst thing was he had no clue he was about to be outsmarted. Overconfidence blinded him enough, to disarm and disable him.

Greg looked very much like the boxer who just knocked out his opponent and instead of showing a loser some respect; he stood over the defeated fighter and spat on him. I recognized the sore-winner in him.

Now it was my turn to do some damage. The time came for great white lies; for which, I was so intensively prepared during my medical training. For almost ten years of my education, I was the soldier preparing myself to become a general. A big part of this curriculum was to learn how to talk, how to soothe, how to cure. I was also acquainted with the art of deception. For many years I was encouraged to lie to my patients, when of course there was a need for those kinds of lies. Many times, I would tell them they would be all right, even when I had known for sure that they only had a matter of minutes to live.

These lies had the magnitude of life and death. These lies were the ones that Mr. Hippocrates himself would not call inhumane. He would have considered them perfectly human. I had Mr. Hippocrates' approval to lie. Kissing Greg's ass by telling him the things he wanted to hear did not appear to be a big obstacle in my plan. Too much would be lost by not kissing his ass.

"Greg, ever since I have known you, I have admired you. I recognized in you a superior mind that was unmatched, probably the best mind I may ever know... near perfection, when it comes to sheer knowledge, cleverness, and analysis. I learned a lot from you and I thank you for that. Though tonight you treated me kind of rough, that's okay. I'm a big boy. I take things like big boys do."

He just stood there. He did not stop me. By allowing me to continue, he let me deliver the poisonous sweet nectar to his ego. I tried to deliver a tone of voice denoting acknowledgment of my defeat as well as my overall inferiority.

"I envy you. I really do. Things come so easily for you. I just wonder how you do things so smoothly. About me knowing myself, you are right again. I put a lot of pressure on myself. I complicate my life unnecessarily. You are perfectly right. I need to reevaluate myself and my plans. I need to know who I am. So in the future, I will choose my goals very carefully. Just like you said, I'm not born a child of a king or queen. So how could I play the role of a prince? I never meant to compete with you. I might not be a bright person, but I'm a survivor. I understand I certainly can't survive in this life, if I take on people like you."

I continued massaging his ego. It wasn't just big. It was huge. To be adequately massaged, it needed more time, more energy, and more deception. I was only hoping that I had in me enough skill to do the job. With ecstatic pleasure, I felt he enjoyed my concession speech very much.

Studying his shadow carefully in semi-darkness, I could not miss the moment, when he pulled Mary back in the room, closed the door behind her and in a minute was sitting very close to me. Mary did not give any indication that she liked the where this was going.

"Greg, I don't like this. I really don't like any of this. I want to go to sleep. Take me home please."

"Mary, Al still has some time with his power as the birthday boy. I wouldn't leave him alone now. Not after he was just given bad news like this."

"Thank you Greg." I sounded appreciative. "Mary couldn't understand this, could you Mary?"

"Oh, I understand this all right." Mary made a desperate attempt to clear Greg's cloudy head. "Greg, be careful. He's up to something."

But, it was too late for Greg to listen to advice or to follow advice he could not hear. He was doomed. He was in the worst situation imaginable. At this time he was convinced that today was his day. Therefore, he acted, felt, and presumed things would go accordingly. He looked like a gambler with an incredibly lucky night with all the confidence one of those nights brings. An athlete would refer to the condition as being "in the zone". Greg would not give up the opportunity to enjoy watching and listening to a humiliated opponent.

Mary's weary pleas were ignored and dismissed.

"Relax Mary, little Al wouldn't try to trick Greg Entel. Is that right

Al? All he wants is some comforting moments from us. He has also learned a very valuable lesson. In the future, he will think twice before he decides to go after something he can't handle. Now he understands that his ability to sit on his behind and read, that doesn't make him any smarter. You have to have it in your genes Al, in your genes. Then and only then can you have everything, I mean everything."

"You're right Greg. I know you're right." I did not argue with him. On the contrary, I let him feel and know that I continued to be under his superiority spell.

"Greg, watch out. He is playing games- dirty ones. He is up to something very nasty. I can feel it. Take me home please. I had enough of this guy. I want to go home." Mary now was standing in the corner again. She was smart enough to sense that something very wrong was about to happen in this room. But she was not a prophet who could predict what was about to come. And even if she did predict it, she did not have power to prevent anything that was about to happen.

"Mary, twenty nine more minutes, I said twenty nine more minutes. Don't worry, your boyfriend has everything under control."

He was wrong. He didn't have everything under control. He underestimated me. And I was about to demonstrate that underestimating me could be very dangerous to his health.

Payback time finally arrived. Payback for everything. For the job I was losing. For the insults I took. For my father that died so young. For my mother that had to bail out in desperation from our family's sinking ship in order to salvage her sanity when I was twenty months old. For the love that I wanted and needed, but was denied over and over again. Payback time came for all the hardships that I had to endure during my uneasy life.

I was ready to be vicious. Now Greg stopped being just Greg. He was everything that was wrong with my life. He was the consolidation of everything sinister that happened to me. He was the reason for me to be vicious.

"Greg, it just occurred to me, what it would feel like to beat you in something." I started.

"Like in what?"

"In anything. I mean anything."

"You must be kidding." He sounded surprised, that a thought like this had even crossed my mind. "Al, do you really think there is something you can possibly beat me in?"

"I don't know. But I can't help wondering how it would feel, seeing you actually losing to me in something."

"Al, you know this is still your birthday. If you come up with any worthwhile challenge, I might even accept it."

"It's funny, me beating you, me being a winner and you being a loser. I never thought about that."

"So think now. Or should I insult you more? Don't you want satisfaction? What kind of man are you? Tonight is your night. Now or never, Al go for it."

I could smile now and that is what I did. In the darkness we were blanketed, I could afford a well-deserved grin. My plan was cruising smoothly. The final stage of it arrived with remarkable ease. I could not dream of a better set up for the final insult. I was calmly delirious.

"Greg, come to think of it, there is something in which, I might be more successful than you. Of course there must be something. You're no Jesus Christ! You can't be infallible."

"Jesus Christ, I am not."

"Then yes, I know what I can beat you in. Drinking. I know how to drink, vodka in particular. But I'm not sure, if it's fair to you. This thing is only for manly men. You probably never sat with friends like that, sitting, talking, and drinking. I don't want to be unfair to you. Besides you wouldn't accept this kind challenge anyway. It's probably too macho for you. You're too brainy for that."

I was playing with him now. This time I was telling, I was suggesting, I was advising. He was just listening. He was the one that had to make a choice. He did not argue, did not object. His silent figure stood motionless for a moment.

"So, what do you say? Do you want to go for it? How about accepting this challenge? You would not deny a birthday boy's request, would you?"

I came out swinging. I felt, I did not have to pretend any more. Greg was on the hot spot primarily by his own repartee. Of course he got some help from me too. He trapped himself in a mirage of omnipotence. Now he had his pride to save not only from me and Mary, but primarily from himself. The latter part was more troublesome for him. I really believed he thought of himself as invincible.

I did my part. Now I could relax. It did not really matter, whether he would accept the challenge or not. Either way, I would come out a winner. Either he would accept my challenge and I would go for a large-scale victory or he would not, and I would know that he was frightened of me. But something was telling me; I was going to go all away. I had that feeling. His hubris would not permit him to back down. I knew a big victory awaited me.

Greg paused to consider the circumstances. His decision making process certainly took time. A few times, I heard him sigh. I could see him struggling on whether to accept the duel. To choose avoiding the potential loss and to live with himself in shame was ultimately unacceptable. He did not want to damage his pride. Eventually, he succumbed to his inevitable acceptance.

"Al, you didn't really learn much today, did you? So, you are habitual loser." Greg's natural conversation was trash-talk.

"Greg, I can beat you. I will beat you senseless. And I think you know it. Something tells me you are not a big drinker. I got you Greg. Now I have advice for you. Go home and take this beautiful girl with you. You don't really want to get embarrassed. I made my point and I'm satisfied."

I continued to play with him. He did not appear much of player now. If he was a bully a few minutes ago, now he was barely hanging onto his machismo. As a gambler, I knew his cards; and above all, I dictated his behavior for the last few minutes. The last one was the big one. As two psychiatrists, our ability to manipulate each other's behavior was a significant factor in our level of skill.

Greg finally committed to the contest. He stared at me, studying me through the darkness with only the city lights providing us with thin islands of light around the room. He never saw me like this before. In my face, he saw something he had never accounted for. It was a test of my street smarts against his all around polished intellect, my average memory that remembered enough to survive, against his phenomenal memory that was so desperately trying to remember something that could carry him to victory yet again.

I could feel from the jerky movements his shadow was making that he considered leaving my place a few times. But his rigid pride would not let him make the move that would have proven to be the smartest move of his life. In fact, his ego would contribute to the biggest mistake of his life. A combination of the above and a deep seeded cry for respect produced the mistake. No matter how offended or embarrassed your pride may feel, that offense cannot be rectified with sheer stupidity because stupidity may lead to disastrous consequences, which would in no way preserves or restores pride. And, Greg was clearly confusing his pride for his integrity. His stupid mistake made me feel very smart.

"Okay, Greg. This is the way we'll do it. Each of us will take a big glass full of vodka and chug it at the same time. Whoever finishes first and maintains his faculties wins. We will record a one-sentence victory speech that will be tape-recorded to decide who has more control. I have no objections if your girlfriend referees this game. You wouldn't object her decision, would you?"

I did not hear him say anything for a few more seconds. I could see his eyes on the two cups that I had brought to the table. He was measuring the size of the cups. They were the largest cups I had because I knew that the bigger the cups were, the bigger my advantage. Each cup was nearly the size of a bottle. Then I saw him swing his right arm in a decisive manner. I interpreted this as him finally making a decision and committing to the contest. Just like I expected, he fell for it. He, as an adult, made his choice. Now he had to live with the consequences that come with every major decision in life.

"Okay birthday boy. Let's go for it. Only let's do it with class. Let's make this more interesting. Let's do it for something big. I'm sure you wouldn't mind getting something out of this." He still sounded confident.

"That's fine with me. But be careful. I will not do this for something. I will only do this for someone." I was gradually unfolding the last page of my complex multifaceted plan.

"What do you mean?" He was curious but not concentrating. His voice was still firm, but now it was teeming with uncertainty.

"What I mean is that if I lose, anything you ask me to do, I will do it without question. If you ask me to go out in the street completely naked for a very embarrassing and very uncomfortable stroll, I would do it. Basically, you get one free dare. That would make you happy, I guarantee it. I hate the cold. That's why I know I won't lose."

"And if I lose; I would do the same thing or anything that your pedestrian imagination might suggest. I'm that confident". At this time, Greg continued to sound confident. He still could fool a lot of people, including Mary, but I was not fooled. How could I be fooled? I was the one who designed and staged the last ten minutes of his life.

"If you are that confident, you wouldn't have a problem with my wager."

"And just what would that wager be?" He asked with concern.

"If you lose, I get your girlfriend for the rest of the night." I couldn't believe that I actually went through with this whole thing. The coolness, with which I carried myself, frightened me. But this

THE BALANCING GAME

scare was not powerful enough for me to abandon my drive to obtain the satisfaction I was seeking.

Mary cried out with disgust.

"Greg, let's get out of here. You don't have to do this. You don't have to prove anything to him."

Greg didn't say anything for while. His shadow remained still. Only the sound of frequent and heavy breathing was revealing his anxiety and concern. He continued to think. After about twenty-five seconds, his thoughts produced this;

"Mary I believe in success. I believe in life. And I believe in people who believe in me. You don't have to say yes, but I do expect you to believe in me. So, if I lose, which I won't, I expect you to honor your word."

Even now, she continued to believe in his success. Maybe that's why, when she said "all right," I sensed her support. She was like a cheerleader who really believed in her team. Maybe, she was expecting something more, as if her ascent and his eventual victory would get Greg to propose as if her grand romantic gesture would induce one of his own. It is tough to figure out exactly what she was thinking, but she was very confident in his success.

This unusual game was about to be played out. This game had no winners, only losers. Each of us was doomed. Maybe because we both crossed that invisible line, into realms well beyond taboo with our competitive intoxication. Greg was the defending champion, who was about to be beaten by the underdog so badly that it would change both of our lives. Mary, standing in the corner of the small room, was about to be sacrificed to the stronger gladiator of the night.

Now, that game was about to begin, I would be remiss not to set the stage. When I got those two glasses, I got them from my "dining room" table {which was also the living room and basically the entire apartment save for my room}. That table was full of leftover food, and I dug out a bottle of vodka. But then, I returned to the chair where

Greg was sitting. The two large glasses were not traditional glasses, they were collector's cups from some convention or another and they were meant to support various other beverages that can be ingested en masse. They each had a logo on them, but in the darkness, neither of us could see the logo, and I like to think it was the jolly roger, the old skull and cross bones, but I cannot attest to that.

I proceeded to fill both glasses to the top, the absolute top of the glass, so much so, that I spilled enough vodka that the outside of the glass was probably highly flammable. But I had my reasons for that. I handed one glass to Greg. The other one I took for myself. Everything was set for Greg's fall. But now, I wanted him to know that he was doomed and to wallow in it. I wanted him to feel the anticipation of his own demise. My education in drinking the clear poison, was far superior to his. I got my education from the best professionals in the field. He deserved to have some kind preparation for this unfair match. The deep-seated honesty in me demanded to give him a crash course in drinking, to offset unbalanced odds.

"Greg, I think you should know something. A few years ago I lived in a place full of drunkards. One of them, a Russian guy, with no family, no friends, and no name, noticed the way I was handling his drink of choice, and volunteered some pointers. Greg for fairness sake, I should give you the same pointers. You might want to use them."

Greg let me talk. He mellowed as I spoke. He was letting me do the talking without interruption. He was a passenger in this ride. And that wasn't like him at all. In fact, this totally uncharacteristic action gave me further insight into his mindset.

"He was taught how to drink vodka in Siberian camps where the ability to drink was the only way to avoid being taken advantage sexually or even at times to be eaten for dinner. So I listened to what he had to say."

"First of all, look at the drinking process as a confrontation between two antagonistic parties. From your part, you want to literally swallow the drink, so that you can enjoy the feeling that the alcohol brings once it reaches your brain. From its part, alcohol has a goal. It wants to get in your blood and play on your wishes, and it wants to play on your balance. If it is not handled with the proper respect, it does more to you that you bargained for. It pushes your life out of perspective. It changes your mood, and helps you escape from reality far further than you might want. If you don't realize this, you are vulnerable, like any person that ignores his opponent and doesn't give him respect. Respect, Greg, he was talking about respect."

Greg was listening without interruption. He looked like a student who came to class to learn his favorite subject- one of those classes that makes you forget how useless it will be in real life- one of those classes that just starts to make sense in an almost spiritual way. This was a time of great need and the need was the knowledge of drinking. He stood up in front of Mary, showing her his backside. Mary was not my concern, but I was paying attention to her nonetheless. For all his great intellect, Greg did not appear to be a quick learner. He was showing slight signs of vague respect to me as an opponent, but certainly there was no true respect. That is why I liked what I was observing.

"First of all," I continued. "You take a good look at your opponent. You bow down to it, just like a martial artist would. Give it the respect it deserves. Then measure your glass and the alcohol it contains. Calculate how many gulps it would take you to finish the glass. The fewer, the better… but you should never make a rookie mistake and underestimate the number. That would be a disaster. That will make you choke and it would get pretty ugly. Go easy. Maintain your cool. Take an extra gulp if you have to. And again, don't ever allow yourself to lose the rhythm and grace, or the respect of your enemy."

I finished my sermon and still Greg didn't move… didn't say anything. He just raised his hand with the glass, signaling his readiness for the event. Mary continued to observe the events from the corner of the room.

I looked at Greg, and then one more time at Mary. The supernatural vibrations I was receiving, were taking me to a higher level of consciousness. My mind was set on one goal, one purpose: on anticipation of beating Greg.

Neither of us even considered salvaging the evening. There was still time for time to freeze. There still was enough logic hidden somewhere to stop the madness. But we chose not to interfere with fate. So, the plane started to plummet to earth and it had no chance after this moment. Only something bigger then fate could change things, but there is nothing bigger than fate.

Then it began. There was no gunshot to signal the runners, but this was more like a chess match than a race. We held the glasses filled with the mind altering spirits, and were observing each other's shadows. For me, this was not the first of these games I have played in my life, and I had been successful the last... well, the last many times I have played. For Greg this must have been his first.

I observed how tightly he held the glass. With that amount of force, there was no grace at all. Then he made another mistake that I warned him not to make. He tried to drink it in one gulp. I have heard of people being able to open their throats to allow the fluid in, but this amount of this coarse a liquid, it would be nearly impossible to maintain that. He did not count, he did not bow. He did not show the proper respect to his opponent. In a matter of seconds, he started to choke, and couldn't get his breath back for while. Suddenly, he felt the urge to throw up, and he ran to my bathroom. This time he was using my bathroom without asking my permission. Soon, he was bellowing out inhuman noises, actually unfortunately they are probably all too human noises. These noises were very much indicative of his suffering.

My part went smooth. Taking a deep breath and a number of equal swallows slowly made me light headed, tight cheeked, and narrow eyed. But it also made me very much a winner. I was still on my feet, and more saturated with alcohol, than intoxicated. I could feel the alcohol rushing through my bloodstream, but even more disgustingly I could feel it oozing through my pores.

For a while, I tried to concentrate on the noises coming out of the bathroom. I thought I deserved the pleasure of hearing the sweet sounds of vengeance. For a few seconds I let his pain be my trumpet. Then to my surprise I found out, that I had more pleasure from anticipating the victory, than from the actual victory itself.

After I lost interest in Greg's musical performance, another matter, a matter of sexual nature this time, had to be finalized. I was very much on top of the situation.

My prize, Mary, walked out of the bathroom. She was in shock seeing her Greg so soundly defeated and not his usual controlled self. And evidently, he must have muttered through his vomiting that she had to fulfill her part of the bet because she was utterly dazed and defeated. So, she moved back into her corner, waiting to be taken by the winner. With my finger pointing at her, I summoned Mary to me. I can't say she ran. But I also couldn't say that she had to be pushed towards me. Pretty soon she was standing very, very close to me. I pulled her body, pressing it firmly against mine. For a moment, she resisted, but I felt her resistance fade into an acceptance that was hardly reluctant. Greg's nauseating sounds had captivated her attention. She was looking in the direction of the noises.

"Relax. Trust me. You don't want you to hear this."

I don't know if she heard what I said. She had obligations to meet and promises to keep. And she was ready to do anything for her love. I was caressing all of the curves of her body. This raised the speed of my blood flow. It also aroused the interest of my sexual organ. I knew that Mary knew it. I compelled her to feel it.

"It's hard, isn't it? Just like life." I said. The alcohol probably influenced my words, as the rapid blood flow carried the toxins throughout my body.

"Listen Al," she finally said, breaking the trance before mumbling something incoherently. An innocent victim caught in between the male ego's bloody competition, was about to pay her price for being in love with the wrong person, in the wrong place, in the wrong time. "It has been a disastrous party for me. I want to get this over with. Just tell me what you want me to do."

I put my head on her shoulder and whispered in her right ear;

"I'm going to my bedroom now to sleep and I mean sleep. You take care of your boyfriend. I hope he learned something tonight."

"You mean I don't have to go through this?" She sounded surprised, but to my chagrin, not terribly disappointed.

"No, you don't have to go through this, not tonight. Can you hear your boyfriend? Do you think a few minutes of you would give me more pleasure than that sound? I don't think so. Not tonight for sure."

Only one thing remained for me to know. – "Yes, I can drive"-- was Mary's answer. Now I could leave them; him and her.

It was now time to be in the sole company of my thoughts. With no Mary and no Greg. Without papers that now seemed valueless. On my way down to the land of dreams, I encountered drowsy thoughts. There was a considerable degree of wondering, what would makes ordinary people happy; fights that they win or fights that they are not able to win yet. What brings more satisfaction; the feeling the pleasure itself or the anticipation of upcoming pleasure? I did not remember what the old Greek philosophers had to say about it.

I knew I was dreaming. I was in a different world, in the world full of anger, alcohol, tiredness, satisfaction and sleep.

Chapter 3

"Hi, my name is Al Letne and I have a problem. I feel guilty all the time. This is really bothering me a lot. I think I need help, doctor."

Very rarely do I feel the need to talk to anybody. When I feel like my head is heavy and is full of thoughts that must be unloaded. I feel that discarding things is somehow important.

I always thought that wasted anything; be it body, garbage, or even old or smelly thoughts should be eliminated. Only then does everything new, fresh, clean, and innocent have a chance to emerge.

Being a very private person, I would not just share the most intimate and bothering thoughts with just anybody.

In my study, at the opposite side of the table, right across from me, I clearly see a person sitting. He looks younger than his occupation would suggest, and older than his age would indicate. He has thick dark brownish hair neglectfully combed in a hurry from right to left. His face seems pale, very pale. Too much analyzing sleepless nights, I guess. While he most certainly wears clothes that are expected from a man of his occupation; like suits and ties, while talking to me, he is very casually dressed. His height must be about five feet and ten inches. He does not strike me as somebody with important professional degrees by his last name. He appears to be more of a jock than an intellectual. His speech is clear and firm.

I always wanted to know his religion. It is very important for me to know the person that will know almost everything about me. He should have my trust. Looking at him, I really quite could not decipher, which temple he would attend or which holidays he would observe. At times, I would think he is a Catholic descendent of Italian ancestry.

At other times, I would be convinced that he was fifth-generation Protestant from a northern European country. A few times, I could bet, he was a son of Jewish parents. I guess I would never know. There is no sense asking him. My guess is he does not know the answer neither.

I watch his every move carefully. I observe his lips flutter about. I notice that he only talks when I am talking. He always smiles or frowns simultaneously with me. The resemblance with looks is also remarkable. It was like he is me and I am him. That may be why, I trust him so much. That is why I tell him everything.

"Doctor I can't understand this. I don't know why. Any time something goes wrong around me, I immediately assume responsibility for it. If a car in front of me gets in an accident, I won't sleep that night, thinking that somehow I contributed to somebody's tragedy."

Then I'll stop. So will he. Then I will resume talking. So will he.

"The other night I saw my father in my dream. He died at forty-nine years of age. He was a chronic alcoholic. He also held two jobs to support my education. Now in my dream, he shows up at my doorstep. He looks just like I remember him. When he sees me, instead of being happy, all he does is shrugs his shoulders and spreads both his arms. Then I see a sardonic smile on his face."

"In my dream, I witnessed this. I also watched him go away and disappear in a foggy darkness. I can't say I know what he meant. But what if these gestures were signs of disappointment of a person who sacrificed his life for me while giving me everything he could, even if that was not so much. And how did I repay him? Sometimes weeks pass by, before I even remember him. Maybe he is angry and disappointed."

The doctor never says anything before me, or after me. He never makes any different moves... only ones that resemble my movements. He always wears the same clothes I do.

In short, he is my mirror image. That's me, relaxing, confessing, discussing, and complaining with the closest person I know. And all this without leaving my room, without wasting my time and money.

After every session with my mirror psychiatrist, I feel lighter. The sack full of guilt, which is carried on my back like a hump, gets a hole, and guilt pours out.

As soon as I get a little relief, I give a little smile to my doctor. I usually forget to be grateful. Without thanking my psychiatrist I get up in a hurry and disappear.

So does my psychiatrist.

Chapter 4

A terrible loud noise woke me up from what was a very sound and deep sleep. The process of awakening helped me realize that this five o'clock wakeup call could only bring discomfort to my emotional state of mind. Even hearing Mary's voice did not calm me down a bit. She was calling from Greg's phone. Her crying and screaming voice sounded ominous. She was not saying much, just kept repeating my name a few times and then she remained silent for awhile. This concerned me.

"Mary, what the hell is going on? Are you all right?" I asked in anticipation of hearing something very wrong.

"Al, it's about Greg. He isn't all right." She continued to cry and scream.

"Mary, I want to be frank with you; Greg's well-being is the last thing that would worry me this early in the morning."

That is what I said trying to keep my cool. But something was getting to me- something heavy and unpleasant. Anxiety made me sit up on the bed. I could feel a major tide coming and the survivor in me was bracing myself for the impact.

Then it came. On the other side of the line, the messenger was giving me the bad news.

"Al, we had an accident. Greg is paralyzed from the waist down. He has a broken back. He will never walk again. Al, you son of a bitch, is this what you wanted to happen? Are you happy now? Is this what you wished for on your birthday? You planned this, Al, you planned this, you son of a bitch!"

"When did this happen?" I managed to ask.

"Two minutes before midnight. It was still your birthday!" The screaming voice answered.

THE BALANCING GAME

I thought I was ready for the worst thing that I could hear. This was bad. I was not prepared for something this serious. Suddenly I lost my balance. I felt like something very mighty picked me up and dragged me back to reality or even beyond reality. There was no sky above and no ground below. I could not see or hear anything. My numbness began resembling the miserable and abundant distraction that my patients frequently had on their faces.

But this state of mind would not last forever. This escapade, which was initiated by my instinct of survival, trying to help my shocked mind, ended with great participation of the same instinct, fearing that long departure from reality could also damage my sanity.

So I had to come back to the realization of the terrible truth; Greg was paralyzed and I played a part in it. The last drink in my house was filled with incomprehensible consequences. It was a terrible night. Guilt was being born in the most painful of ways. It was about to be delivered naturally with no need for physical force.

And when the guilt flowed in, I met him completely unprepared. I was unaware how much the guilt baby weighed and I chose not to weigh him. I just knew he was heavy. I did not know how tall he was and I chose not to measure him. I just knew it was tall. I could not see his face. I could not hear his cry. I just felt him inside of my head. He was there. He chose to reside in the room at the top, the penthouse. Soon, he would become much more mobile, or shall I say much more malignant.

That night I became an unwitting parent to this monster. The monster that would occupy room in my spacious mind without paying me rent and that would consume my life from within.

So it started. My life would not be the same from that night on. From then on, I coexisted with a great guilt.

I managed to put down the phone. This literally disconnected me from the outside world. I had a new obligation... I had to care for my guilt. I could not handle anything else that day. I did not even bother to call work to let them know, I was not coming in. The new priorities in my mind did not have work on the list. I had to feed this growing emotion, and guilt knows how to suckle.

I ate nothing and drank nothing. Terrible thoughts flashed through my head. I remember telling myself again and again, that I did not mean to hurt Greg this much, that it was not my intention to cripple him. But, maybe it was. Knowing he will be drunk while driving his expensive fast Porsche, I increased the chances of his driving to a crippling fate.

Every time I would tell myself, that it was not my intention to hurt him this badly, something in me would issue a question; "Are you sure?"

I was busy nursing my newborn guilt the whole day and the whole night. Then I came to the realization of one very simple and universal rule; no matter how significant a tragic thing that might happen to a person, life still goes on, with him or without him. In each of us, there is a survivor that awakens in trying times and in turn wakes us up. He will tell us things we want to hear. He will point out to us, that much worse things could happen and asks us to consider another rule of life, the positive one. This rule clearly states; in every tragedy however terrible, something good will arise. You've heard the adages from silver linings to lemonade.

And suddenly I remembered; with Greg paralyzed now, I had a clear shot at that assistant professor's job. On the twenty-fourth hour of my grief, forgetting conveniently the guilt for a second, it struck me like lightening; that I would survive anything and I was emotionally invincible.

With this knowledge firmly in mind, I felt another visitor in me; shame. This one I had no problem handling. I just showed him my back and kept on walking.

Chapter 5

1

Professor Fisher did not look cheerful. His usually smiling face was now a picture of immeasurable sorrow. Routinely he would crack a joke before, during, and after every meeting with his staff. Not this time though. His long roundly protruded nose appeared reddish in color. Knowing him for years now, this could only mean he was angry- very angry.

This was a time, when each of us was supposed to be very much preoccupied with heavy thoughts; predominantly what we would be doing in two months and in turn, the rest of our lives. When this meeting was called for the whole department, everybody thought this would be kind of farewell party or at least a very cordial gathering.

Even though it had some elements of the typical farewell atmosphere, this was clearly not a farewell party.

"Soon, you'll be leaving this place," the chief of the department, a world-renowned psychiatrist was addressing his senior fellows "and you'll be taking with you, everything we taught you here; good and bad. We hope the ratio between good and bad will be overwhelmingly in favor of the good. We tried our best to give you the best."

He was kind of out of it. He was staring straight into nothingness, his speech was monotonous, and his head was totally motionless.

"I don't know if you have noticed or not, but there is one big thing missing in this room. It is of great concern to all of us. I'm talking about Dr. Greg Entel. As you know, he isn't doing well these days. He is crippled and is not in much of a sociable mood." He stopped, sipped water from his glass, and then remained silent. It was obvious how much Greg's absence troubled him.

"I know for a fact that none of you likes him. All twenty of you hate him... because he was the smartest. You didn't like him because he always told the truth. You didn't like him because he demanded and he expected. You had problem with that."

"How many articles did he publish? 20? 25? How much genius did he dispense? "The God of the Mind," "Psychological Profile of a Leader," "Manufacturing Revolutions," "Measuring Guilt" were a few of his papers. Each is more dynamic than the last. What have you done?"

Professor Fisher was becoming angrier. He was not blaming any particular person for what happened to Greg. He blamed a whole generation.

"I always thought of him as your conscience. And I felt like you'd be okay as long as he was with you. But you didn't want him with you. He was in your way, in all of your ways. You tricked him, you got him drunk, you put him in a car, and you destroyed him. You put him in a wheelchair. Now he is immobile and now he is... not sober. That's what all of you dreamed of. Now you have your unsupervised freedom."

"One thing I personally guarantee; healthy or not, you will need him. He can't come to you. You better go to him, whenever you can. Please, for your own sake, please visit him as often as you can."

The famous psychiatrist broke down. He couldn't hold back his tears, which began to flow abundantly down both sides of his face. He was old. His brain arteries were sclerotic and narrow. Not enough blood was getting to his brain. That is the way the representatives of this new generation interpreted the break-down of this old and famous man. The new generation was coming... with noise, confidence, and new values. Professor Fisher, a renowned worldwide expert in human behavior, had problems understanding these modern young characters.

THE BALANCING GAME

Dr. Fisher finished his speech and looked around. He looked like he knew that he could not reach the audience. After shaking his head a few times with disgust, he left the room. His exit was somehow more rapid than you would expect from somebody of his age.

2

When I was in seventh grade, our social studies teacher gave us homework. We had to construct our family tree. Everybody started to complain; they had to go so deep in the ground to look for their roots that it would be time consuming to complete the homework. In the midst of heated debate and discussions, a boy, sitting next to me, filled with great hatred towards me screamed at me.

"Hey Al, you lucky son of a bitch. I'll bet this is the easiest homework you ever had!"

Unfortunately, he was right. This was the easiest homework I was ever given. My family tree was very short; it had no roots whatsoever. My alcoholic father easily could start and complete it.

My mother according to my father's story, left us when I was two years old. "It was very hard on her, having you and me around." He would say, not in a very distinctive voice. No blame and no anger was ever expressed.

As I grew a little older, I realized she did the right thing. She did jump off of a sinking ship. There was no sense in all of us going down. She probably thought we had no chance to survive. I am sure if she thought otherwise, she would have never left us. I know that is what she would say if she did show up. I knew one day the most amazing woman on the earth would approach me and tell me; "Hi, I'm your mother, and I miss you."

I don't know where I come from. Which part of the country, my parents called home. Which country my ancestors came from. The only person who could possibly enlighten me in this topic was my alcoholic father. But, he never bothered to fill me in on the secret. He never mentioned the past. Maybe it was so bad that he was afraid to associate himself with it.

My poor father. He spent most of his adult life facing the world, his world, with his brain overflowing with alcohol. Maybe instead of escaping his past consciously; he should have dealt with it, so he could face the present and fight for a future with more of a life. I would not know how intelligent he was. I did not know how smart he was either. He spoke with drunkard's stammer, a constant slur in his speech, and he never had any clarity of tone. The funny thing was his speech would become the most clear, when he was the drunkest and was about to pass out.

My conversations with my father could never last long and were never very substantive. Whenever he would initiate a discussion about life, he would usually end up talking to himself because while he was mumbling, I would hit the books viciously, thinking the books would help me become less like him.

Almost every night, he would pass out, but, he would invariably wake me up and in a very, lucid and comprehensible voice ask me if I did my homework. Even though I was barely old enough to think about his life, I realized just looking at him, that he was pathetic, and yet his only preoccupation before he ultimately would lose his mind was whether I did my homework.

Maybe, in his fatherly way, he was giving me a powerful message. He knew I had to find some other way to live. And in his alcoholic mind, the books were my passport to a different life, different than his.

I got this message every single day.

I walked around with books, regardless of whether I was reading them or not. Even carrying these tools of knowledge without using them, was giving me the kind of satisfaction one usually gets, from completing a day's work. The neighborhood I grew up in was not really established or prepared for boys like me. Constantly walking with books in my arms, and with no time to hang out with the local bullies, I quickly became a favorite target for harassment.

It did not take much time for those bullies, to learn a few of life's funny rules, not to mess with people with books. Those thugs would hang around without any purpose in life, waiting for some opportunity for some easy fun to come by. Then they would see me. Coming from school, my arms were filled with books and my brain was preoccupied with the future, minding my own business and my minding my own present.

"Here comes the little bookworm," somebody would scream and a group of five 'tough guys' would jump me. I would end up badly beaten. And I mean badly. But one of the least lucky of the five would end up sharing in the blood loss. This would be the one that I would grab at the beginning of the attack, when I would try to choke him or bite him. I would barely feel pain that the others would try to inflict on me, but I would always feel the pain I forced on my stunned adversary.

They learned what I already knew. I was not scared of them. I could take a few punches relatively easily. It was hunger that I was scared of. It was failing that I was petrified of. They got tired of their little games. Besides almost every one of them had scars that I had delivered.

They left me alone. They did not want anything to do with a crazy bookworm like me. The only confrontational episode I would have with them was, when somebody would make fun of me carrying books. That was also a mistake on their part. They could joke about my past. They could disrespect my present. But no way, could get away bad-mouthing my books that represented my future. The future was the only healthy thing in my life.

Never touch a person's sacred scrolls with an intention to insult. This is a message that those bullies received from me. I just hope they are spreading this message wherever they are now. That is of course if they wised up with age.

The neighborhood where I grew up was very diverse, like many of New York's neighborhoods. You could easily learn geography by merely knowing where most of your acquaintances were from. While it was diverse in appearance and ethnicity, almost the entire neighborhood was typical blue-collar workers. Most of them were simple unpretentious, honest working people, living their lives the only way they knew how.

Their daily struggle for physical survival, their lifestyle of pride and decency, and their dedication to their families are some of a few bright spots that enhance my recollection of this area of my childhood memory.

3

Life in university did not really change much, just because Greg could not walk any more. Greg's seemingly irreplaceable leadership was easily substituted by David Axel; a genuinely nice and competent character. He was well liked by almost everybody around, including myself. His presence kept the usual daily routine in a smooth flow. I could not help but notice one thing; mainly that it was David and not me, who was chosen to carry out the chief fellow's duties. That was a strong indication that despite Greg being out of my way, I had to look for a job outside of this place. It was becoming obvious that I was not the only one who blamed me for what happened to Greg.

Ten days after that inauspicious night, I was summoned to Dr. Fisher's office. Usually warm to me, the chief of the psychiatry department this time tried to keep things on a strictly professional level.

"Dr. Letne, the department reevaluated things after what happened to Dr. Entel and decided not to consider your candidacy for the job you applied for. We thought it wouldn't be fair to keep you in suspense and give you the wrong impression. Now that the chances of Dr. Entel's return is almost nil, you would be the next logical person for consideration. But, circumstances require that we bring somebody from outside."

Dr. Fisher was not just cold to me. He was completely ignoring me. For whatever reason, he did not think it was necessary to look at me while delivering the message of this importance to me. It seemed like he was reading a rehearsed speech as he was giving me the information.

"I understand Dr. Fisher. I understand"-- I managed to mumble. Then turned around and went for the door in a hurry.

"I don't know what exactly you understand Dr. Letne. But I want you to understand this; he is a genius, he had a chance to fly high, very high"— an angry Dr. Fisher's words caught me at the door and literally iced me. I stood there for a while. It must have been over ten seconds.

"I'm sorry, very sorry," I whispered. I continued to whisper the words in the corridor and in the street.

4

Through our mutual acquaintances, I was well updated about Greg's condition. He remained hospitalized for two months. After, as doctors put it, "remarkable improvement," he remained paralyzed from the waist down. It was clear; a person who as a world-renowned psychiatrist stated "could fly very high," would never be able to walk again. The irony of life was busy working on Greg, putting the finishing touches on his misery and sealing him in an electronic wheelchair, a very advanced one.

I tried not to think about Greg. Every time my mind would wander upon his name, my guilt would start flaring up, stirring things inside me and upsetting my inner peace. Life was tough without this inner turmoil, and I definitely did not need an extra heavy load to deal with on a daily basis.

Meanwhile, I succeeded in finishing that fifth required, but now somewhat insignificant paper and started to apply for jobs around the country. My chances to get something even remotely resembling my dream job were not good. In fact, my best estimate placed my chances at approximately zero percent. Because of the events that took place and because of my state of mind; I found myself in an undesirable position. I was beginning to panic; with only two months remaining before the conclusion of my fellowship, I still did not even have a clue of what I was going to do. Traditionally, my mood vacillated with ups and downs , but I did not have any ups for quite some time. I knew with my qualifications, I would get at least some kind job, but I was afraid that I would accept a job based on my desperation for survival, not my aspiration towards my goals.

In the midst of my anxiety, I got a telephone call from Greg. That is just what I needed; a midnight call from Greg to calm me down. Frankly, I expected this call because I knew he expected me to call him. And after not receiving my anticipated call, the next logical thing was to hear his voice.

"Al, this is Greg"-- said voice that resembled Greg's.

"Greg, is it really you?" I was remarkably calm, considering who I was talking to.

"That's right Al, it's me. How are you doing Al?"

"Are you asking me how am I? I'm okay Greg. You tell me how you are."

"I'm okay I guess, all things considered. You probably know by now that I can't walk. But Al you can hear me talking, I still can talk Al."

There was a few seconds of awkward silence before Greg said something.

"Al, be a good sport. Come and see me tomorrow night. You wouldn't say no to me, would you?"

"Of course Greg"-- was my answer. But while it was me who said those words, it was guilt that was making me say things without thinking. That surprised and scared me the same time. The idea of having guilt as my spokesman felt kind of creepy. But I would not yet know what practical implications this chaos inside me would cause.

I did not go any deeper into analyzing anything in the conversation. I tried to be practical; after I got directions to his place, I promised him I would be there the next day. I did not know what to think and what was behind this; but I realized that going to Greg's home meant more than traveling a few miles. I had other kinds of traveling to do; I understood that I would have an emotional journey too. But this kind of transportation that was causing me headaches.

Chapter 6

It took about forty minutes to get to Greg's home. I did not have a car; courtesy of my poverty. So I had to transfer three subway stations just to get within walking distance from his place. It was about nine o'clock on this spring evening as I approached Greg's house. Quiet streets were lit up by the city's neon lights. I could see a different world; a world of wealth, endless possibility, confidence, and this world was oddly tidy. All this was producing an aura of privilege for everything and everybody that resided around here.

I found the house where Greg lived. It was just as I expected. Architecturally designed in a manner to emphasize to visitors that inhabitants would never have to stand in an unemployment line. I did not go to the main entrance.

Instead, as I was instructed, I found the driveway, by-passed a few fancy cars to get to the service entrance on the side of the house. The door was ajar. A little nudge swung the door open. And suddenly I found myself in a small, cold, and dark room.

"Hello Al"- Greg's voice beckoned me. I saw him, or somebody who was probably him. He was sitting with a new discomforting posture, on his electric wheelchair. I stopped in the middle of the room. I could not move anymore. Nor could I say anything. Greg for whatever reason was very helpful. He reached out his right hand. The gesture encouraged me to take a few more steps towards his likeness and eventually to shake his hand.

"I'm sorry Greg. I'm really sorry about what happened to you." I managed to blurt this out sincerely.

"Al, I don't want to hear any apologies. It's not your fault that I'm

THE BALANCING GAME

talking to you from this wheelchair. I wish I could blame somebody for my condition. Then all I had to do to feel better would be, to follow that person's life. Statistically speaking, within two-three years, that person like any other average character, will come across some major trauma of their own to appease my vengeance. At that time I might be in better shape than him. This would give me some kind of satisfaction for awhile."

I continued to stand and watch this shadow of a man as he spoke.

"Unfortunately, no such luck. There is nobody I can blame, not even you. How could I? I would have done the same thing a thousand times, if God had given me a thousand chances."

His proclamation sounded sincere. His calm relaxed me. I believed him. For some reason, I think people in wheelchairs are more sincere. Besides he did not have the need to lie or deceive, the way I might have to.

Initial contact was made. I leveled with him. Now it was easier: first, because of the obligation that guilt was bringing, second because he did not project himself as a winner anymore. He looked more like an underdog now, trying to fight when he did not have much of a chance to win. People are always excited to support this kind of under-privileged fighter, especially a come-back story.

Suddenly I felt some kind unexplainable urge to help him, make him comfortable. I looked around. There were a few things I could do for him. I could easily eliminate the cold, by simply closing the only window that was widely open. Then I noticed the lack of light in the room. The only source of it appeared to be the lights that city evenings bring into all urban homes when nobody is home. It is the city version of natural moonlight.

Greg saw me looking around. "Don't even think about bringing logic in this place." It was obvious. He definitely preferred to stay in the cold, dark room.

I sensed that the atmosphere he chose was chosen more for

communicating symbolic meanings more than for his own comfort. The open window symbolized his connection with the outside world. It was like the connecting life magisterial that is so important to keep the inside and outside world in harmony. The darkness represented the foul mood of the inhabitant. The darkness also left a lot of room for imagination- something that a person with very limited mobility needs in great quantity.

Greg appeared surprisingly calm and in good spirits for somebody in his condition. Maybe it was because of the help he was getting from those bottles on the table that looked like bottles of vodka to be exact.

After the first few minutes of insignificant chatter, Greg offered me a seat on the chair across from the open window and handed me a little glass full of some noticeably heavily alcoholic liquid.

"Vodka" he said, while reaching out his right arm with the drink. "Your favorite, isn't it?"

"Yes, it is." I answered.

By now, I started to wonder, what exactly Greg asked me to come here for. There had to be more Greg wanted than just to see my face in the dark. And mine was the face of a man who consciously or not, contributed to or even caused the miserable state of his body and soul. While there was no obvious or visible animosity between us, we could not really spark a conversation. I could not ignite any topic and neither could Greg. My brain was still preoccupied with a strong desire to be helpful to him.

"Is there anything I can do for you Greg?"

"As a matter of fact yes, there is something you can do for me. It's funny you asked me. Actually, that's why I wanted you to come."

"Anything and I mean anything Greg. Just name it." I was happy he actually was asking me to do something for him. I knew this could be very healthy to my inner turmoil.

"Al, I really need you to do something for me, but before I ask you for a favor, I have to know if you will be comfortable with the idea of doing something for me."

"Greg, I said yes and I meant it." I was getting impatient. Now, I felt like I needed to do something for this guy. I felt like I needed to do a favor like diabetics need an insulin injection.

"Okay Al, I want you to do me a favor; I want you to make an appointment with Dr. Fisher and try to see him as soon as possible," Greg was plainly straight. I was not happy about what I just heard.

"Greg, I don't think, this is a good idea. We already had a very unfriendly chat the other day and I don't remember parting on the best of terms."

Greg remained silent. Or maybe his silence was a sign of disappointment. I did not want to disappoint him.

"Listen Greg, if that's want you me to do, that's what I'm going to do. What do you want me to talk to him about?"

"About that job."

"About what job? The job most likely is taken already."

"No, it's not." Suddenly, Greg was angry. He expected more obedience from me than he was getting.

By now, I thought I knew what he wanted me to do. He called me here, so I could do him a favor by going to Dr. Fisher's office and ask him about the possibility of Greg getting the job. Walking is not a prerequisite for the job of a psychiatrist.

"Of course Greg, I'll go to him and ask whatever you want me to ask him."

"Thank you Al. Somehow I knew you would do this for me. Just go to him, and tell him that you have a very good candidate for them. You know what? Don't even ask, just demand the job."

"Sure Greg," I continued to be obedient. I was kind of relieved. He could have asked for a much greater favor and I knew I would have it done for him.

Soon I was ready to leave. I got up and headed towards door. Greg did not offer me to stay. When I reached the door, he tried to remind me about his favor.

"Sure thing Greg, don't worry about it." I did not let him finish his sentence.

"Of course I'm worrying. You even didn't ask me who the job is for." He sounded upset.

"What do you mean for whom? Of course for you. And you know what. This is a very good idea. It's a good idea for you Greg. You've been cooped up in here for too long."

"What?!?" exclaimed Greg with obvious disgust. "Al, are you crazy? You must be kidding. Did you really think that I would ask for this kind of job, in the condition I'm in? You are really crazy Al." Greg started to laugh. He was making a strange noise; it almost sounded like a cackle. Or maybe it sounded strange to me because the whole situation was awkward.

"Then, who should I ask for?" Greg lost me completely.

"For Al Letne." Greg's serious serene voice replied. His laugh faded quickly to leave room for his statement.

"You should demand the job for Dr. Al Letne."

Something big, incredible, and pathological was taking place in this small room. The guy who sat on the wheelchair, who had his quality of life damaged by almost hundred percent; now was demanding me to go out there, and get this job for myself. And as far as I was concerned, I put him in the wheelchair.

I started to suspect that Greg was not in his right mind. I was curious to know, why he sounded crazy; because of his blood alcohol level, or because of his recent traumatic experience.

Still I had to go through this. I wanted more practical advice.

"So Greg, how should I do this?" -I asked.

"Very simple. You just tell him, that you are the best candidate for the job, and it would be a stupid mistake for them to bring some outsider for the job. Don't ask me any more questions, just do it for me, will you? Good night now." He began to laugh again. "You made me laugh. I haven't laughed like this for a long time now. You thought I wanted the job, me in my Rolls-Royce wheelchair?" I could hear his invasive cackle echo in my head long after I left the room.

Chapter 7

1

The next day I was sitting in front of Professor Fisher's large messy desk across from Fisher himself. This was in an attempt to make good on my promise to Greg. I knew it would be hard and that I would be nervous. But I did not know I would go completely mute. Dr. Fisher was very patient, looking at me with obvious curiosity. But when a whole minute passed and there was no opening statement from my side, he exploded.

"Dr. Letne, the way you barged in my office, I thought you had some important point to make. I remind you that I am a very busy man and I'm not here to revisit your past."

His nose was turning red quickly, which meant his level of anger could reach a fury any second in the immediate future. Maybe his last words made me more aware of why I was before him. Alertness visited me suddenly and the next thing I knew I was talking. I was doing Greg a favor. I was in the process of demanding something from my boss, from the man who could very easily withhold my future from me with all the achievements that would come with it.

"Dr. Fisher, this is about that job. I was told it's still available. Is that right?" I heard a voice of a very confident man.

"Yes, it is," was the answer of a very surprised looking professor. "But I thought I made it perfectly clear that nobody from the new graduates is under consideration."

"Dr. Fisher, I think you are making a big mistake." It was I who said that and it was a piece of cake. I was not sweating, nor was I trembling. I was decisively aggressive. I was stupid.

THE BALANCING GAME

With widely open eyes, and an even wider open mouth, Dr. Fisher now appeared more amused than insulted.

"Doctor, let me understand this. Are you telling me that I'm making a mistake?"

"Yes, I believe so Dr. Fisher. I was brought up in this place as a thinking psychiatrist. I acquired values that I cherish dearly. Whatever I have and will do, I attribute to this place and to the people I blindly followed, and I mean you Sir. I also learned to tell people I greatly respect and admire, what's on my mind. You deserve this much from me. That's why as a sign of great respect to you, I demand your consideration of two people for that job."

My near-sighted speech brought me the result of great short-term satisfaction, which also by all probability would be disastrous for me in a long run.

Dr. Fisher continued to look amazed. He gazed around the room in astonishment, almost like he hoped someone else was in the room to witness this moment. He did not interrupt me and let me finish my courageous, but silly speech. Then he became curious.

"Doctor, I just wonder, who would you think should be considered for the job? Could you name names?"

"The first person will be Dr. Greg Entel. Just because he can't walk, it shouldn't mean, he won't make a brilliant professor. I strongly believe he is the best you can get for the job."

Dr. Fisher was quiet for a few seconds. This was a good sign. I thought I made him think. At least he was not furious, as I envisioned he would be.

"And who will be the other one, whose consideration you demand?" He asked.

"As a second choice, I request that you reconsider my candidacy. I might not be as bad an option as you think after all. I earned this consideration."

I could leave now. I did this favor to Greg. I would not know the consequences of this irresponsible action yet, but I was not really thinking about consequences. I was just happy that I went through this whole ordeal.

I stood up and took a close look at Dr. Fisher. He was not moving.

"Dr. Fisher I might continue to shock you with my last statement. I won't apologize to you for my loudly pronounced beliefs. Because, I think it was you, who taught me not to apologize for my loud thoughts, as long they were coming from my heart. And these thoughts Sir, I can assure you come straight from my heart."

I gave Dr. Fisher an opportunity for rebuttal, but with considerable surprise, I noticed no anger in him at all. He even sounded like he was rationalizing his actions for me. This was very unusual. I expected nothing of this kind.

"Your loud thoughts are well taken Doctor. Now you have to listen to my loud thoughts. I want to be as frank with you, as you were with me. Dr. Greg Entel is the best man we can get for this job. And I don't care if he is in a wheelchair, or on respirator, as long as he can issue some kind cognizable signs of life. You see we agree with you on this one. But forget it. This is impossible."

I wondered what Dr. Fisher meant by impossible.

Dr. Fisher was a tall man. And when he walked around the desk and stopped beside me, I realized I had to look up to him in order to listen to him. And he demanded the attention.

"Now about you Doctor... Some people, and those are people that are participating in the decision-making process myself included, don't think you are a suitable candidate for the position. For whatever reason, known or unknown, things changed recently... not in your favor."

Then he turned around, went back to his chair, sat on it, and without looking at me said something that could not mean much to me.

"Doctor, your papers aren't in the garbage yet. I might take another look at them."

THE BALANCING GAME

My audience with the man had concluded. Dr. Fisher did not say this. Nobody really announced it. Dr. Fisher just forgot about my presence. He went directly to a phone call.

I left the office with a satisfactory feeling of accomplishment. Not because I significantly improved my chances to better my future. It was obvious, there was no chance that I would get the job. My satisfaction was derived mostly from accomplishing the mission, doing the favor itself.

2

I got home early that day. Maybe because I had a terrible headache. Two tablets of Tylenol helped me with remarkable swiftness. They took away the pulsating pain that was making my head heavy and uncomfortable to carry around. But still nothing could remove the burden that I carried with me.

And the day was not done yet. There was one more little thing to digest that night... a telephone call from Greg. He did not say much. He just said "thank you" and hung up. The call was short and strange. It was very creepy. I do not remember me telling Greg, when I'd be meeting with Dr. Fisher. Something very super-natural hung in the air, full of mystique. How the hell did Greg know I talked to Dr. Fisher, and why didn't he ask about the discussion itself? What was Greg's plan? So far, the plan looked disconcerting and I was an active participant, a pawn, in this larger game.

Heavy thoughts tired me soon. I decided not to try to solve the puzzle that Greg created specifically for me that night. I just had to let things flow in their natural course, or whatever way the prime mover steered them.

3

For the next few weeks, my major preoccupation was checking my mailbox. A terrible fear of being unemployed in a few months, was hanging over my head. I was definitely panicking. In six weeks to be exact, my super-training was over. My studying would end at last. There would be nothing more left for any university to teach me. It was up to life to take it from there. Somehow I got carried away with the overwhelming problems that I had no control over.

Soon I would have to leave my place, which became my security blanket during my fellowship years. I became familiar with thoughts of me being without a place to stay and without pocket money for food.

I was also about to lose my fellowship stipend, which was by no means a great sum of money, but was enough to keep my basic needs satisfied. It was not that I was afraid to stay unemployed forever. The mailbox was full of letters, all kinds of them. But they were not the ones, I was waiting for. And I was still frightened and defiantly unwilling to take a job out of necessity.

It's amazing how things work out sometimes. You look in front of you, thinking that things you are waiting for, should come from somewhere within your field of vision. And you are completely taken by surprise, when they come from another direction.

The answer for my future problems came from my past. It happened.

The time came for me to take a job, any kind job. The first offer that I have received, I had to accept it. I had to survive. But it turned out; that the job I took was the one that I dreamed for many years. A rare combination of need and desire united to play things my way. Well it happened to me.

About two weeks after that dreadful audience with Dr. Fisher, I received a letter from his office. Considering the nature of the

THE BALANCING GAME

conversation I had with him, I had a pretty good idea what the letter would be about. Therefore, when I read Dr. Fisher's name on the envelope, I threw the letter to the garbage basket immediately, without even opening it. Being exceptional at the game I had entitled trashball, I was surprised that Dr. Fisher's letter missed the basket, and instead, ended up in the corner, under a small table. This was kind of a tease. This missed letter, deserved to be read.

I got down on all fours like an animal to recover the letter and after retrieving, I opened and read it.

This letter was not a rejection letter. It was offering me the job.

I took this long dreamed fantasy job with remarkable calm. And this shocked me. It was like a person that is about to be executed, pleading for mercy, for his life, and suddenly when the mercy is granted and he is informed about it, he becomes numb. He finds out the terrible truth. He is not happy at all. Maybe he did not value his life all that much.

Suddenly I was an unhappy man. Or maybe I was a pig asking and dreaming for something so badly, but upon getting it, I spat on it with my inappropriate emotions. Then I saw a reflection in the mirror. This creature was kneeling down holding a letter in his hands, very close to his face. I knew that somebody was me.

I forced myself to get up, and as I assumed an erect posture, I experienced an extraordinary pleasurable rush. The success was reaching me now from inside my body and soul. The language was very loud and shameless. I experienced the highest degree of the ultimate pleasure of life. The climax itself... was something like an orgasm, only of a higher caliber of joy, much higher. The interesting thing was, it didn't happen until I straightened up onto two feet and reclaimed my human posture.

Dr. Fisher's letter was very official and very formal. It also was very instructive. Dr. Fisher was informing me that after careful and extensive consideration, the department of psychiatry decided to choose my candidacy over many other applicants, for an assistant professor's position in clinical advanced psychiatry. Then there were the standard congratulatory elements and a few words on the faculty's excitement about welcoming me to the team. You cannot just lift the whole world. There will be neither you, nor your world for you.

I started to walk from one room to another. A few times my pacing ritual took me to the bathroom. I did not stop walking; I felt that I had to talk to somebody. I often feel the urgency to share monumental events with somebody, whether the event is good or bad. And this message was a big one because it was granting me a sunny spot in the world. That is why the next thing I knew; I stood in front of the mirror talking to Dr. Al Letne.

"Doctor, I feel different. I feel respectable now. I feel like somebody just opened a door for me and invited me in a VIP room to society's elite. I feel like somebody standing by the door is announcing my entrance. He calls my name. Then he reassures everybody, that nobody should be scared of me because I'm not sick anymore. I successfully cured myself from some contagious infectious disease."

One thing was getting to me. "They are letting me in." I said. Then after a long pause, a person from the mirror, resembling me, looked at me with respect and congratulated me;

"Congratulations, Dr. Letne. You are a big man now."

"Thank you, Doctor."

4

In two weeks, all the necessary papers were signed. I officially became what I dreamed of for the last two years. Most of my friends and acquaintances were happy for me. People that I disliked congratulated me anyway. That was not easy for them. I could see and feel, an obvious discomfort emanating from them while they were performing the congratulatory act. One faceless and nameless competitor asked me, how did it feel, taking away something of this magnitude, that which did not belong to me.

On my way to maturation, from boyhood to adulthood, I learned a few important lessons in life: I learned how to cross the streets of New York City, the capital of the world, how to survive and scrounge for the bare necessities, and I also learned how to live with all kinds of people, and all kinds of negativity directed towards me. It is amazing when we discover the depths and the reserves of human patience and adaptation we possess to survive.

With time, things would cool off in my favor. And this in combination with my prestigious status would put things in proper prospective. I always thought that success could act as an antidote to the animosity around me.

Now that I lost my fear of uncertainty for my future, I was again surprised by how this much awaited and welcomed success failed to deliver inner peace. Maybe because that place in my mind was already occupied by a more powerful presence than peace, by guilt. Peace cannot reside in your head as long as guilt is there. I came to this realization; that peace and guilt had problems coexisting, and this smelled like qualitative trouble not only for my present, but for my future too.

Shortly after signing all the necessary papers, I assumed my new position and the responsibilities that came along with those papers. I made rounds with students, residents, and fellows. It was a little awkward in the beginning being the boss over the very group of people I was so recently a member of. But I understood perfectly. Every group of people needs a teacher and a leader. And I would fill that role for them from now on.

A few times a week, I delivered lectures on different topics. Twice a week I would see my private patients in my small but cozy office. I could not dare to dream of doing anything better than this for a living. At night, I did extra reading and writing. The Department of Advanced

Psychiatry expected me to increase my number of publications. For a while, I forgot my private life. In fact, I did not maintain a social life. There was no woman around me to share my thoughts, my feelings, or my bed. But I understood very well that there were priorities in life, and at that particular time, my private life had to stay in line.

About Greg- I forgot him, or I thought I forgot him. A simple telephone call from Greg, a month after I started the new job, reminded me how little I had forgotten. The way this call affected me, bringing back all kinds of hidden philosophical anxieties, I realized how firmly chained I was to this immobile person that just would not go away.

Greg asked me to visit him. Of course, I agreed before I realized what I said or even thought about it because the answer was instinctive. Again, I was scared. When things are beyond your control, you can do little to affect your own destiny.

Greg's call shook me up. With his first words, I heard the rattling noise that chains make, when unpolished links of steel violently clang with other equally unsavory steel links. I tried to freeze my body, and by doing so, I hoped to decrease not only an amplitude of my motion, but also the pain, noise, and suffering, that result from the moving chains. I continued to breath, but even this was a luxury that I tried to limit.

The call came in the depths of the night, when my sleep was soundest; when my REM was at its peak.

"Al, this is Greg, your best friend." That is what Greg's voice said. It was *his* timing, *his* style, and *his* sound.

"Greg, are you all right?" I asked in anticipation of something upsetting. I prepared myself for the call that a soldier gets at dawn, when duty calls for him to activate and serve his country.

"I'm not alright Al. I don't want to lie to you."

"Anything I can do to help?" I asked.

"I think you can do something for me and I know you will."

"What is it? Tell me."

"You can't do this in absentia Al. I need your physical presence for the thing I want you to do for me."

"So when do you want me to be in your place?" I asked without giving it a thought that I could have plans made for tonight. Even if I had plans, I knew I would change those plans to accommodate him.

"At eight tonight."

"Okay, at eight tonight," I repeated.

Only after I hung up the phone did I remember that I did have to change my plans for tonight. This was going to be my first date in quite some time. A few people at the hospital set me up with a woman whose image was decorated with glowing referrals. I liked what I was hearing about her from the several people that knew her. I also liked her telephone voice and what that voice was promising me.

But we change things in life, plans included. I hope my blind date would never find out I had to drop her for another blind date; and it was not even a woman, not really; unless Fate is a woman.

5

I do not know if it is normal to dream at night and recall it in the morning with amazing accuracy, but this happens to me often, quite often.

Mr. Dreamer woke up with a heavy head. He realized this when he tried to lift it. It was the same kind of heaviness that a previous night's alcohol abuse brings the next morning. This was the kind of discomfort that invariably is included in hangover syndrome.

But Mr. Dreamer did not drink last night. In fact, he did not drink the night before that either. The last time he consumed alcohol of some significant amount was at his high school prom. That was years ago.

There was some other addiction forming stimulator Mr. Dreamer was addicted to: dreams, constant dreams, all kinds of them, small and big, good and bad, night and day. At night while asleep, he would dream about anything that he wanted to be in real life or anything he wished to have.

His favorite dream was to be the king of the night. With remarkable persistence and luck, he would have no problem seeing himself in this role. All he had to do to become a king at night was, to retire to his bed with his king sized mattress and fall asleep.

And then he could become a king, just like that. He would surround himself, with those advisers around him. He would go to war to restore his country's pride. He would issue decrees that would improve his people's quality of life. He would try to provide them with food, clean air, and shelter; under which, they would be safely protected from all kinds of insults, be it from nature or fellow human beings. He would also help his people get a good education. Those who could learn would be sent to the best schools to get the best education for free and those who were good with their hands would be provided with adequate and respectable jobs.

Mr. Dreamer would not forget to treat himself as kings are treated. He would be accompanied with a good-looking, royal, and loyal noble wife. He would also surround himself with a few other young and beautiful female companions. His "live and let live" attitude was very obvious in his daily royal life.

In short, at night he was a real king, maybe for just a few hours. But it did not really matter. "Big things are always short lived," he would say. What mattered for him was that he was happy. Every day he had something to look forward to. He was waiting for that time every night, that moment he could assume his royal responsibilities.

Significant numbers of normal people would go to sleep just to retire from their daily burdens and in so doing get away from their bodies and minds for a few hours. They would accomplish this by being unconscious about real life. With Mr. Dreamer, sleep was somewhat different. He had a night shift job.

But nothing is ever perfect for anybody. And there was a little problem in the other half of Mr. Dreamer's life. Dreams would occupy his mind during the whole entire day. His head would become a loading dock for all kinds of dreams. There was not a real favorite one Mr. Dreamer would single out and strive to make come true. Maybe that is why while he was successful and in command in his dream-world, he never really took off from the earthly ground.

He was like a hot air balloon that needed to unload cargo to maintain its flight. From time to time, some objects had to be discarded in order to cut down the balloon's weight. Mr. Dreamer had a problem. He loved his dreams very much. "Those are like my children. I created them. I gave them life. I nourished them. How can I get rid of them?" He would rationalize with himself about the need to keep them close to him.

So he lived the way he lived. In the daytime, he was nobody that wanted to be somebody. And at nighttime he was that somebody. One part was real. The other one was not.

But he was content. He was in harmony.

Chapter 8

1

I went to see him that same evening. This time I drove to his place in my own car, courtesy of my much-improved financial situation. I did not have a problem finding the place. It was an August evening and somehow an unusual cold front was beginning to reveal itself in a fresh and chilly way. The door of the side of the house was unlocked. After a few taps on the door and receiving no answer; I gently shoved the door to gain entrance to Greg's place.

In a matter of seconds I found myself in an already familiar room, dark lit only by the city's neon lights that stretched into Greg's space. Greg was sitting in a corner of the room, conveniently closer to the table. The position enabled him to reach for bottles of vodka that looked like drunk marching soldiers. Actually, there were so many bottles that it looked like Greg collected them. The window was widely open, just like last time. And the light was not switched on, also just like last time. Somehow, even in the depth of the summer, the place managed to feel cold.

Greg did not respond verbally to my greeting. He just lifted his right hand, with a glass of vodka in it, and drank the whole thing in one gulp. By doing so, he acknowledged my arrival and welcomed me. Greg looked glad or at least more emotional about my visit. I could sense his enthusiasm by observing few extra involuntary movements he made with his body.

"Sit down Al. There is a chair for you." His voice was not the voice of an intoxicated person. His speech was well controlled and his words did not fail him. But the way he kept pouring alcohol in his system, it was only a matter of time before the body and mind would give into alcohol's whispering sweet nothings.

Soon I was sitting on quite a comfortable chair, right in front of the open window. With an unpleasant realization, I noticed that I could not afford to feel at home in this place. And not because this was not my home, but because it reminded me too much of where I came from and I did not want complacency to settle in. I did not hide my shivering, maybe because I could not.

"So Greg how are you doing?"

The courteous query was all I could manage.

"I'm doing just fine Al." With these words he reached out his hand to give me a small glass full of vodka.

"Al take this, it's not really hot. It's not August in here. This will warm you up."

After a few seconds of consuming alcohol, I felt temporarily warmer and more relaxed. I could see Greg's profile; his shadow on the wall was sitting on the wheelchair and holding a glass of vodka in his hand.

After a few minutes, Greg started to appear impatient. He wanted to know how I was doing. He was becoming annoyed and demanding.

"Al, tell me how are you doing? Tell me everything, Al. Have mercy. I don't really get much information here."

"I'm doing fine Greg. By the way, I never really thanked you for that favor you asked me to do. I really don't know what happened, but as you probably know, I got the job." Greg's degree of participation in me getting my job, as I would realize later, would turn out to be greater than I originally thought.

"How is the job?" He asked me with a sad voice. That was easily explainable. The job he was asking about should have been his; but it was not.

"It's fine Greg. Are you sure that's what you want to talk about?" I tried to avoid this touchy topic. "Maybe we could talk about something else?"

"Like what Al? You know we don't really have much to talk about. Remember? We come from two completely different worlds. So what would we possibly talk about?"

"Then may I ask you, why am I here? You didn't call me here just to tell me how different our backgrounds are." I was curious. There was something Greg was building up to and I was anxious to know what he brought me here to ask of me.

"What is it? What you want me to do?" I did not sound like I had any reservations about doing him another favor.

"Are you sure you'll be comfortable doing me a favor? Are you really sure Al?"

"Yes I am," was my firm answer.

"You're right. I didn't call you to remind you where you come from. I called you because I want to ask you a really a big favor." Now he was collected, confident, and authoritative.

My heart started to palpitate. Cold sweats covered most of my skin. Another favor? Last time I had to do him a favor, I ended up almost screaming at my boss, at a person with the power to destroy my life, if he so desired. My heart rate slowed down considerably after remembering, that as a direct consequence of that favor, I gained much more than I lost.

"I can handle this, what is it? Give it to me straight."

"Listen Al." He was slow in talking and appeared depressed. I could tell that whatever he was about to say, was very painful for him. "I'm having a tough time nowadays, getting adjusted to my new life. I thought I could handle anything. And with time, I will probably be fine. But right now, I have to live with what I am. I had to do some thinking about what I'm going to do with my new life. Things changed a lot around me. Accordingly I should make changes myself. These changes will affect my relationships with people; both those that are close and those that are distant. Fortunately, I didn't have many close people around me. But there is one person I want you to help me to get rid off. I do need your help in this Al."

I had no idea what he was talking or whom he was talking about. "Greg I think you need more support and understanding now, more than you ever needed before. But listen, you are the boss of your head. You know what you are doing. The only thing is Greg, when you said to get rid off somebody, you didn't really mean... something terminal?" I expressed my legitimate concern. You never know what is in an emotionally disturbed person's head.

"Relax Al. Don't start killing anybody just yet. Nobody did anything so terrible to justify murder. The death sentence is the ultimate punishment. What I'm about to ask for has nothing to do with crime at all. In fact, it has something to do with pleasure- a lot of it."

The shot of vodka I ingested was probably my fifth. So when I heard the favor Greg wanted me to do for him, I met it with a relatively clear head. But, my stomach started to act up, giving rise to all those chemical reactions that eventually might cause actual vomiting.

"Al, just listen. Don't try to understand me. You have to be on this wheelchair to understand me. So, just listen and don't try to make any smart remarks. I don't need them." Greg's self-control was melting by the second. There was a detectable crack in his voice.

"Greg, just tell me what you want me to do, and I'll do it." I was set up and ready. This was another brief moment of peace; knowing that I was again about to help Greg, once again psychologically alleviating the guilt, but once again only temporarily.

"You remember Mary, your prize for winning the little competition we had? Now here is what I want you to do for me. I want you to collect your prize tonight. I want you to do this favor for me Al. Don't even think about excuses. You'll do this for me Al. That will help me a lot. I want to be alone Al. I just can't handle her being here every day. I can't throw her out. I don't have enough strength to do this emotionally or physically. She just won't leave. Al you have to help me. You have to. I can't carry her around. I don't want to be loved. That luxury is too much of a burden for me. It's too much pressure."

Greg was not as emotional as I would expect from somebody delivering this monologue. His sentences were well formulated, and his words carefully chosen. And oddly enough, the idea and the message were delivered with clarity.

I did not throw up. The chain of chemical reactions was interrupted at some level, causing severe nausea, but no actual vomiting. There were severe tremors, but no actual earthquake.

I could not understand him. How could I, a walking person at the peak of my life, flying so high, understand somebody who came down from even greater heights, who even after landing on his two feet, ended up on this wheelchair. He had a right to be left alone, without somebody hovering over him, making his life more miserable.

"And how do you suppose that might happen Greg?" Suddenly with cool precision, my voice was asking a very practical question.

"Very easy Al. You'll be surprised how easy it could be to screw a beautiful woman; unless you're crippled like I am; sitting on a wheelchair. Al, just tell me you're going through with this."

Greg knew my answer already. The rest was just plain psychology; preparing me mentally and most importantly preparing himself for one of the cruelest moments he had to endure. And suddenly I realized what Greg was trying to do; by making me to go to bed with his loved one, he was counting on this extreme measure to help him hate a woman he loved so much. He knew that somewhere near his love for her, hate resided. And if he could just manage to cross that invisible bridge from love to hate, powerful energy could be created, capable of doing extraordinary things. Then he could leave her.

I did not have to think much. I knew that he needed help and he was asking me to do him a favor. I knew that I had to deliver. I also knew that I would. After all, nobody was asking me to sleep with a cow or an elephant. We were talking about Mary, whose nude silhouette still made me blush.

"Greg, if that's what it takes to help you, that's what I'm going to do. I'm not questioning your motives Greg. You probably thought about this enough."

"Thank you Al. I knew I could count on you." He sounded reservedly glad now. His hand with the glass was lowered and somehow tilted. I even saw and heard sounds of spilling alcohol on the floor. This was a distressing scene to watch: a man terribly beaten by life, trying to reorganize his new life by destroying the closest things he possessed; his job, his love, and his self-respect. On his way to freedom, the way I understood it, he stood to lose something more in addition; not only as a person, but as a man as well.

"She should be here any minute now and please Al, don't drink any more alcohol. Save yourself. Somebody in this room should be able to perform."

I did not know about performance anxiety. I never had any problem before. But this situation might be different; I never did a favor for somebody by screwing his girlfriend in front of him.

For another ten minutes or so, we did not even exchange a word. There was just the silent breathing of two men heavily preoccupied with their problems and the liveliness of the August evening. In a way, those two men were conversing with their silence... that no one could understand but each other.

I took Greg's advice and did not pour any more vodka in my stomach. I rarely drink too much, except in stressful situations, and by definition this was a stressful situation.

2

The harmonic symphony of silence was rudely interrupted when someone opened the door without knocking and entered the room.

That somebody was very much female and very shapely as well. Without saying anything or expressing any kind of emotion to the stranger in the room, as far as I could make out in semi-darkness, she went straight for Greg, bent over and tried to hug him, after kissing him on the lips. I could see Greg starting to pull away. She was not giving up. She made an attempt to follow his squirming body by throwing herself on top of him. Again, he tried to escape and in the process began shoving her away.

I had to witness all this. It made me incredibly uncomfortable. Inevitably, my lack of control over the situation was making me frustrated. It took a simple comparison of my situation to Greg's for me to relax. I remembered what Greg planned to witness and endure. My "discomfort" now felt like a pleasant trip.

"Stop this Mary. We're not alone". I heard Greg's voice. "You remember Al, don't you?" Greg's voice cracked a little or so it seemed to me. Maybe I just heard it that way. He definitely did not sound like a man who had everything under control. Mary turned around and now she was looking in my direction.

"Oh, Al. Sure I remember Al. This is the guy who is specializing in replacing you." She sounded very sarcastic. She had every right to be. Her voice was full of anger and bitterness. "Why are you here Al? What do you want?"

"Hi Mary." I managed to say , but that was all I could muster. By now I realized that despite the cold temperature in the room, I was sweating profusely through my undershirt.

"Al is here for two reasons Mary." Greg's voice was monotonous and very sincere.

"Then let me guess, Greg, let me guess." In contrast with Greg's voice, her voice was more colorful. There were a lot of vibration in her tone and a lot of emotional charge in her voice. "So Al wants to know, how you are doing. Is that why he's here? Greg is doing fine Al. No thanks to you."

THE BALANCING GAME

"That's not the only reason Al is here, Mary." Greg sounded like a businessman now, who wanted to close the deal he has set up.

"Okay. Now let me take another guess, Greg. So far I was successful in reading his mind. He apologized, feels guilty and offers you help. Anything he can do for you he'll do, or so he tells you now. But for all this time he not only was hiding from you; get this, he was busy taking over and doing your job." Mary was extremely hostile to me. That was obvious. But whenever she would turn her face to Greg's, she was full of warmth and love. That was even more obvious.

"Mary, Al didn't come here to apologize. He has done nothing to apologize for. He didn't come here to see if he can help. I don't expect him to do that. He owes me nothing. In fact we are the ones that owe him something. And he came here to collect that something." Greg made sure Mary heard his last sentence, and made sure she was looking at him.

"Greg, we owe him nothing. He can go to hell." She continued to speak to Greg as if I wasn't even there.

"We just can't just send him to hell, Mary. Me and you; we owe this guy something."

"I don't remember you mentioning any debt to this son of a bitch. And me, I don't remember me promising him anything." Mary was screaming now, saturating the already dramatic scene with more tension. This was too much for me to digest. My stomach was sending me signals, growling and turning. Suddenly Mary stopped screaming, like she remembered something and apparently she did. Then she approached me really closely. With all the light the room was offering, she took really a good look at me.

"You son of a bitch. You didn't really come to collect your night, did you?" She asked me directly.

"Yes I did," I answered equally directly. I could not believe I said that or that I had said it with such poise and confidence. I rose to the occasion. I picked up where Greg left off. He needed help and he got it from me. We played these adult-games and this room was too small to disappoint Greg, whether his motives were childish and naïve or calculated appropriately. And all this was happening in front of my wide-open eyes.

"I always wanted to know what a son of a bitch looks like. I always wanted to know what you people breathe. I already know how you people act and what you say." She stopped looking at me. Natural darkness prevented this calling; of learning the anatomy of a son of a bitch.

She went to Greg and pleaded with him with whispers, but his heart had hardened and he was resolute in that this is what he wanted. I could see her rationalizing his decision in her head. Perhaps, she wanted to honor his wager, the last wager of the man she once knew… or perhaps she felt his frustration by his inability to have sex with her, so she needed to do this for him.

So, reluctantly she went to the bed. The small bed was quietly playing a role as a very important character in the upcoming event. She sat down on it. Her head was down almost to the point where her chin was leaning on her chest. She looked like a high school girl, who was about to learn a heartbreaking lesson. That not just life and fate, but people are also capable of causing great pain. Often, the people you love can hurt you infinitely more than those you hate. This was a valuable lesson. The degree of value was very high, but so was the degree of pain, hurt, and humiliation. Each of us makes decisions every single day; based on our beliefs, judgment, and advice that our heart directs. And she made hers.

She did not look like she was thrilled about what was about to happen. Her semi-shadow looked uncomfortable and her breathing sounded confused. Then I saw her get up and take off her coat, signaling that she was going to participate. The time and situation called for my more active participation, than merely sitting and watching her undress. That was not why I was called here. And I responded. I got up. And trying not to look towards Greg, I approached Mary.

THE BALANCING GAME

She was standing by the bed. I could hear her shivering; and not necessarily because she was lightly dressed or the room was very cold. In a second, my coat was lying beside hers. After relieving myself from the coat that was so necessary in this environment, the cold was hitting me hard; and everything looked real.

I made the first move. I pulled her down towards me. Close enough to touch her face with my lips, and my chest contacting hers. Then she stepped back. With a quick movement, she pulled up her dress and what I thought she did, took off her underwear. I could see it landing on my coat, negligently finding itself in the corner of the bed. In a few seconds, she was in the bed. I did not really know what clothing was still clinging to her body, but I knew for sure that only a thin blanket was between her as a woman and me as a man. The blanket was not meant to be an obstacle to performance and it did not prove to be an obstacle. Soon I was under it, and on her.

The bed fortunately turned out to be the least lit area in the room. This little lucky gift was greatly appreciated by me. We could not really see each other. But looking is the last thing you are expected to do and darkness was not impediment to performance.

Suddenly, the word performance gave me an idea that could save face in my eyes. I proceeded immediately. I managed to pull my pants and underwear down. I could feel how my shameless sexual organ awoke, feeling a woman's body, especially one this attractive so very close to it. It is amazing how low a degree of consideration our primitive physiology possesses. Even in this kind of psychologically charged atmosphere, there was no hesitation of any kind, from my most aggressive organ to indulge in the anticipated pleasure.

Her legs were widely spread; I started to look for her right hand. I found it far from my body, somewhere beside her head. I tried to pull it down. She resisted. But with a little more force, I eventually succeeded. I positioned her hand in a manner that would cover her vaginal entry to her body. Now I could lean against it, or against her body. This was what

I meant by performing. My hard, and angrily disappointed member, had no way to have its way. To my surprise she picked up the idea of the performance piece, with remarkable quickness, and made sure, that there would not be any actual intercourse.

Suddenly I was hearing this woman so close to me moaning. It sounded exactly like I would have imagined making love to her would have sounded, had all gone smoothly. I had to follow her lead now. I could not just lie on her, without making any kind of noise, without making any kind of movement.

With my body on hers, with my sexual organ pressed against a fully open Mary's palm, assurance was obtained that this heavy, wet foreplay would not end up with a home run for my aggressive member. This actually was fulfilling dual functions: policing my key and at the same time, covering her lock; and by so doing, we minimized the chances for temptation on both sides.

An unbelievable thing was taking place in this room. The survival instinct of our morality was taking charge in this bed; where there was very little distance and time to cover from good abstinence to sinister pleasure, from the joy of self-respect, to the degradation of succumbing to temptation.

We were dancing like lovers and we were singing like lovers. With this going on and without any guilt in our heads, I felt relieved. She also appeared relaxed. Her body no longer felt tense to my touch. I was finding this out as I would accidentally, or not so accidentally, fondle her breasts, or other accessible parts of her body, not covered by clothing.

There was no perception of time, place, or even Greg for us. That is why, when we heard Greg's awakening scream, we needed some effort to come out from a different world and taste reality.

"That's enough! Stop it!" Greg shouted with desperation in his voice. "The rest- you can do somewhere else!" I completely forgot about him. Maybe because there is a limit in the mind, as to how many people your brain can think about at the same time.

It is like saving two desperate people from drowning. You cannot save them both at the same time. In a split second, you choose somebody closer to your soul and body and try to save that person first and forget about the other one for awhile. While you are saving the first person, you should pretend there is no second person. It was clear to me that on this occasion, I certainly chose to save myself. And I succeeded. I did not have to wash my body with lye to get clean.

Greg was demanding attention. He got it with little delay on our part. It was not easy to get in under the blanket. It was harder to come out of the blanket. But whenever our attention was given to Greg, it was certainly complete.

"I want you out of here right now. You sons of bitches. Leave me alone immediately." Already on our feet and fully clothed again, we stood there and listened to his tirade for a few seconds. Mary tried to calm him down. His whole plan was to make himself angry- very angry. He wanted to be angry enough to execute his decision. Now, we had to leave him immediately. We did just that.

3

We left the place in a real hurry. Greg's screaming voice followed us for awhile. I was leading the way. Mary followed me obediently. In no time, I was in my car, with closed eyes and behind the wheel. It took about a minute until I could think or speak logically.

But soon, I was collected enough to realize the importance of what had happened. I turned around, when I noticed Mary's presence in the car. I opened my eyes, switched on the lights and looked at her. She was quiet, very much preoccupied with her own thoughts, but she also was very beautiful. I had seen a head similar to this one in my imagination, when I put it on her beautiful body.

"God, Mary you look good." I could not help admitting that, though I knew; this was not the time, mood, or place for complimenting her appearance. This was the first time I had a prolonged opportunity to evaluate her looks. I do not remember exactly what struck me most; her long hair, or maybe her blue eyes, or her lips, the innocently protruded lips of a disappointed child. What I remember for sure was that I was taken by the looks of a woman with whom I shared quite an intimate experience. And only now had I the opportunity, to notice this womanly woman.

She said nothing- just looked at me with inspecting observation and returned her head to its previous position, facing forward. She was in the process of recognizing that there would be no Greg in her future. This understanding, coupled with the dark sky and empty streets, were not encouraging signs for her immediate future, from where she was sitting.

Her silence and preoccupation were contagious. I lost my appetite to talk. And like always, when you don't talk, you think, especially when you have so many thoughts to sort out. This particular night offered a tremendous amount of quality material to analyze.

The night was really remarkable, I admitted to myself with a calmness that surprised me. In a matter of a few minutes, I staged the whole night's scenes in detail, in my head. Soon I was ready to draw conclusions. They were obnoxiously pleasant.

The night was a complete success. The main objective was achieved. Whatever had to be done was done. Whatever had to be achieved was achieved. Of course there were a series of ugly scenes that took place, but the long-term ramifications of the events went as well as it could have and everybody delivered with flying colors.

All three of us participants, were beneficiaries of this costly success. Greg got what he wanted, his freedom. Even though he sacrificed a lot of his valuables, he came up unhappy, but still a winner. Considering what he obtained tonight, we could conclude; his calculated investment paid off.

Even Mary, although she looked traumatized, upset, and severely depressed, in the long run, she could only benefit from departing Greg. For a twenty-three year old, gorgeous, naïve, yet intelligent girl, she would eventually realize Greg was not much of a future. Fortunately for her, she was cruelly beaten by life, so her future would not be negatively affected with her senseless commitments to unnecessary obligations.

And as for me, I was supposed to be happy just doing a big favor for Greg, and serving my mind with a piece of peace, the thing, that I so desperately needed.

In short, the night was a smashing success. That is what mattered. It is human nature to forget, or to ignore how things are achieved. What is conquered is what actually sticks out for everyone to see, with a lot of colors of honor painted on it.

After I convinced myself that things worked out in everybody's best interests; I felt like my body became much lighter… just like the last time, after doing my first favor for Greg.

I am still not sure how long we sat in that car. At some point, practical reality had to return to us and when it did, I asked her where she lived.

"Eighty-second and Broadway," she answered. She still continued to stay in her trance.

This was on my way. The drive was uneventful. While driving, no thoughts or words were exchanged. Soon we got to Mary's place. I pulled the car in front of the building.

"Is this the place?" I asked.

"Yes" she said. But that was all she did. She did not move or demonstrate any sign of leaving the car in the immediate future.

"Al, do you think Greg believed that we actually did it?" She asked a few seconds later. She continued to torture herself, searching for rationalizations and not finding any.

"Does it matter?" I tried to downplay the night's significance. There was no benefit for any party involved to relive what was lost; when we were forced to leave the past behind.

"Do you think we fooled him?" She insisted.

"Apparently and fortunately- yes," I said.

Mary was not in a hurry to move on. She remained far from the real world. That is why she was so far from Greg.

"Al, Can you take me back to Greg? I don't want him to be alone, not after what happened tonight. I want to tell him; there was nothing between me and you- that nothing actually happened. I know how important this is for him."

"Mary, are you crazy? Don't you realize, after what he witnessed today, he would never want to see you again? Besides maybe this was his way to get rid off you." The truth, the cruel truth, was brutally delivered.

"What are you talking about? Why on earth, would he want to get rid off me? I am the only one he has left!"

"Mary, Greg is desperately trying to build his new world, where he will feel comfortable. Don't you think he is entitled to his place, the way he sees it?"

A few minutes silence calmed her down. She had no questions left to ask. Now she remembered that it was time to go home. That obviously scared her.

"I don't feel like staying alone. Could you come up and spend some time in my place?"

"Of course." I did not want her to stay alone either. Her emotional state was not giving me any clue about whether she might try something foolish. It was a good idea to accompany her, while she was returning home with a completely new outlook on life. She had to endure unpleasant thoughts and residual memories of terrible experiences that the last few hours of her life brought her.

Her room was much smaller than mine. It barely had enough space to hold a simple table, two chairs, and a small bed. We sat at the table and she started to talk. She told me about her rich and obnoxiously pompous parents. She mentioned how ashamed she felt, when they would come to her college campus to visit her. They would proudly tell her friends about the wealth they possessed, about the cars they were driving, about employees they employed and how important it was to be tough on them, so they would always know who was in charge.

She continued her angry and rebellious rant and I listened. Then she continued to talk and I was no longer listening. I just couldn't. It was probably very, very late and besides, I had my own thoughts to wrestle with. Eventually she stopped talking. Now I could see her head on the table. She fell asleep. Everything together; her late night, physical and emotional exhaustion took over. I managed somehow to pick her up and put her in bed. I did not undress her. I thought it was a bad idea.

4

It was two o' clock a.m. before I got back to my place. I was extremely tired. Vivid memories kept me awake. There was one more thing to do. Without doing it, I would not or could not go to sleep. Already in bed, I dialed his number. The telephone rang a few long rings, before it was answered.

"Greg," I said. There was no answer. On the other side of line, somebody was just holding the receiver.

"Greg, this is Al. Are you all right?"

"Of course I'm all right," his sad voice replied. But even so, I was surprised; I was expecting a much sadder tone in his response, considering the things he had to experience a few hours ago.

"Al, how is Mary. How did she take the whole thing?" Despite the caring nature of the question, his voice did not reflect empathy.

"She is a little shaken, but she looks like will be all right."

"I wouldn't worry much about her. She is several years younger than we are. Her wounds will heal faster."

His last statement confused me a lot. I wanted to ask him a few questions, some filled with anger, some saturated with only curiosity. But I was too tired to ask, to listen, or to digest any more explanations. Besides I was not sure if I would get any.

"Good night Greg," I said and prepared to hang up the phone.

"Wait a minute Al. I didn't ask you how you are doing? Sorry I had to use you. I didn't really have much choice."

"I know you didn't."

"Al, I want you to know how much I appreciate what you did for me. You came through for me today."

"Good night Greg," I wanted him to go away. He had no plans of doing that though. It was so easy for me to do this to him. All I had to do was to accidentally drop the phone and than pretend, I was asleep. It just looked easy. It was not easy at all. It was very hard. If I could just do this…

"One more thing Al."

"What is it Greg?" I asked with heavy heart.

"If you just could come and visit me sometime that would be nice Al."

"I will Greg, I will."

"That will be nice. Good luck Al. Now you can go to sleep."

He let me go on his terms, again.

This was one of the longest days in my life. I wanted to close my eyes and in my sleep to see better things and have better experiences. With this in mind, I let a power that was beyond my control take over me. I also let this power take care of me. I was taken far away from heavy thoughts and heavy people. But for only for a few hours. I expected the same power to bring me back to the same heavy thoughts and to the same heavy people.

Chapter 9

1

I like to teach. I get tremendous satisfaction from teaching; I enrich people with knowledge and make them better human beings. Not everybody is up to learning though. Not everyone is born to be taught. That physiological difference is understandable. Human power distribution is such that there is need in many other fields, for those education-haters, or people who prefer physical force over mental calculation.

Here, in this teaching institution, it is assumed that everybody is capable of learning and wants to learn. They are often born privileged, talented, and rich. They were admitted in this elite medical school and could afford to pay the very expensive yearly tuition. Tuition fees for one year is roughly equivalent to the income of an average working family. In short, this is a place for the rich and smart. This was not a place for a poor person or an idiot.

I looked at the auditorium crowd. It was made up of fellows, residents, interns, and medical students, supposedly the smartest group of young people in the country. They proved this to be true going through multiple grueling selection processes that tested them at every turn. Now they came here to learn. And it was me, who was to teach them. I was the teacher and they were the students. This was exciting!

When I sensed the students were ready to listen, I started to talk. I introduced myself as an assistant professor in advanced psychiatry and introduced them to the science of psychiatry.

I asked the audience if anybody knew what psychiatry meant.

Some boyish looking face gave me a correct answer but using incorrect words.

"Psychiatry is the science that deals with the deranged person's behavior and the mood swings of the insane."

The student looked and sounded satisfied. He thought he was right.

I was not satisfied with the imprecision of his answer.

"Saying the right things in the wrong way is still wrong. We all are people, regardless what kind of deranged or crazy things we do. Therefore, our vocabulary shouldn't contain expressions like a crazy or deranged person.

I believe in thinking, discussing, listening, and arguing. I believe that opinions of only those who believe in these kind of things should be heard. I also believe in conversing with myself. This is perfectly sane and normal thing to do, as long as it goes unnoticed. While we have just one face, it definitely has a few sides. Often times, the opinion-making process involves a great deal of consideration. That is when conversing with yourself is logical- to embrace different facets of your personality and come up with the best opinion, the most suitable to your most prominent face.

Talking about different faces and mood changes, I want to discuss a topic that was fascinating to me since my early childhood. Depression and maniacal mood swings are something we all experience in some degree, every single day of our lives. And it's very much considered a normal part of life. It's extreme amplitudes that we consider abnormal and that is what attracts our medical attention."

I was enjoying the thrill of the lecture, but the students could tell I was nervous. But, I continued on anyway to maintain control over the room.

"When I was a kid, I would envy the person who was never in a bad mood. In the same vein, I would pity the person who constantly appeared depressed. I would empathize with these people, without knowing the reasons for their constant good or bad mood.

THE BALANCING GAME

As my maturity arrived and I learned a few things in life, I started to realize that what you see is not an accurate reflection of these observed subjects; you also have to listen to them. I mean, you also have to use all your senses, a combination of looking, touching, smelling, listening to properly analyze their situations to determine the proportions of their emotions.

Who would you rather be? The man... or woman that has everything they want, but at the same time have something unexplainable inside you that makes you unable to appreciate those gifts and thus makes you extremely unhappy all the time or the person that appreciates the nothing that he has?" I asked the question for which I still don't have an answer.

"This person might have to suffer scores of tragedies in life and constant misfortune, but for whatever unexplainable seems happy. People might feel sorry for you, but you wouldn't care because you feel good, really good."

I looked at the listeners and felt that I did indeed get their attention. Now I could proceed. First I asked to bring in Mr. Fred Gansk. He was very energetic, cheerful, and ready to answer my questions without hesitation. In his mid-forties, Mr. Gansk was balding, but in a dignified way and he was well groomed from a clean shave to sharp clothes. He looked like he had everything under control in his life.

Confident and talkative, he sat in front of the class and acted with a briskness that clearly was demonstrative of his character. He was observing students, who for their part were observing him. Then he started to stare at me with a grin that would not leave his face. Even after I began questioning him about his life and revealed a few facts about his life, that was making the status of his cheerful mood fall under strong clouds of suspicion like something was wrong; that all was not well in his head.

"Mr. Gansk, would you tell us, how old are you?"

"Forty six, Doctor." He looked amused about having all this attention.

"What do you do for a living, Mr. Gansk?" I continued to ask him simple questions; the ones he was not supposed to have problems answering.

"I run a small architectural firm." He was quick with answers and showing definite signs of enjoying the situation.

"How has business been lately? I heard you had some kind problem. Is that right?"

"Little problem? It wasn't a little problem. Actually the problem was and still is big enough, for me to apply for bankruptcy. But that's okay. I'll start a new company, bigger and more powerful. I will get the best people in the field. I will make it work Doctor."

"Mr. Gansk are you telling us, that your company is going under? Is business that bad?"

"Yes Doctor, but just like I said I will..." And he repeated his previously stated optimistic, utopian statements about his big plans for the future.

"Mr. Gansk, could you tell us about your family. Are you married?"

"Yes Doctor, I am." His tone did not change much, even though I was asking him about the people dearest to him. His wife and his only child, his daughter, were recently in a car accident, that left his wife comatose and his daughter dead.

"My wife is just having a little problem, but I'm sure she will be all right soon."

"And your daughter Mr. Gansk?" I asked cruel questions deliberately, in order to call his senses back to reality. I had to use a powerful stimulator. It was the practical equivalent of pinching comatose patient in order to determine the level of unconsciousness.

"My daughter unfortunately died in a car crash. There is nothing I can do about it. We still have to go on living, don't we?" He responded with an inappropriately cheerful tone of voice, considering the topic. Emotional cheerfulness could be explained by nothing else, other than that something terribly was wrong with Mr. Gansk.

I thought by this time I made my point. Mr. Gansk was a perfect symbol of walking happiness and he certainly would have fooled a lot of people, making them envious of him, making them think, that he had everything in life going his way.

2

Next, I introduced to the auditorium, Mr. Phil Cosset, a symbol of walking misery. This unfortunate patient was the complete opposite of Mr. Gansk. He was strikingly different in appearance and behavior from Mr. Gansk. He moved slowly, answered sluggishly, and did not appear happy at all. As much as Mr. Gansk projected himself as a symbol of happiness, Mr. Cosset was very much the opposite.

"How old are you Mr. Cosset?" I started to ask him the same questions that were given to Mr. Gansk.

"Fifty-one," was the answer of very tired and unhappy man. You could see that he did not enjoy being among people. He would rather be left alone. He probably wished all these unfamiliar faces and questions would disappear.

"Mr. Cosset I heard your company is doing remarkably well."

"Yeah. We just recently acquired few new smaller companies, and this move turned out to be very profitable. Actually this made us one of the biggest and most successful companies in paper industry." Mr. Cosset was telling us about his company's incredible achievements, but the way he described them, you could tell he was not happy about this success at all.

"How about your family, Mr. Cosset? Is everything all right?"

"Everything is fine. My wife just informed me, we are going on some kind of trip. This would be for our twenty five year anniversary."

"Wow, twenty five years. That's great. How have those 25 years the marriage been?" I asked.

"I have great wife. I'm the luckiest man around." He answered.

"And how about your kids? You have two children, don't you?"

"Yes, I have one son and one daughter. They are fine. They are nice kids. I'm very fortunate, having children like these."

"Mr. Cosset what you are telling us here is, that you are a very successful businessman, the luckiest husband and a fortunate father. You have everything that it takes to be happy. And yet we know that you know you aren't happy at all. Why?"

"I just don't know. I just lost interest in everything. I don't want to wake up. And when I do, I don't want to get up. All I want to do is lie in bed with my eyes closed and do nothing. I don't want to eat, walk, or talk. I'm so depressed, when I have no reason to be. You asked me why. You tell me why. I'm not a doctor, you are."

Mr. Cosset's mood did not improve at all, even after he had already received all kinds of treatments, including a few sessions of the barbaric electro-shock therapy, without any visible signs of improvement.

I could not answer his questions. He did not look satisfied. But in a teaching hospital like ours, the patient's satisfaction is not always considered a priority. Sometimes, the focus was only on the students and doctors learning and improving. At that particular time, that was our goal.

The students had no more use for Mr. Cosset. He had to be dismissed. His mental condition was presented as a classic example of a person with a deep severe depression.

"The two very unfortunate people presented today were complete opposites of each other. Their fate brought them here, and even though their outlooks were different, they were both similar in that they are ill." Looking at the listeners, I realized that they were deeply touched by the human misery that was presented before them.

THE BALANCING GAME

But this was not what I wanted them to learn. You do not go to medical school and pay tuition, to learn human misery. This kind knowledge could be easily acquired outside of this medical school.

I wanted them to hear and to understand. People are like books in that they cannot be judged by the cover. We could envy people just because they look enviable, like Mr. Gansk and we could pity somebody like Mr. Cosset and in both times we might be very wrong.

The human mind possesses a tremendous magnitude for empathy. But, there are no boundaries that cannot be surpassed.

"The most significant thing I hear from patients, is how they react to unbearable life pressures, and how they escape from those empirically established boundaries of normalcy, liberated by a depression or mania. Those states are the best compromising escape destinations. Feeling they could not go on with "life as usual" any longer, they use different vehicles to arrive to their compromising destinations. One uses a negatively charged vehicle to arrive to a happier station and the other a happily charged vehicle to arrive to a station full of misery."

I could tell I was losing the crowd. So, I retreated.

"My question to you would be again: who would you rather to be, if you had to make choice? A person who has everything and everyone around him is happy, but at the same time you feel miserable all the time. Or would you rather have the world's pity because of all the tragedies and mischief's you might have in your personal and professional life, but at the same time feel good, inappropriately good all the time? Isn't everybody's dream in life to feel wonderful?"

"Personally I see something intrinsically fascinating in the way we react to negatively or positively charged situations. We are not always appropriately responsive to them. At times, we are very inappropriately perceived, when we cross those invisible borders of normal mental reactions. All of our escapades end at the stations, that are fashioned in a very balanced manner. While giving you this question, I would have to admit, I would have a problem choosing either scenario."

"But that's me. I want you to think. I want you to share your thoughts with each other."

With this, I left the class. But I didn't remove myself too far from the room. In fact I leaned against the door, which I intentionally left ajar, so I could overhear voices from inside.

The class was noisy. It looked and sounded like everybody had an opinion and wanted to make it known to the rest of the group. The opinions sounded different, but they were all expressed and accepted.

I was satisfied that I caused this kind commotion. Now their minds were occupied thinking about finding answers to unanswerable questions. But my motive was not about finding a correct answer. The fact that they were tackling the complicated and deep topics of thinking science was gratifying.

Now I could leave and I did just that.

Chapter 10

"Doctor, I dream a lot at night. Even when the day wasn't exciting, I would still have a dream of some kind that night. They aren't really nightmares. And the most weird thing about those dreams is, I remember every little thing about them. And they are stories, strange ones."

The doctor makes the right decision and says nothing. This is his patient's time. He wants to share his story, dream or whatever, let him talk.

"A confession booth was fully occupied. On the one side, there was a priest, loved and respected by everyone. On the other side there was a young man with a bad reputation, as the town's people would characterize him. The young sinner was about to give confession and the priest was ready to receive it.

The priest was known as a saint in this place because of the way he was and the way he lived. The young character despite his young age, already showed everybody; how a young person should not behave.

The priest was not rushing the young man. He knew there was somebody on the other side of the booth in desperate need of cleansing himself. He also knew that person would not talk yet. As an experienced priest with many years of service, he had seen all kinds of people and heard all manner of sins; he realized the other person in the booth, always needed a little encouragement.

"We all sin, and God knows it. We all do and say bad things. There is nothing in you and in what you do, that isn't known to him. So, this confession is not about God finding out what you did; it's for you to purify yourself, to breath easier and feel free."

"I'm a born sinner," encouraged by the priest's words, the young man started to talk. "I hate myself, maybe because people hate me. Some nights, alone, I ask myself, what did I do to deserve their hate? So what if I drink a little and I'm nasty sometimes. Yeah, I get in some fights, and when I do I fight dirty, I fight to win. So what? They do the same things to me too."

By now the priest had a good idea, who was on the other side of the booth, what kind of person the man was to want God's forgiveness.

"Whatever you have done, whatever you do or whatever you will do in the future, God still thinks of you as his son. He still loves you." The priest said in reassuring manner. "But you have to ask for forgiveness for the sins you committed. This is a very special place. He comes to listen to you... to really hear you. You have to be more remorseful about the way you live."

The young person said nothing for awhile. He was clearly sorting out the sins worthy of confession. Then when he thought he had something to say, he said it;

"Father, there is something I want to confess. There was a beautiful girl, the kind that looks innocent and was as innocent as she looked. She was a girlfriend of a friend of mine. After what I did to her, she isn't that beautiful, or innocent any more. And that friend of mine isn't a friend of mine no more."

There was a long silence; a sign of regret, or remorse for whatever took place that caused her losing her innocence and him losing his friend. The priest remained silent, allowing the young man to continue to talk without interruption.

"Once after a wild party, my friend asked me, if I could pick his girlfriend up from work. He didn't feel good, and had to stay home. She worked as a secretary in some kind of law firm, and at times had to work late. She was paid double for overtime, and would overtime hours all the time.

I stood by the open door, while she was getting ready to leave. I was drunk and she was naive. I knew she wanted to change clothes,

THE BALANCING GAME

but I didn't know why she was doing this, knowing I was watching her. What I saw was a beautiful woman getting undressed in front of me."

He stopped again. When he resumed, he sounded remorseful.

"She resisted for a little while, but she didn't want to fight. We all ended up losing. She lost that innocence, my friend lost his girlfriend and I lost my friend. And all this for a few moments of pleasure. Why, why did she have to get undressed in front of me?"

The priest continued to be a priest.

"God still loves you my son. He will forgive you anything."

"Father I feel so dirty. I wish I was clean like you."

Later in his dark room, he would wonder how he would feel in that situation. How he would react if a beautiful woman would get undressed in front of him. He really wanted to know. And suddenly he realized that there was some strange feeling in him that wanted to act out. Now he had that feeling of envy towards that young sinister character, that would not resist the temptation; enjoying all the pleasures life brings. The strong feeling of envy now was bringing in the room a very beautiful, innocent looking woman.

The priest refused to admit it even to himself. But he did really wish that he was that dirty young man without any inhibitions.

The priest tried to sleep. It was a late night already and he had to get up really early the next morning. The priest had a very busy schedule to keep; conducting morning services, meeting with community leaders, talking to local business associations, receiving confessions and so on and so on. But the father could not fall asleep. There was a woman, innocent looking beautiful woman carelessly getting undressed in his room. Slowly in no hurry, and with no regard to his presence, his fatherly presence, she removed her clothes, and soon she would start showing the most intimate parts of her body.

The priest got up and shook his head a few times, as if trying to send the sensual half-naked female image away from his field of vision. But she would not go away. She continued her strip-tease, now reaching to her bra.

The priest was sweating now. With cold moisture on his face, chaos in his mind and the heat in his body, he was finding out a great deal about himself the hard way. He was very much human, with human needs. His sexual arousal came as a shock to him, at a time when he thought he was beyond of all these earthly temptations.

The woman was completing her exposure. The priest was very much in the middle of awakening as a man and as a sinner. And now he no longer minded the transition. He did not wish this image of the female beauty go away.

Then she was gone. Actually, she never was physically there.

"Forgive me God. Forgive me for my weakness. Forgive me for failing your trust."

Then he knelt down, looked up towards the cracked ceiling and initiated his confession. He did not forget to mention the dream that would not let him sleep. When he finished, he got up feeling relieved.

As a person devoted to God, he was sure he would be forgiven. The father would see him as a whole person with a lot of credits on his side, and not merely as a man in a moment of weakness.

Was he forgiven, really forgiven? If he was, why did he need to repeat his pleas for forgiveness so often?

"Forgive me, though I'm a sinner, I'm your son too.""

The patient finished the tale of his dream and sat up straight. He looked directly at his doctor and asked, "what does it mean?" His therapist looked back at his patient who had just shared something so meaningful with him. Bewildered, the doctor took a moment to compose himself and asked, "what do you think it means?"

Chapter 11

1

In general, I kept my distance from Greg; I avoided him for months at a time. On my birthday, I knew I would certainly make an extra effort to pay him a visit. He was surely expecting an appearance. But, it was more than that; I needed the visit for myself.

On those days, I could hardly wait until my working day was over before rushing to his place like a desert-wanderer dying of thirst. I would sit in his small, dark, cold room, in front of a widely open window, fully clothed, assuring myself maximum coverage from the night's air.

Greg would greet me with silence from his headquarters located in the corner of the room, conveniently close to the table. This strategic point was vitally important to Greg. On the table, on his side of it, lay a few bottles of vodka. Some of them would be full, some of them were already drained. But they all appeared alike before him, like obedient soldiers awaiting their general's command.

Although he never stated it outright, I knew he was always glad to see me. I could tell by some of the extra involuntary movements he would make. His hand holding a small glass of the drink would shake with a little more force when I first walked in. A few times I heard the very familiar sound of liquid dropping to the floor. I also noticed how the glass in his hands was tilted, letting the spirit flow out of it.

I interpreted this as a reaction of a weakened man to a minor joyous occasion in his life. Somebody was visiting him.

Pretty soon, we would start to talk, laugh and drink. Then we would continue to drink, laugh, and talk in that order. I would tell him everything; I mean everything. I would tell him what I lived for, whom I lived with and why I lived at all. Of course I would also mention what I did or didn't, what I dreamed of and what would make me happy. So it was only natural, that after few visits, Greg pretty much knew Dr. Al Letne almost as much as I did.

We would not forget to discuss the cases of my patients. I would ask him for professional opinions and advice. This would make his night. "You think I still got it?" He would ask facetiously, but would wait for my answer. He would repeat the question if my answer would not come quick enough. "Of course you do." He would hear it from me.

Then he would ask me about one particular patient- the one with the strange notion about everything in life being equally balanced. He would ask me how the man looked and whether he was spouting anything new.

After these pretty routine topics, he would propose a toast to Medicine, the most human science.

While still in a sober state of mind, he would invariably discuss The New York Times Bestseller list. This was surprising to me, because I never saw any book newspaper, or even a computer in Greg's room. And yet he was very much updated, informed, and well-read. While I did follow The Bestseller list, my knowledge of those books were limited. I did not pay attention to these books beyond an occasional jacket cover, and I rationalized my ignorance by blaming it on lack of time. So while I knew the names and authors of those books, I would have problems participating in a meaningful discussion about them.

When I would complain to Greg about a lack of time as my main reason for not reading those books, he would assure me that I was not missing out on much. "Don't worry," he would tell me. "I don't know how people can read all this garbage." He was angry at almost everybody. He would call the bestseller authors stupid, because of the stupid topics they would choose. He cursed publishers because of the way the books were chosen for publishing. And finally he was amazed at the low intellect of the average reader.

After repeatedly hearing Greg trash authors, blabbering about how easy it was to top those average IQ bestseller authors, I jokingly suggested, "Why don't you try it?" He almost always said nothing. I said almost, because once he did say something, "I'm thinking about it."

I did not pay much attention to what he said. But later I would find out the hard way that he had been thinking about it a lot.

All that nonsense was the easy and entertaining part of my visits. There was another part though. This part was more depressing. It was also awkward. The room would become a classroom. The people in it would assume academic appearance. Greg would transform into a professor and I would become his unwitting student. Our transformation would invariably coincide with our level of intoxication.

As alcohol would saturate more and more of our brain cells, our talk would become silly and we would touch on increasingly ridiculous topics. That's when Greg would take over. He would become more open and would spill his crazy balancing theory and the balancing formula.

At first I would not pay much attention to this silly theory, to this crazy formula, and to these weird views Professor Greg formulated and expressed. But as time passed, I would be persuaded and forced to listen, like a good student.

2

I believe it was my fourth visit to Greg, when I really started to listen to whatever strange theories, he was saying. The first couple of times, I wrote it off as the gibberish of a drunk madman. By the fourth visit, I realized that it was important to him and I had no choice. I had to listen to Professor Greg. He was demanding my full attention, and with time I succumbed to his power over me. I had to cede my undivided attention. I fought fiercely to avoid this discomfort and I tried to ignore him. But rationally, one ought not to fight after one no longer benefits from the fight.

And when I was defeated and overpowered, I had to listen to this;

"You should know by now, what I think about life. Altogether it's a fair thing. It treats you in a strangely balanced manner. Even at its worst, it still gives us something that would allow us to adapt and adjust. You don't have to be physically strong to counter-balance the misfortune that we so often face in everyday life. Too much strength without accompanying a minimum of wit, very easily could be catalyzed to self-destruction."

"You probably expect me to give you an example." He paused and appeared to wrestle an example from his mind. He also continued to be alertly concentrated and focused. He wanted me to ask questions, to participate.

I wanted to leave this place with its unusual inhabitant. I wanted to block my awareness, from every sensory nerve I possessed. I wanted to order my eyes not to see. I desired my olfactory not to smell the odorless odor of nothingness. I arranged my posture on the chair in a way that would avoid my skin touching anything, and in the process, I curled into the fetal position. And most importantly I wished I had my ears plugged, so I would not have to listen to this lecture about life, coming from this man in a wheelchair.

There was not much I could do but be this baby, hearing a noise and directing my attention to the noisemaker.

"Do you want me to give you an example Al?" He asked.

"Yes, I do," I answered.

"Okay then, how about those dinosaurs, looking so powerful and mighty and having hegemony for centuries. How come you don't see them around much? You know why you don't see them? There is a simple logical explanation to it. Because they were wiped off the face of earth. And you know why? Because they failed to counter-balance to changes, the constant changes of nature. In so doing, these creatures succeeded in signing their own death certificate. They accumulated a lot of mass in their bodies, but they couldn't move fast enough. They developed big mouths, that could eat but couldn't speak and most importantly their under-developed brains couldn't think fast enough to prevent their disappearance.

I listened to him. The only way I could effectively kill time was to follow the leader's instructions. Power was speaking and I was a follower not in position to rebel.

Greg continued to lecture. My undivided attention fueled him. Empty vodka bottles, modestly standing in the corner of the small table, had served their master well, making him totally drunk. His brilliant but twisted mind continued to solve the problems in his head. And beyond his brilliant mind and analytical personality, he had time… plenty of time to think. The combination of his love of teaching, having a loyal student, a friend he could trust by the name of vodka, his undisputed academic talent and an enormous amount of time had to produce something. This production was something large, something unusual, something unique and it was debuting before me.

"Al, I have a theory that I call "THE THEORY OF HORRIFYING BALANCE." I believe everything in life, and I mean everything is equally balanced. As soon as life is born, there will be death matched to it. Big balances small, beauty deals with ugliness, tall with short, old with young. A beautiful woman will suffer from losing her beauty, when she gets older, and the degree of suffering will equal her pleasure from her youth's beauty. Rich people will have problems departing from their wealth and at some point they all do lose their wealth."

I was listening to this and at some point caught myself actually liking what I was hearing. It was interesting and amusing, logical and smart, insane and somehow plausible.

"When a person is born, his natural life span is expected to be approximately a hundred twenty years. That's what the best physiologists tell us. This is true only under one condition; if only we will preserve the person from every possible insult that he so often suffers from the outside world; big or small. Hypothetically speaking the whole physiological process can be divided into a few stages.

First the infancy stage would include the years from birth to puberty. The next stage could be named a teenager age and it will contain years from fifteen to forty. Then will start the young age from forty to sixty and middle age from sixty to ninety. Only after this will come real old age. But this is only in the ideal. In reality though, because of the numerous pains a person must endure, those years will reduce with every single insult.

Imagine how it works. God or whatever power governs us, gets a yearly register, pretty much like a cash register used in supermarkets and starts balancing things.

The countdown starts at one hundred twenty. Then something happens when an infant he wasn't cleaned fast enough. Wasted material remained longer than it was supposed to. So he cried and cried from psychological and physical harms; caused from neglect and physical discomfort caused from dirty wet smelly wasted material. And there goes a few minutes, or hours trimmed down quick.

Then how about those school years, with all kind of pressures on a child? To compete, to achieve, not to fail, to live up to parents' expectations, to jump longer than everyone else, to run quicker than the other guy. Years full of failures, deductions and rejections... the cries of his unsatisfied parents."

I was listening to him rant for what seemed like hours and I did not know what to think. Some of his points seemed like drunken babble, but the main points resonated with me. He could tell as he continued to gain steam.

"Then peer pressure. First love coming in and going out, with

THE BALANCING GAME

roaring, tearing, crushing, exploding. First sexual experience, first night of drunken revelry. First dream crushed.

All these translate into years, could make your count down snowball, trimming more and more skin from life, from what looked like an eternity."

"That register must be very busy and that supermarket must be very busy one," I chimed in hoping that Greg would notice that I was following him closely. I was really fascinated by what I was hearing. While I could argue very enthusiastically about the amount of years Greg would take away from the poor person for any one of life's particular foibles, the idea of balancing down life according to the amount of harms a person suffered was at least interesting and amusing.

Greg would go on to mention a person's younger years, and struggles he had to endure to establish his place in a world of the jungle, where he would acquire skills to adjust and accommodate, to fight and retrieve, to hit and run, to cheat and lie, to love and hate, to trust and distrust. He used silly, but meaningful examples like the time when a person shows up at a party uninvited, when all the good seats are taken.

"So in order to better his condition, he uses what he learned. To get a better seat, he has to unseat somebody else. And he tries. He works and talks, he fights and cheats, he steals and bribes. He betrays and or is betrayed. And if he is mad and if he has it in him, he kills, or if he has it in him, he is killed.

If he survives, he continues a rough bumpy road. The dirt impairs our vision, but the register has no problem seeing the damage done.

When the dust clears in his life, he reappears dirty and tired, used and abused, or user and abuser, conquered or conqueror. But regardless which side of fortune, he would be attached; his account will be damaged. Punishment for life experiences for bad or good would be equally damaging, and that will reveal themselves through his appearance. He would look and think as an old man."

Greg definitely got carried away with his crazy thoughts. Though the topic was extremely interesting, it also was quiet tiring for me. I got the general idea of what he was talking about, but I was ready to leave.

He continued to talk. I continued to think. I could not stop admiring the analytical power of Greg's thoughts. I looked around and felt like I was sitting in some kind scientific laboratory... almost like that of the deranged Dr. Frankenstein. But instead of that monster, the doctor tried to create, he was working twenty four hours a day, seven days a week, developing a balancing theory, and some kind balancing formula, so he could use this theory and this formula in practical life.

Greg was not finished yet. When he sensed I had some room left in my brain to receive more information; he went further, much further!

"Al, people are like children that need guidance. Like children, people keep asking questions. Every day they learn so much. But like children, people remain helpless. They are easily manipulated, misled, taken advantage of because they never have enough information needed to be strong, independent and happy. They are like sheep led to the slaughter. They go to wars where the chances of their return is minimal, they choose lifestyles that would almost certainly make them unhappy in life."

I knew Greg was drunk, but how drunk? Or was he just plain emotionally disturbed?

"They don't really have much of a choice," I angrily suggested.

"They will." That was his response. I let that linger as I hoped he would leave me alone with this weird theory.

But, there was more to come.

"Al, when Newton saw an apple falling from the tree, he realized there had to be some physics law. He found that law, that now we call the Newton's law. When Helmholtz observed that no energy, regardless of source, would just disappear, rather it would change shape, face, and name, but never total amount of units, Helmholtz

THE BALANCING GAME

found that law of physics known nowadays as Helmholtz energy conservation law.

Why should we assume that people aren't guided by my laws of behavior. After all, we are part of nature. So that's what I came up with. We can improve the odds of a person's success in life by giving him the tools to succeed. And I'll give them my formula.

H+O+P+E=S. H stands for homework, O for organization, P for performance, E for efficiency and S for success.

Everything starts with H. Homework. There will be no success if the proper preparation is not done. In order to achieve something, the person should determine what exactly it is that he wants to achieve. A clear objective has to be identified. Strong and weak points have to be realistically evaluated. All the information pertaining to achieving the goal should be obtained.

Then comes the O. All the homework material should be organized. Strong sides reemphasized and clearly spelled out. The final plan must be chosen.

Now the person has to P. Perform. By this time, he is knowledgeable about what he is doing and why he is doing it; he is prepared. This would definitely increase his chances for success.

Every action taken should be the E. Efficient one. Extra effort and time wasted can be easily avoided, if every part of the formula would be conscientiously followed.

All the above would lead to S. Success. I would guarantee it about ninety per cent of the time.

This formula is simple enough for people to understand. That's why I'm so sure people won't have a problem using it.

By my estimation millions of people would benefit from this very primitive formula. All they would have to do is to live with H+O+P+E=S. It would also be free. It won't cost anything to anybody. All the most important things in life are free: AIR, WATER, LIFE, DEATH, LOVE, HOPE."

On any given day, more than ninety percent of people are unhappy for whatever reason. And if it is so, then on any given day there is a huge market for Greg's formula to apply. It could be applied easily to more than billions of people, in need of some kind of improvement in their troubled lives.

That is, of course, if Greg's formula had some practical implications.

Meanwhile, the inspired shadow was delivering a formula that could positively affect billions of people, at least in his own mind. His blood alcohol level was probably ten times the legal limit to drive. But he wasn't going anywhere. Or maybe he wasn't just drunk. Maybe he was mentally ill. I see people with these kinds of grandiose notions in my office often, very often. The only difference was, none of them was Dr. Greg Entel. This one was.

He honestly believed, that his year register idea, his balancing theory, and his balancing formula would reshape modern human being's approach to destiny and fate and clearly would put more active emphasis on individualism and individuals striving to participate, analyze, think, equalize, and succeed.

He believed that if there are laws in physics, that no energy is lost in life, that it transforms into something else equal in intensity, so at the end the balance won't be disrupted. Why should we assume that there isn't something similar with everything we do in life?

Rather than allowing me time to process these ideas, he rambled on; "The deal is nobody is born to live forever. As soon life as life arises, a death is looming to match. It's only fair. Life would be balanced with death. If person will live to eighty years, when he dies, his eighty year gain will be evenly matched with a loss of eighty years of life. He also will have taken evenly what was given to him; One head, two eyes, one mouth and one tongue, the blood, the brain..."

As he continued, I started to lose focus.

THE BALANCING GAME

3

Nothing lasts forever. Even Greg's lecturing stopped. A teacher exhausted the material to its most minute detail. He had to rest. The student needed time to digest and retain. This student was not just good; he was very good. And the teacher knew it. That is why this student was actually his favorite.

"Greg, something tells me, there is more to this lecture, something more practical, something that requires my active and direct participation."

"You are right," he said and paused.

"Then, can I have it please?"

"Al, today is your birthday, isn't it?'"

"Yes it is."

"Okay then, you wouldn't have a problem, doing me a favor, would you?"

The last question was given to me in a familiar fashion. An anticipation of a positive answer from my side was obviously expected in his tone.

Here we go again. Again with this favor thing. This would never end. I felt angry, helpless, frustrated. But there was something else- it was hardly explainable and it wasn't just curiosity. Another chance of self-cleansing? Is there such thing?

"Sure Greg," I answered calmly, but was detached yet again.

"Al, as I told before, I wouldn't ask you to do something that I wouldn't ask of myself,"-- Greg said reassuringly.

"That I know Greg. You don't have to go through these pleasantries. Just tell me, what exactly you want me to do." I was anxious to hear, what kind favor Greg wanted me to do for him this time.

And then came this roaring rush. No preparation, no previous experience made me strong enough, to meet this coming thing.

"Al, I want you to marry Mary."

I was pretty sure that's what he said. My head started to pulsate loudly. My eyes widened enough to see nothing around. My hands stopped moving. My tongue suddenly did not have enough space in my mouth to move. This obviously sick person continued to be obviously sick.

Helplessness and anger, surprisingly were soon replaced by obedience and a strong urgent desire to do something good for him, so I could erase something equally bad from the past.

"Greg, are you really asking me to do you a favor by marrying Mary?" This was not a question of disbelief. This was more question of clarification.

"That's right Al; that's what I'm asking you to do for me. And I have a very strong feeling; you'll do this for me. Won't you Al?"

"Greg, before I give you my answer, I want you tell me what makes you so sure, I'd this for you."

"A combination of things. First of all, this is something I wouldn't have a problem doing myself under other circumstances. Then I know your head. I know the anatomy of your thoughts. Some of those thoughts are active, some are dormant. Those passive thoughts, unused and unfamiliar to you, can be activated very easily. That is of course if one knows how to mobilize them, which I do, and knows what to do with them which you know I do. If you didn't want me to control your behavior; you had to be more careful, much more careful. Which you weren't. You showed me your guilt. You didn't hide it from me. That was a big tactical mistake. It's so easy, to appeal to those guilty thoughts. Al, you have no chance. I know all your cards. It's so disgustingly unfair. But so is the fact that I'm sitting on this special electric chair for special people."

It was scary to hear, what I heard. It was not news for me, what Greg just told me, but clearly hearing it from him, how I was under his mercy; was horrifying. I deserved it. That is what happens when you show your strong emotions to the people around you. And I mean any strong emotion; be it love, hate, or guilt. You will be surprised how quickly volunteers show up to take advantage of this unfair poker game that we call life.

I was a survivor by nature. I had to survive this too. In order to do this, I had to push away all the thoughts that would distract me from doing practical things; the things that had to be done. And I was good at isolating and repressing. I swept those distracting thoughts under a long rug. I understood that this was not a solution. But without doing this, I would not have been able to function. After all, I was not really sure I wanted to lose any of my thoughts, regardless of their value, their purity, or their unpleasantness. Maybe I wanted them in an accessible place, so I could get them back any time I desired.

Then I remembered Mary and everything associated with her... The night, when my life changed, the night when my dreams were revisited. I also remembered the night, when any kind relationship between me and her, should have ended.

"And how do you suppose I do this Greg? Just call her up and tell her, that Greg wants us to get married. That Greg has that crazy idea creating or rather continuing his life through me. Using my guilt, as a manipulative tool, asking me to do unusual favors for him?"

"Al, don't give me an answer now. Go home and get some rest. I'll think of ways to make Mary to marry you. But first I wanted your assurance from your part."

"I don't have to wait until tomorrow. Yes, I'll marry her- that is of course if she agrees," I couldn't think straight. I was overwhelmed by my helplessness. Then again, even if I thought with a calm head, there was guilt lurking somewhere, governing and censoring all my answers.

"Thank you Al, I knew you wouldn't say no to me. I just knew it." Greg sounded delighted. As if, he just heard the "yes" from his fiancée, whom he just propositioned.

"Sure Greg," however sickening the answer was, I probably meant it.

Once again I left the place in a familiar state of unrest. This time it was not that I had to go to my boss to demand that particular job to be given to me. Or that I had to screw his girlfriend in his presence.

This time it was different, very different. This time he wanted me to marry a girl, I had met only a few times under very stressful circumstances… the girl who thought of me, as the cause of her misery.

"She probably hates me a lot," I told myself before retiring to sleep that night. This statement comforted me somehow. Sleep came easier, much easier than I thought it would come.

Chapter 12

1

A few months passed by, after that night. I continued my daily routine in quite a dull fashion. I would get up in the morning to get ready to report to work. I would make rounds with my staff and residents. I delivered lectures and taught. I would see my private patients in my office. I would work on my scientific papers. Twice a week, I would go out on very successful dates, even though they were more like one night stands than romantic relationships. I would make sure those women would be of a certain caliber; with good looks, reasonable intelligence, and a level of sophistication. Their marital status did not really matter much to me. It was my position that whoever was ready to go overboard, would do this me or without me. And if so, it was stupid to pass up such really good opportunities.

I led the life of a successful bachelor. And while I would whine occasionally about the dullness of my life, like we all do, I was reasonably happy with my lifestyle. The only thing I would admit to myself in full secrecy was that there was no love in my life. But I did not worry about that much. I did not think it was impossible. I actually could see it coming. After all, I was giving myself a lot of opportunity to meet someone special. So, it was just a matter of time.

Just when I thought that nothing would surprise me in life, after my extraordinary experiences I acquired from hanging around with Greg, I was about to be proved wrong yet again.

Two months after meeting with Greg, I started to believe he was leaving me alone; I received a message on my answering machine. The message was left by none other than Mary herself.

She requested a call back and she left her telephone number. My common sense was telling me to erase the message. We all have common sense, but we do not really use the sense routinely. This time was no exception. I got closer to the telephone and did the opposite of what I should have done; I dialed Mary's number.

A very sweet voice answered the phone.

"Mary?" I asked nervously.

"Yes."

"It's Al. How are you Mary?"

"Of course I'm okay. So how you have been Al?"

She sounded fine. She also sounded cheerful.

"I'm doing okay." The conversation was not really shaping up well. I did not know what to say. A quiet pause followed, after which, I hoped Mary would disclose the purpose of her call. Somehow, she sounded like she expected me to start any meaningful discussion.

"Mary, is there something you wanted to tell me, or did you just want to know how I am?" I had to interrupt the silence.

Suddenly her voice became angry and before I knew it she started to scream at me.

"Wait a minute! What the hell is going here? For last two months, you've been sending lilies, my favorite flower, every day with passionate notes of how much you love me and how happy I could make you, just by acknowledging your existence. You wrote how much you would give up just to hear my voice for a moment. And now after fighting with myself for last two weeks, deciding to call you or not; all I hear from you is if I am all right. You are a joke Al. Goodbye. Don't bother me with your expensive attention."

She hung up and left me very confused. I had to admit to myself, this call was one of a hell of a strange one.

I did not understand, what she meant. Then I remembered Greg and his favor. Things started to be clearer. I remembered every detail of that night's events including what was expected from me. I also remembered the statement Greg made that night; "Al, you don't have to do anything. You just wait. One day she'll just call you."

"Just like that?" I asked.

"Just like that," Greg answered with remarkable confidence.

I remembered this. I hoped that Greg's requests would evaporate as the months passed.

The same night as expected, I visited Greg. He could not hide the pleasure of hearing my voice.

"Al, let me guess, she called you, didn't she?"

"Yes she did."

"A few months after she lost 'the best thing that ever happened to her.'" He was laughing and laughing loudly. Somehow, I started to feel, this was a different type of laugh, a bitter laugh. After all, he was just told, his love was calling the person she presumed was Greg's mortal enemy.

Then he stopped laughing. I could hear the loud moaning of a suffering person. "One year, that's all I'm worth of. She waited a few lousy months! That's all I'm worth?" Then he screamed cheerfully. "She did call, just like I said she would, am I good or what?!?"

I was confused. First, I thought he was happy. Then, I thought he was angry that Mary's love withdrawal syndrome lasted for only a year, and that put the price tag on her love for him. He probably thought he was worth more.

Eventually he settled down on the happier side, and understandably so. While sitting on his wheelchair, he still possessed a power, that could make people swoon on his command.

"The funniest part of all this is that she really thought and maybe still thinks, that you are the worst son of a bitch alive. Now you tell me, if life isn't funny."

He could not control his emotions, whatever kind; good or bad. This was entertaining for him. In fact, any kind of emotion was okay with him. And he wasn't hiding it.

"I still did not get an answer about what the hell I wrote in those letters," I was losing my patience.

"Don't worry, she will tell you things, you will get the idea. Listen, you sweat a little. Move your brain. Have some fun in this relationship."

"So what happens know?"

"Not much. You said she hung up the phone on you in anger. So, you call her back. Just lie a little. Tell her you lost hope, that she would ever answer your letters, and when she did call, you freaked out, which was the truth, by the way."

"And then what?"

"You have to pick it up from there Al. I told you enough. There is only one more piece of insider information that I think you should get from me; she likes to be touched a lot. She doesn't much care about the actual screwing. She is satisfied when she is touched. And being a doctor you should know where a woman wants to be touched. And by the way, if you ever have a problem and want her to cum, bite her right ear."

"Come on Greg. You're pulling my leg here," I said but somehow I believed what he was saying.

"I wouldn't lie to you Al, trust me. I don't know why. Once it happened by accident, and she came with violent spasms. Then it happened deliberately and every time she came a few seconds after I bit her right ear and little blood started to ooze from it. What can I say, maybe this is her Achilles heel."

Greg stopped talking and looked in my direction. He probably wanted to make sure he did not give away his beloved's secrets in vain. I did not give him any reason that tonight I was any worse a student than he knew I was. My attention span was long enough, my retention ability was good enough, and my loyalty to him was proven enough to assure him that he did not waste his, not so busy, time for in vain.

THE BALANCING GAME

"Al, please leave now. I'm tired," he said while drinking another glass of vodka.

When by the door, I was given another valuable piece of advice.

"Al, don't make a stupid mistake. Don't bite her left ear. It will make her angry, very angry."

"Later Greg and don't worry."

"Don't screw this thing up for God's sake."

"Don't worry Greg I won't," was my answer. I knew this kind of answer was better for Greg than that shot of vodka. That told me, how much he liked the answer.

But, I was left in silence. The quiet was extremely distasteful. The silence was ominous. And while you are perfectly aware of the danger and you should get out its way or you will take it, in whatever comes.

"Al, are you okay?" Greg was asking while trying to bring me back. "You didn't change your mind about that little favor, I asked." There was no way out and it was smart not to argue or fight. That would consume my time and energy; and it looked like I would need plenty of both very soon. I had to follow the flow.

"Of course not Greg. We all should keep our promises, and I will keep mine."

"By the way Greg, would you mind telling me, what made Mary to call me?" I sure wanted to know.

"Elementary Doctor Al, elementary. I simply used my theory and formula. By my theory nine out of ten woman succumb to a man's persistent attention. Then I just applied my formula. A few things should be emphasized; attention should be in the right dose, the time should be right and some necessary homework should be done; just to learn what she likes and how she likes them. In my case, I already know what she likes, so it was just a matter of time." Then he paused a little and started to laugh.

"A few measly months. Ha-Ha-Ha."

"Greg tell me one more thing; if you are so confident, how come your statistics just mention ninety percent of women? How about those other ten percent, what about them?"

"It's again elementary Doctor Al, because one of out ten women could be mentally sick or retarded, blind, unable to read, or not interested in men at all."

"So what's going to happen next Greg?" You probably have this whole thing mapped out. What am I suppose to do now?"

"You are right; I have all this worked out in great detail. That is why I don't have any suggestions for you at this time. Because I trust you enough. You told me you'll do your part and I know you will. I have that much confidence in you."

"I will, but just tell me one more thing."

"What is it, Al?"

"Why are you doing this? I want to know what motivates you to do this." I meant to ask him this for long time now.

"I have my reasons and don't ask me that question. I'm not asking you, why you are doing me these favors."

2

The next evening, armed with a scouting report about Mary's strengths and vulnerabilities, I dialed her number. All of the information was inside info, and this was making me a card player that knew his opponent's cards. The rest was just a technicality. I cleared her suspicions very easily, by simply lying to her.

In this unfair game, Mary had no chance. She was completely manipulated and outplayed. From me she heard the things she wanted to hear. That she has been the object of my affection for awhile now. That I just could not force myself to call her earlier, because I knew her poor opinion of me.

If you want to accept someone into your heart, there are plenty of rationalizations, things that our mind will emphasize and other things that will be overlooked. She remembered for example, how I could have, but did not take advantage of her sexually, when by her estimation, most people would have. She also remembered how I asked, if she could drive on that unfortunate evening, when Greg was drunk and insisted driving, despite her teary pleas. And if it is so, it was Greg who chose his fate that night. This justification cleared me in her eyes, in having even remotely contributed to Greg's present condition.

"He didn't listen to me, that jerk. He didn't let me drive. He asked for trouble and he jeopardized my safety too. It was irresponsible of him. And also it was Greg that forced me to sleep with you, like I was a trophy. It was you who graciously saved me from humiliation."

I let her think that way because that is how she wanted to think. Things worked out much smoother than I could have anticipated. It took me quite awhile, before I realized that I was not doing any favor to anybody. I knew she was young and beautiful. I knew she was sexy with a great body and every part of her was the perfect size and shape. What I did not know, I learned with time.

She turned out to be not as naive, dependent and helpless, as I originally thought. Despite her youth, she was principled with established convictions. She already knew coming from rich roots that she would soon flee from wealth and privilege, in favor of helping the poor and disadvantaged. She was fascinated with my miserable childhood and thought of me as a model for disadvantaged children.

In other words, she was very much prepared to fall in love, and after a few other tidbits of insider knowledge, like blowing in her right ear and biting her right ear was used, she would be completely under the mercy of Greg's twisted and merciless mind.

Soon, I found out her other sexual secrets. I was much more intimate with her than I was with anyone I had ever been with before. Poor Mary was very much set up and ready for whatever I could offer.

It was only a few months of dating, passionate and intense dating that I knew I actually wanted to marry her. And when my offer came as a proposition, the answer was wholeheartedly and resoundingly "yes."

So within 8 months after we started seeing each other, we were married. That means 10 months after Greg asked me the favor, I completed my task. I married her. I did Greg a favor.

The only time I was unsure about Mary is when I would think about Greg and her passion for him or his manipulation of me into this situation. I was in love before, many years ago. I still remembered the sleepless nights, jealousy, anger, nervousness, anxiety, and feeling completely detached from reality. This time I did not feel these emotions. I was planning, listening, calculating and being in complete control of her. Few other people might call it love, but the situation felt right.

"What the hell?!?" I thought to myself. You never know. Sometimes things work better, without the heavy emotional attachment and investment in a relationship. Besides I was following the order of a very powerful force, namely guilt and I was satisfied that things worked out this way. When you only follow somebody else's desires worse things could happen, than marrying a very intelligent, beautiful young woman, who was in love with me.

After two weeks of being married, right after we came back from our Venezuelan honeymoon, we were sitting in the living room of our Manhattan condominium and going over all kinds of congratulatory letters and bills that had to be paid.

"This is strange Al, look at this," Mary was showing me a card that had neither mentioned congratulations, nor had a name on it. The card just said three words, to be exact.

"Thank you Al."

For Mary, this was a card that some forgetful well-wisher sent us. She just passed it to me and forgot about it in a second. I had a good idea who sent this card, and that thank you was for me for doing a certain favor for him. She was lucky she didn't know about this favor.

We were keeping this new address a secret, so the other cards were received at a PO box, but this one was sent directly to our new apartment. Getting a card at this address that I thoght nobody knew about, was a reminder that something very watchful, very determined, and very involved continued to follow me. I also knew it was not God.

After our whirlwind romance, things returned to a new, but remarkable similar repetitive routine.

I continued to succeed at my job. The list of my publications was expanding and soon; there was a well-founded rumor in the department about me getting a clinical professorship.

As for Mary, she graduated from law school cum laude, and found a job dealing with civil rights. She immersed herself in her work and was getting satisfaction from helping the underprivileged.

I had everything, that my father would call a place under sun. I had money, the power to dictate people's minds, a beautiful wife, and a lot of warmth coming down from being close to sun.

I could live like this forever. But nothing is forever. And I knew that. I had no illusions about it. Things change in life, but like in that law of physics, while changes take place all the time the collective intensity of life doesn't change at all. It just changes faces here and there.

3

The new routine that Mary and I established led us to barely see each other. It wasn't miserable at all for me. I was alone again, but without many of the pitfalls of being alone.

Both of us were carrying intrinsic differences we possessed and our frequent separation exacerbated those differences. I had different things to pursue. I wanted to be rich in the future, because I was poor for so long in past. I knew I would not be ignored by people, as I was oftentimes in my adolescence. I also wanted to be powerful. Powerful enough to make people not only to listen to what I would say, but would also follow the power of my words. This power thing, had something to do with my failure in past to attract people's attention to my softly spoken thoughts.

I did not think I wanted something unusual, something unique. I was just like any other soldier that wanted to become a general. With me, I wanted it more. Is it not natural to dream about those things, when you never tasted them? When you cannot remember your mother's face, you never saw your father sober and you do not have anybody on this earth with the same last name as yours, what are you supposed to want?

And I could never forget that horrible fear of starvation, hanging over me during my helpless childhood years- the fear that my alcoholic father would forget about feeding me. Because every single day, he had a choice to make. More than a few times, he would choose his addiction over my survival.

In one of those hungry nights, when I was not the chosen one, I gave myself a promise that I would never be hungry again.

I did not like to be hungry. When hungry, I would hate everything and everybody around me. And I hated this in me. When hungry I would always become angry.

I was smart enough to realize, at a relatively young age, what would make my stomach full, what would make people notice me, what would make people listen to me and what would make people love me.

I had plenty of evidence, accumulated from daily life experiences, that with money, power, and recognition, love will come too. Because love is a hobby, a rich person's hobby.

Mary was born rich, in a powerful and recognizable family. Her parents, being very prominent lawyers, they were very active in the

THE BALANCING GAME

political arena. On a daily basis, for many years she saw disrespect to food, to people and love, because she grew up saturated with excess.

I wanted to climb up the social ladder, so I could be part of a group, who tries to look up to the sun from the highest point. She was born there. Now she wanted to come down and mingle with those pale faced people who, for whatever reason, avoided the sun on a daily basis.

We were both young and restless. And we both felt guilty. My guilt was different though than hers. An alcoholic father raised me alone. Being chronically debilitated, he still held two jobs and pushed me forward with my education. In my mind, the money he could use to cure himself from his chronic alcoholism, he was instead spending on me. And when he died, somehow I attributed this at least partially, to my existence and my aspirations.

I felt too much was invested in me to fail. I had no right to fail. I wanted to prove to my father that his investment paid off.

Her guilt was different. It was born in a spoiled rich girl's mind. Every time she could, she would avoid anything that had a luxurious look about it. She would rather stay in a cheap hotel and have dinner in places, where she would sit closer to the working people.

She became a typical liberal with strong convictions, believing in human equality. I had great respect for her strength of character and beliefs.

She grew up a lot, since I met her the first time. From a helpless, naive, gorgeous follower, to a strong, independent, almost revolutionary woman. She forcefully defended criminals, whom she believed became criminals because of the system.

With the ideological differences we possessed, gradually we started to avoid each other. This was easy to do. Each of us was so busy, pursuing our goals that we even did not have to come up with excuses.

When together, instead of discussing our absences, we argued or remained silent. This was not a positive sign for a new marriage.

Once I got married, I made even more frequent trips to Greg's place. Whenever I would mention my marital issues to Greg, he would avoid the subject and say nothing. He would just pour another glass of vodka and drink it with remarkable speed.

Finally, one day, I started to whine about my marital problems and he did say something. After pouring another glass of vodka first in a glass, then in his stomach; he shook his head a few times and mumbled something very unclearly.

"This is not good. I have a problem. This is not working at all." I thought that is what he said. While I still was in the process of confirming Greg's words, another statement came, but much clearer this time.

"This is not good for my career." This was very creepy to hear. My marital disharmony was very bad for his career. But by now I was desensitized enough not to make a big deal out of his mumblings. The first moments after these kinds of statements were stunning to me, but had become accustomed to recovering from them remarkably.

He did not make any suggestions. He did not give any advice. And most importantly he did not ask for any favors. The last one was the one that surprised me. From the statement Greg made, it was obvious he was personally touched by problems in my marriage and because his future was threatened, he would come up with some kind favor-oriented solution. But he did not.

Later, I would think of a reasonable theory why he did not waste a favor on this matter. He was smart enough to know, that the end of this marriage was very near. He was very right.

To obey my guilt and feel good, I had to succeed, advance, achieve, conquer. For her to obey her guilt and feel good, she had to sacrifice, give, and disobey.

THE BALANCING GAME

On my birthday and the second anniversary of his accident, we discussed my flailing marriage. But he did waste some extra drops of his holy spirit. This time, he was celebrating something within his mind. Then he paused for a few seconds. That is when I froze and stopped breathing; during that pause, he was creating his new project for me. This was very scary.

During our previous visits, I would report to him with great pride my progress. I would detail for him how many papers I published, how much more I was charging for a visit and how many good looking women I slept with, but not this time. This time, he had something to report to me. I felt like he was not excited about my achievements. He would not ask me any questions that would encourage me to elaborate about my boastful statements. But, he always asked me, "Al, are you happy?" That is what he asked. "Are you happy?" Was all he would say.

Greg did not appreciate my bragging this time at all. He did not comment, nor did he ask questions regarding details. What he did instead was, he asked me the same stupid question again, just like last time.

"Are you happy Al?"

I generally would not answer these questions. Maybe, because I was not sure how to answer the question. Who knows what happiness is? For some people happiness is having a full stomach, for others having sex with a beautiful woman would put him in paradise. Yet for some people happiness is, if their enemies get hurt badly. There are many people with different priorities in life. Go figure what makes each particular individual happy. As for me, I was dressed better than before, was more respected than before, with bigger sums of money in my savings account than before, more...

But, about me being happy, of course not. I was not wired that way. Happiness is a trait that only people with under-developed brains possess. How can you be happy being in the right state of mind, when at any given day there are things to achieve, obtain, conquer, and destroy? And if that is true, how would I claim to be happy, if at any particular moment, there is so much to pursue, to achieve, and to juggle.

Part 2

Chapter 13

1

Even in no logic there is logic enough. Whatever begins should end. And the end did come to nothing, to silence, to motionlessness, to ignorance.

I could see a person on the wall, his silhouette in the shape of a crippled man in a wheelchair. He moved. I could hear the ruffling sound that his move created.

Suddenly, the silhouette which was nothing a moment before became nobody; presented itself as something, that developed into somebody, that chose to say something. That's when I heard this;

"Al, I want you to do me a favor". Then a pause followed- a long pause. These extended seconds created a false hope that comforted me. There was a possibility that my brain, occupied heavily by a mind-altering liquid, willfully deceived me.

But then again I heard this, "Al, I want you to do me a favor. I know today is your birthday. That could only mean, you wouldn't have a problem doing me a favor. Am I right?"

I said nothing. I did not want to believe he was saying something or that I was hearing that something.

"I want you to write a book for me." He took a shot, as if for dramatic affect and then stated, "a bestseller." And suddenly the trance was disrupted, alcohol started to lose its power over me and let me go. Darkness hit me and the cold saturated my bones in a rapid electric current.

There was more to all this; the room wasn't really empty any more. There were people in the room.

Greg awakened the slumber of our deep dark past that was so profoundly rooted, it could only be summoned by something powerful. Greg's statement had that kind power.

"I'm not really asking that much of you, am I?"

I heard enough and I knew enough to realize, what was happening in this Frankenstein-esque laboratory. The decision was made by Greg, that he would write a book and I would take credit for the book. The book most likely would be about Greg's BALANCING THEORY and the BALANCING FORMULA he always raved about.

This book idea was another scheme in an obvious attempt to continue his life, with all his dreams, vicariously through me.

I did not know where all the alcohol went. Cold and darkness so unboundedly rushing in this small room, were not really causing any distraction from Greg's latest attention grabber. Unexpectedly, instead of running away from the cold, I unbuttoned the top two bottoms of my shirt and instead looking for more light, I moved my head in a way, to the scattered light from reaching my eyes.

"Al, I'm not talking about a mediocre book. Me and you wouldn't really settle for one of those. You and I would settle for no less than a New York Times bestseller. I guarantee it!"

His voice was firm, dictatorial and confident.

"Al, trust me. I wouldn't want you to do something, that in good conscience, I wouldn't do myself."

Greg sounded sincere. In fact, he sounded very sincere. Deception was not one of Greg's flaws. His honesty was a major flaw. But, there was not much for me to do. Once again, Greg had me in panic mode, mainly because of how trapped I felt. In a matter of seconds, I experienced an unbelievable degree of anxiety, the type that comes with one's uncertainty for his or her future.

The powerful commotion did not last long. The first and the worst tremors of my internal earthquake passed with remarkable speed and soon I was occupying a small space in a light daze and clear confusion.

"Thank you Greg," I said. Then I said something else. That something else amazed me very deeply. I do not exactly remember what I said, but whatever it was I said, did not include the word "yes". However hostaged and blackmailed, used and misused, ransomed and enslaved I felt; my answer was a little different this time.

"I have to think about this one Greg" and by saying so, I pleasantly shocked myself, for the first time in a really long time.

2

It was about eleven o'clock p.m. When I got to "Laity's". I felt down, really down. This bar helped revive me a few times before. For the last few years, each birthday became a new Judgment Day for me. Maybe because this is a day, I easily found time to look back; and collect unfulfilled dreams. This is when I look around to make sure I am alone, so nobody would witness my confession to myself. The possibility of my dreams failing would be conscientiously analyzed and I would be witnessing how my house of thin dreams with swollen brick walls could be flattened.

Realization of a fact, that I never grew up to a size, that could measure and match the original, miscalculated, naive and primitive dream-bound height. Only after I recognize the mismatch, I relax and quietly resign to a darker part of day, and whatever that part brings.

"Do you come here often?" A much younger girl with bad teeth and a flat nose wanted to know. I scanned her thoroughly. Her body was not on the decent side either. I completed my innocent observation with an impartial conclusion; she was not a blessed creature. Then I looked around. It hurt me to realize, that there were several good-looking women around and I had to be the object of attention to this unattractive woman. Being a little insecure, I immediately suspected something was wrong with my age, looks, or luck, or it was combination of all of them.

"Not really, why?" I asked her in return. While I was not here to flirt, I could benefit confidence-wise, if a better looking girl would come on to me with the same question. But for practicality sake, it really did not matter who was giving me the pick up lines.

"I didn't come here to pick someone up, or to be picked up." My answer was whispered, with an unwelcoming face. It really was not for her to hear. It was for her to go away. Surprisingly she did hear, what I said. She did have after all something going for her; hearing and nerves. And age too, which was irrelevant in her case.

"Then what exactly did you come here for?" She continued to be persistent in pursuing whatever she had in mind. She was becoming an annoyance. I had to turn my back on her.

"Your loss" I heard her say. I also heard a sigh of relief but I knew it belonged to me.

Whatever my loss was, it quickly became somebody else's gain, proving that physics law about energy preservation. No energy is lost in nature; energy is merely converted from one form to another. A chubby, balding guy with a lot of family problems written all over his face, came alive after he heard the already familiar line addressed to him this time. This made me smile. I was sincerely happy for my right-sided neighbor. He looked like he needed some break in his life and in all probability he was going to get one.

I was left with an unanswered question. If I did not come here to drink, to meet women, then what was I doing in this bar? This place was famous for drinkers, and sexually charged adventure seekers.

"Why are you here Al?" Now I wanted to know.

A few minutes and two shots of vodka arrived to help me answer the question. I like to watch people talk. I like to listen to what they are talking about. Maybe this is merely a matter of professional curiosity. I am not a participant. With a few exceptions, I would rather drink and smile alone. It is much easier for me. Nobody expects me to comment on, or analyze things. I am not paid to observe people and things here. Maybe that is why I feel free. No obligations and no expectations make me feel lighter. "Is this why I'm here?"

I looked to my right side. The fat neighbor appeared much happier and relaxed now. The ugly girl looked satisfied. She thought she found a companion for the night.

Now I turned to my left. Two younger guys, misguided by their age and the physical strength they possessed, were getting obnoxiously louder. Alcohol was beginning to get to them. They acquired the common mirage of invincibility. This conclusion was reinforced, after I experienced few forceful pushes. To me those pushes seemed unnecessary. They believed their actions were justified. They succeeded in their quest for geographic expansion.

Well they both were on the heavy side. I did not mind. Actually, I understood them. They were trying to improve their territorial position in this overcrowded bar. They could not do that by asking nicely. They had to use a little force. "Just like everywhere else," I mumbled to myself with a smile.

The guy with a big head and a very hairy face was in the middle of making a big statement. What I understood was, he was painting himself as a smart, good-looking Valentino smooth talker, who wouldn't take 'no' from a girl. And he of course, would succeed in any romantic adventure.

"She told me," he was telling some victory tale to another loser, who was unlikely to be romantically linked with any walking creature, "I was in love with you all along. I just didn't want to give you the impression I was easy." "Come on!" I said loudly. This guy was full of it. I could feel this professionally. He was also a drunk with bad belching habits. The totality of his lies, hallucinations, and belching, made his departure from the bar imperative. But that wasn't my problem. It was his. He was a big boy and I hoped he knew what big boys were supposed to do in this kind situation. I closed my eyes and opened them again moments later.

"You aren't drinker, are you mister?" I was brought out from my drowsy state of mind by the bartender Bill; I think that's what his name was. I checked the time. It was twenty after one, of course in the A.M. I lifted my heavy head and looked around. Fewer people remained in the bar. All the familiar faces were long gone, from the left and from the right. They staged their brief appearance in my life's stage and then quietly disappeared.

I saw the bartender standing very close to me. I guessed he was talking to me.

"Did you ask me for something?" I lifted my head.

"I said you are not really much of a drinker, are you?" The bartender repeated his question to me.

"You are right, I'm not a drinker; I'm a people watcher."

Now, I clearly was in the position to have a reasonable conversation with a bartender, who was still standing very close to me and appeared to be in a talkative mood. His name was, in fact, Bill. He was about my age, well built and well-mannered. With his hair nicely combed and his clothes neatly ironed, Bill projected trustworthiness. And people with plenty of problems to spill, would line up for his attention. Before I dosed off a little, I observed him serve people, not just alcohol. I was amazed with his ability to remember the majority of his clientele by their first names. He would ask them about their work, wives, kids, mistresses.

This guy possessed a very special talent, the one that I as a psychiatrist would appreciate. He had to listen and digest so many things, happy and unhappy day after day. People would open up to him without any extra pressure on them. There was no fear of spreading their secrets. With confidentiality guaranteed and unlimited amount of alcohol allowance, almost everybody felt the urgency to talk, confess, rationalize, blame, promise, and threaten…

I noticed with an ironic smile, that the situation for open and pressure free talking was better here than it was in my office or any

THE BALANCING GAME

other psychiatrist's office. People are not encouraged to have alcoholic beverages before or during the sessions, so they maintained their inhibitions.

"My boss might not like this trait of your character, we don't do much business with watching clients, but that's okay with me," Bill was laughing now. He was in a good mood. The bar was only scarcely filled in this very early morning hour and he probably still had good few hours to kill. He looked happy now; this rather brought me around.

"Listen Bill, that's your name is, isn't it?" He didn't answer, but did confirm it by nodding his head few times. He was all attention. You could see he really wanted to hear what I was about to say. "I'm a psychiatrist. People come to my office and talk to me about their problems. And God knows they have plenty. I was watching you. This place and you. The same things happening here. They are opening up to you even more than they do to me. Then you give them alcohol and I give them drugs. We both do the same things. Medicine is drugs, so is alcohol. Drugs alleviate people's fears. They become lousy thinkers. That's what the goal of treatment is. When you think straight, that's when you pick up all kinds of problems and that's when you feel something is wrong. But when you are not in a position to notice things, you don't know or feel half of the problems, that's when you could feel happier."

Bill listened to me carefully. Then he had comment to make;

"Maybe you're right, maybe not."

"How can you handle all this on a daily basis? You must be full of it by the end of your shift?"

Bill summoned me closer, looked around. It was obvious; he did not want anybody to hear what he was about to say.

"I asked the same question to my friend, also a bartender the other day."

"And what did he say?" I asked with great curiosity.

"Nothing. He didn't answer the question."

"That's all? He didn't say anything and that's all?" I was persistent in my quest for getting the answer.

"That's not all... Next day-he just went up to his boss and quit." "Why?"

"I guess he just couldn't take all this."

Bill became sad. Now he looked like he needed a drink. I lifted a nearby bottle and poured it in a small glass. He didn't have to be verbally offered. He swallowed it in a matter of a second. Then he smiled at me and prepared to move away.

I was not about to let him go without answering my question.

"That's him, but how about you?" I insisted.

"Me?" He shrugged his shoulders and grimaced.

"I have a different approach to all this. If somebody tells me, he just lost his job; I would tell myself, Bill you lucky son of a bitch, that's him that lost his job, just be happy you are still employed. If somebody should lose a job, it's better him than me. If somebody tells me, he has just lost someone, I would scream at myself, how lucky I am. This could happen to me. If some schmo's close person dies, it's better his than mine. If somebody just tells me, he caught his wife cheating, I would tell myself same thing; better his wife should be caught cheating than mine."

Now the bartender's voice was whispering and his face was extremely close to mine.

"Do I sound egoistical to you?" he asked.

"Well what can I say? You are really thriving on other people's misery, aren't you?" I gave him the question, without answering his.

"That's the name of the game, I mean... life isn't it? I believe bad things should be dealt by life like bad cards in a poker game. And if it's for my survival, it's better if those bad cards are dealt to someone else. This way I'll have a better chance to avoid them. It's like playing cards. A good, smart player would watch and count bad cards, so when someone else is dealt those cards, he would know he isn't getting them in future."

I listened to this professionally cool and calculated bartender. I did not know if he was right, but I did not know if he was wrong either. It seemed to make sense.

"I did notice one thing Bill," I said trying to keep the conversation going.

"And that would be..." Bill stopped and asked though he was already moving away. He seemed somewhat annoyed by my efforts.

"I just realized, those people with problems, they are just like strippers. Under the music of soothing confidentiality, they take off their soul's clothes and expose their most private thoughts to people like you and me. After making sure they exposed everything they could, they feel better. Then they leave, leaving you with their messages to analyze. The only difference is there, instead of them getting paid, we are getting paid."

"I don't know about that. Maybe you're right, maybe not. But this is weird, very weird, man." With these words he moved away from me. The next thing I saw him doing was, with a funny nonspecific smile and a shaking head, clean the mess his clients produced. I could not see though, how spotless his glasses looked.

I looked at him and felt some kind of respect toward my colleague. I thought this respect was mutual, and I liked that.

The time came to leave. It is always like this. You go to a place. Find people you get along with fine and then you just have to leave, just like that. It is very sad if we are not accustomed to this changing lifestyle. A "last call" lifestyle.

I got two more drinks on the house, perhaps a sign of "professional courtesy," and headed for the door.

"So long Bill," I waived my right arm to Bill.

"So long Doc," Bill answered in kind.

I left the place uplifted and almost entirely cheered. It was amazing how the little things you need in life can make you feel so good. A place with warmth and somebody with some common ground to talk to, can go a long way in brightening a day.

As I was leaving, I noticed a few people still hanging out in the bar, showing no signs of departing the place in the immediate future. Was that because, they did not have anybody to rush to, or maybe because they found here something they could not find in their homes? For whatever reason this group of people, hardly on their feet, by their own volition remained in this kind of place, with these kinds of people at this time of morning.

3

By seven thirty, I had to be at Greg's place. Then I could find out what I would tell Greg about me writing the book. I was very nervous and wanted the day to pass faster. Maybe that is why the day turned out to be so long.

This rarely happens, but all my patients showed up, making my day fully loaded. Being a psychiatrist is being a good listener, which unfortunately I was. This was my professional liability. The more closely I was able to listen, the more I was exposing myself to numerous human arrows piercing my soul. Every patient was finding my human unprotected wall, widening the holes, and creating new ones.

That is why by the end of the day, I was fully saturated with everybody else's problems. I usually need a few hours to recover. Some nights I recover fully, but not always. And when I am not completely recovered, I probably pay for this dearly. At times, I had a feeling that I paid more than I was actually paid (and I was paid quite handsomely.)

That day, it just so happened that I had to listen to ten extremely troubled people. The degree and complexity of their problems was remarkably high. That is why they did not mind paying big money to a highly trained professional, who would listen to them spill out their infected guts. I had to listen to every significant or insignificant little detail.

I had to listen, because their husbands, wives, children, parents, friends, boyfriends and girlfriends, brothers and sisters would not listen. And it was I who had to substitute for all their inadequacies.

Mr. Killer lived on the twenty-second floor and that scared him a lot. He kept asking me, what he would be thinking while in the air on his way to the ground from the twenty-second floor.

"That's a long way, isn't it?" he asked me with considerable pain in his eyes. He did not just ask. He wanted an answer also. He was paying for these services.

"It's a long way, but it's a pretty short time" was my expensive answer.

"What do you mean?" He was not satisfied with the answer and was expecting further explanation.

"Mr. Killer you are about a two hundred pound man. According to the laws of gravity, this weight would reach the earth from this height in almost no time."

He shook his head in disbelief. This guy wanted to have time for his final thoughts, while flying in the air as superman.

"I wonder what my ex-wife would feel or say, when she hears this news. Oh boy. That will punish her alright. This one definitely would make her feel sorry and guilty. What do you thing Doctor?"

His estranged wife, last year, based on the information he provided; had a few newly acquired male "encounters" and continued to intensively spend money she did not earn.

"Mr. Killer, you really want to know what she would feel or do?" I asked cautiously.

"Yes, I do," he replied angrily.

"Then I have disappointing news for you. She would not feel sorry, and she would not feel guilty. Why should she? It won't be her who actually doing the pushing. That will be you, with all your forty years and two hundred pounds. Your self-destructive act would be labeled as another sick big boy's bad mistake."

He was listening very carefully with his eyes wide open. He actually was hearing my eye-opening comments.

"What she would feel would be how stupid you were, doing this is to punish her, and in the process leave her all the money you worked so hard for, your whole life's work. She might even laugh... a lot, alone: oh wait except for all her new boyfriends."

His eyes continued widen. Now they were expressing disappointment and surprise. I did not sit here and was not paid big money to give him answers he wanted to hear. My job was to stop him from being a reckless pilot, flying an illusion without a plane or a parachute.

I felt no pity for him. You cannot help people when you feel sorry for them.

"Now that you heard my professional opinion about how your beloved ex-wife would feel, when she hears how you ended your life, I'll tell you what she would do next. This was the second half of your question, wasn't it? She would get married much, much sooner than you think. And the only time she would mention your name, when spending your money. Or with a big smile, she would tell her new husband how bad you were in bed, and how heavy you felt when you were on top of her. And then both of them would laugh and laugh."

Now Mr. Killer appeared miserable and in deep shock. And this was perfectly acceptable for me. In fact, it was my intention to put him in this state of mind. With his clearly suicidal thoughts, I had to give him this kind of shock therapy. By giving him straight truth, I was violently banging his head against the invisible hard bricks of the walls. I hoped that these walls were harder material than bricks.

He would not bleed at all. He had no signs of head trauma. In fact, there was not even a tiny scratch on his head. There could not be any.

THE BALANCING GAME

This banging of his head was a different type. What really took place, as a result of this mind shaking; his illusions had become pale and weak. Now for a short time at least, he was entertaining a new idea, not the sickening one that his death would punish her and make her guilty, miserable and poor.

Another completely different theory was introduced into his badly shaken mind. His physical disappearance from this life, would very well make his estranged wife free, happy and a rich woman full of disrespectful opinions about him to share with the world.

"I never thought about it that way." Mr. Killer shook his head many times now. He never did this before. Maybe me shaking his mind had a direct affect on the amount of his head shaking. Before he did this maybe two or three times. Now it was ten or twenty times.

"Are you telling me, she isn't worth of it?" he wanted clear firm, reassuring words from me.

"No she is not. Nobody is." I answered in a clearly phrased reassuring manner, just like he wanted to hear.

"Maybe you are right." He said this with sad face.

I could smell the scent of at least temporary success and this was gratifying. I felt no less happy, then a basketball player making clutch basket and bringing a victory to his team in a basketball game. Or a writer seeing his book on a bestseller list or a smooth talking politician making his victory speech on election night, knowing he got there by only articulating his teasing promises, but these professions do not really save anybody's life.

My victory was more real. More tangible. More human.

When he was leaving, he had a prescription for antidepressants in his pocket and different thoughts in his head. He paid money, big money for the best services he could get and at least for now, those services bought him more life. Money can buy a few things in life. Sometimes it can by life too.

But every success is temporary. Most problems cannot be cured.

We just postpone tragedies. Mr. Killer still had to continue to live in his twenty-second floor apartment, with a very beautiful view. As real estate salemen would say, this place had a killer view and with no pun intended, it did. They would also emphasize location and with his wife around, that is not the most suitable location for him.

Mr. Killer was my first patient, but he was not my most difficult patient.

Mrs. Frazier had a different problem. She had that unexplainable terrifying urge to badger her husband to death.

"Why?" I asked. "Any particular reason?"

"No reason at all. I would be relieved if I had any. Then I wouldn't think that I'm crazy and I wouldn't be here."

She claimed he loved her. And for her part, the feeling was mutual. She lived in constant fear, that one day she might do something terrible.

Then there was Ms. Klan, thinking that she had sex every night, but would not remember with whom. She would not remember his face or what exactly he told her. She would remember going alone to bed and waking up alone in bed. But she would insist that while in deep sleep somebody dressed like a vampire, would visit her and have sex with her. She would even check her neck very carefully, looking for the infamous bite marks that vampires leave. And then she would be both surprised and scared when she would find no marks at all.

Then there was Mr. Genders, who would first visit every kind of hooker possible and only after having sex with them, would be able as he properly put it, to make love to his wife. And it was not that something was wrong with his wife. In fact, with unhidden pride, he would describe her as a very beautiful and sexually insatiable woman. "That's what is bothering me." He would say. "That's why I think I'm crazy."

Mr. Wilmer, a happily married man for years, with four beautiful children, had that preoccupation with strange thoughts, thinking that one day he could succumb to a gay man's advances.

And so on, and so on....

All kinds of people, with all kinds of problems. And I had to listen to them, analyze them, and come up with all kinds of solutions. Sometimes I could and I would keep that guy from the twenty-second floor alive. That woman away from killing her husband, I would also convince the other woman, that she did not have sex with Dracula. I also had to help that guy, with expensive habits visiting expensive hookers. I had to persuade him that in many ways, it was much cheaper to romance his very loving wife. I would convince him that in some way, she was a hooker too, with the only difference that she did not belong to many men. She had just one man to satisfy. I could not forget about that guy with homophobic thoughts. I would explain to him, that in many cases these thoughts would mean nothing, absolutely nothing. I would describe that every man has some amount of female hormones and this could sometimes cause these kind thoughts sometimes. This would calm him down for awhile.

And so on and so on.... And by the end of working day, I felt very tired, very drained, very exhausted, but very satisfied and very rich.

I sat on my chair for minutes on end, thinking about nothing. Then my stomach reminded me I was hungry. I looked at my watch. It was ten to seven. I still had time, about forty minutes, before I would see Greg and inform him of my decision, which at this moment was not yet decided.

I managed to grab some fast food and fifteen minutes later, with my stomach fed and satisfied, I was sitting in a cab with a very talkative driver. The driver repeatedly tried to strike up a conversation with me, but I ignored him. One of the many questions he asked was what kind work I was doing. I kept my answers very short and I did not contribute to or propagate the conversation.

"So, you a writer. Very interesting," I heard him saying.

"A writer, is that what I said?" Suddenly I was sweating profusely. This man just told me that I said I was a writer, and probably that is what I told him.

I was afraid he was telling me the truth. I probably did answer him that I was a writer. Now I knew what I would tell Greg.

Chapter 14

1

By seven thirty sharp, I was at Greg's place. No surprises awaited me on arrival. The room was as cold as usual. The same person was sitting in the same place, in the same corner of the same room. There was one thing I noticed a bit later; more light was falling into the place that I would occupy, the chair. I did look around to investigate where this extra light was coming from. I could not see a noticeable source for it.

I looked in Greg's direction. While I was not able to see his face clearly, I thought I saw something on his face, something that made me think, there was a big scar on his face. But of course I could not be sure about it.

"Don't ever fall down Al. You should watch your steps. There are so many bumps on your walking path, you can trip and fall so easy. But if you do fall, and find yourself on the ground, for God's sake remember this; do not use your hands to avoid injuring your face. You can always fix up your face, but you will have a problem climbing back up to being human, from the four-legged animal position, you will assume."

That is what I had to listen from Professor Greg, when I reported for my next assignment, and next adventure. But this next favor was coming to me slower than the previous ones. He had to earn it. I had to crawl to it. I had to be educated for it. I had to be persuaded.

"When on the ground with your body positioned parallel to the ground and using all your extremities to maintain your posture; you'll look, think, and behave just like animals do. I have two pieces of advice for you. First, never look up to see the people around you. This would be a big mistake. Those people look at you like an animal. Their human nature won't allow them to recognize in you as a fellow human being in distress. Their ignorance will just frustrate you further; something that you don't need in these earthly times. Second, don't think like a human. You should remember, that was what actually what brought you down in the first place. When you like an animal; act like an animal. Without looking at the people around you, try to get up. Use their bodies, bite them. Don't stop if you see, or smell blood. Use them as stepping stones. Forget who you are, forget your name. You should be Machiavellian now. Remember every moment down increases your anger, frustration. That is not healthy Al."

"We all fall down Al. Only those who get up, are greeted with respect. Only hands of those standing are shaken with respect."

I listened to what Greg had to say and heard what I had to hear. I could not understand, if this thing about falling and getting up was metaphorical or whether they literally explained the bruises on Greg's face. And those views were coming from a fallen man's brain.

It would not surprise me a bit, if they were.

Two minutes of silence in the room brought me to an awakening. Now I was realizing, while the lecture was delivered to me, I changed my location and posture, left the chair and was standing in the most remote corner in the room. Like a punished student, guilty of wrongdoing, I had to endure my appropriate punishment. The teacher was trying to give the student a few slaps on the wrist to teach the good student not to rebel.

"Sit down Al" Greg's voice came from his usual corner.

I sat back on my usual chair, occupying my usual area, facing now a lot of fresh air coming from outside through the open window. Being sober, my body and mind somehow were fixated on that extra light, which my eyes noticed. By now, I stopped looking for the source of it. I just felt its presence.

THE BALANCING GAME

Greg was waiting for me with unusual intensity. I recognized this easily. While there were many bottles of vodka on the table, none of them was empty. This meant that, Greg was not drunk and indications were that he was trying to look and sound sober, sane, and credible. This was a mission for him to accomplish.

"Al, I did a lot of thinking before I decided to ask you this favor. You have to believe me." I believed him; but, because he was not drunk, his voice was shaky.

I did not say anything, trying to remain calm and collected. I had a terrible uncertainty hanging over my head, standing at the doorstep of a new beginning and a very unwelcome situation; this man on the wheelchair, whose face I still could not see, had a hobby. He liked to play games, balancing games with me in his spare time and he had plenty of time. With horrifying uneasiness, I reinforced the truth in my head. I was completely under the mercy of this man, who was damaged, not just on the outside, but on the inside too.

"I just don't want you to think, that whatever I'm asking you to do, is a drunk, crippled, man's tantrum. You see, people get used to literally anything. I don't have to show you examples. I'm used to mine. Whatever way, I still continue to exist. I have my ups and downs. I have my good and bad days. Just like you do or anybody else does."

Greg continued to talk. He did not pay attention to my attempts to comment on what he was saying and this was frustrating me.

"Al, I still have that drive inside me to compete. And if I carefully choose an area where I'm strong, I could beat the whole world, I'm sure of it. I'm just like you Al, just like you. You like to compete too. You know what I'm talking about. You competed with me, choosing something you were good at, and look you won, didn't you?"

With these words, his silhouette straightened up and asked me a direct question.

"Do you understand what I'm saying?"

"Yes. I do Greg," was my answer, and this served as motivation to develop his reasoning why he could beat everybody in the whole world in writing some nonsensical book. I could not figure this out, and I was waiting to try to understand his confidence.

As if he read my thoughts, he did just that, he addressed my concerns.

"Because, nobody reads more, than I do. Nobody thinks more than I do. Nobody analyzes more than I do. I have a very unique and twisted mind. I have all the time on the earth. All day, I watch, read, think, analyze. Now you tell me, who can compete with me? Who else in his right mind, can come up with this horrifying balancing theory and balancing formula? Which walking person, name me one able-bodied person who can compete with me, or maybe you want to tell me, is there another cripple who can beat me?"

"You understand what I'm saying Al?" He wanted my full attention and he had it. He wanted me to do something very unusual for him and I was about to agree to do it.

"My thinking is different. It should be different. It is bitter and deranged in some way, because it's coming from a bitter and deranged body and soul. Do you understand Al?"

"Yes, I do," I said. I knew I understood.

"Then you wouldn't have problem doing me this favor Al?" He asked, in a tone that denoted confidence that he would hear his answer.

While my answer pretty much was already formed, I paused. Greg did not take this hesitation lightly.

"I can't do it without you Al." Greg was working on summoning the guilt in my mind, that had slumbered for a short time.

"Why not?" I resisted. "You aren't talking about playing basketball. Writing a book doesn't require walking."

"First of all, the materials I'm using are completely shared with you for the last several visits. They were discussed with you in minute details. Your participation in producing this book is not, what you might call incidental. Every time you showed up here, I tried to remember and analyze every single word you said. About everything; about life and death, about good and bad, about ugly and beautiful."

"Greg, wait a minute," I wanted to interject here forcefully. But he was in no mood to change his mind. He sensed some resistance this time and felt he had to work harder for this one.

"Al, after all, you were my only live contact with the outside world, besides books, newspapers and TV. I listened to you when you talked about your patients. I remembered all of them; including the one that likes to measure his present fortunes with a ruler, so he can find out about the height of his misery in the future. You remember him? You brought that character to me. He is your creature."

He mentioned a few of my other patients that I discussed with him. But I clearly remembered the character with a ruler in his hands, the interest Greg expressed in him. He wanted to know everything about him, how he walked and how he talked. And especially what he talked about. Of course, now, I remembered Greg's extraordinary obsession with this character. I personally did not pay much attention to this weird man. There were so many of them.

Greg stopped punching me. I felt worked over really well. And Greg knew it.

"Are you with me in this?" He asked.

"Yes I am," was my answer.

2

The same night, I sat in my study and tried to read the manuscript, containing hundreds of pages. I really was not up to the task. First, because I did not have much time for reading, and second, while reading the book, I felt I was reading something that was created by somebody with a wild imagination and a twisted mind. I knew it. I was a psychiatrist, and supposedly a really good one. It bothered me a lot that this book was to come out with my name on it as an author.

Since the size of the book was enormous, I knew, I would not be able to read it all. So I would only try to go through select pages and pick up the most important parts of the book. It took me a few mornings before work, a few nights after work and one weekend between those working days to get a general idea, what kind of book Greg wrote.

It was amazing to learn what was going on in Greg's mind while writing all this. He has pushed my brain and mind, every time his brain became intoxicated.

Greg would mention words like balancing theory and balancing formula often. He would also bring up numerous examples of supporting material to whatever, he claimed he discovered or established.

The book urged people, all kinds of them, not to ignore his theory and his formula. Knowledge of them, he claimed, would almost guarantee them complete success in their lives.

First I thought, I would change a lot of things in this book. But later, I had to abandon the idea. It was very time and emotionally consuming. I decided for better or worse, not to change anything. My hope was that the book had no chance to make it in the real world, and if it did not make it, there was no need for me to waste my effort.

Greg was ecstatic, when he learned that I decided not to change a word in the book. Actually, he anticipated this. Right after I told him I did not intend to edit the work, he informed me that the book was actually about to be published by a giant publishing house and Mr. Friedman, a literary agent of considerable reputation, was handling the book.

It appeared that Greg did not think of consulting with me about things that would affect my life. He just assumed, I would go along with his plans, any plans.

THE BALANCING GAME

3

The book was published at the end of February. Mr. Friedman, my literary agent, described by many as energetic, optimistic and enthusiastic; sounded very lethargic, pessimistic and without any energy.

"I have to warn you Al, while I strongly think, the book is very interesting, I wouldn't hold high hopes, if I were you. This book might not have it what it takes to make it." He repeated this mantra to me a few times, to avoid my eventual disappointment, should the book fail.

He did not have to tell me that even once. I needed no preparation. I could not care less, if the book would succeed or not. In fact, it was my firm hope, or perhaps even a wish, that the book would bomb, without even making a splash. I was vitally interested in this book's failure, so my life would not be affected in any negative way. After all, the kind of work I was doing was not supposed to benefit from this manner of exposure.

"Only out of curiosity, Mr. Friedman, what does it take for a book to make it?" I asked.

"Three things; the name of the author, marketability of the topic, and the budget that publishing company would allocate for the book's promotion," he answered.

"Then, I don't really have much chance, do I?" I asked with great satisfaction recognizing, that my name would not carry the book to success. The topic, as it seemed to me, was far from being marketable, and I was pretty sure, not much money was about to be allocated for an unknown author's book promotion.

Maybe because, I did not care; I did not hide my feelings about the outcome of this book's future.

"Al, I don't understand this. I have a strange feeling, a very strange feeling. Being in the publishing business for over thirty years now, I never even once experienced this kind feeling. Al you don't really care what happens to this book, do you? Or even more strangely, you want this book to fail, don't you?" Now he was looking at me.

He was an old man, who supposedly, had seen everything in his business.

I did not answer him. I did not want to lie. I did not want to tell the truth either. There was no sense of telling him a truth that he already knew.

"I knew something was very extra ordinary, when publishers were practically begging for this book. First I got a telephone call, from a very, and I mean very well-respected friend of mine. He tells me; there is a book out looking for a publisher, how about you take this one. I asked him about the author, and he says; "he is nobody and he wishes to be anonymous." Then I asked him how about the book; if it's any good, and he goes; "of course not," so I tell the guy, how the hell you expect me to sell it. He says; "very easy. Get the book. Read it. Edit it. Prepare it and take it to the publisher." I tell the guy. 'You must be kidding. Which publisher?" Then he gives me a name, a really big name. What do you think? I did just that. Got this mysterious manuscript. Read it carefully. It didn't really excite me, to tell the truth. But having a book published without a hassle was too good to ignore. To my surprise, the book was accepted for publication without any headaches, as promised."

"Then what happened?" I asked with curiosity. I was sensing, there was more to the story.

"Then you showed up, as the author. Then I knew the book was doomed."

"I'm not getting this. If you were so sure, the book had no chance, why did you take it?" I wanted to squeeze out more information, but there might not have been any more information in this well.

"I just told you. Because somebody from that publishing house was already in agreement with your people, to have it published. You know the answers to these questions better than I do. You aren't really telling me everything, are you? I really don't care, if you are hiding something or not. The main thing is, that book is going to be out without any big expenses and no hassle. Now let's hope it will make some money."

I posed more inquisitive questions to Mr. Friedman, in an obvious attempt to obtain more information about the people involved in this mysterious process of pushing this book for a remarkably easy publishing.

Mr. Friedman appeared annoyed. He did not want to hear about the past of this book. His preoccupation was with the future of this book. However gloomy a future it had, the agent sought success.

"Now, you are scheduled for some promotional lectures and media appearances." He was strictly business oriented. He was holding a piece of paper with a long list of events, which I had to attend.

"No way Mr. Friedman. I thought it was understood, that there will be no promotional activities from my side. I have no time for this show business hype." I categorically refused to even listen to what he had to say.

Mr. Friedman was angry, upset and tired. His anguished face said more than his words could deliver. But before he opened his mouth to attack me, I succeeded to throw at him my firm look and convincing final statement.

"Sorry Mr. Friedman, but this is something we both agreed on."

"Okay, you are the boss. But I'm telling you right now. This book has very little chance to make it as it is. Without us doing something promotional, we might be seeing each other for the last time."

4

Success came very quickly and in unbelievable quantities. The book that was given to an agent as a mere favor, soared. Critics found the topic edgy while still being educational. Readers were touched, realizing this book was about them. They wanted to learn the balancing formula, so they could use them in the balancing game. They wanted to know everything about the tools, which would virtually guarantee the improvement of their lives.

Greg turned out to be right. The amount of time he devoted to thinking about what ordinary people wanted to hear, the amount of ability he had to communicate to them; all of that combined with his superior intellect put him in the prime position to achieve success with this work.

Within two weeks, the book hit the top thirty and was a suggested read in a special article of the NY Times book review section. A famous book critic critically acclaimed the book calling it "a must read".

"This book promises you things you want in your life, and delivers the tools to build those things by yourself, and for yourself."

"The topic is cheap. Misery and failure shadow our lives. The promise is big. It promises to improve your life."

"Suggestions are scientifically articulated, and improvement is attainable. And the formula is simple, primitively simple. That's why this formula should be a new axiom of success."

"If you think you have enough sophistication in you and if you believe your intelligence is of high caliber, then this book is for you to carry you to the next level of consciousness. But if you think that you lack the above attributes, then I suggest you avoid the embarrassment of misunderstanding."

I do not remember the critic's name. However, it was not Greg Entel. Actually, it would not surprise me if it was.

When I thought the book had no chance to make it, I was encouraged. When Mr. Friedman took me as an agent out of pure practicality, I was concerned. When he strongly suggested to me to do some promotional appearances, I opposed. When the book started to make a big splash in the book market I panicked. I understood that the success of the book would lead to the death of my meticulously crafted lifestyle.

Chapter 15

With the book's success came another chapter of my life. My post-book world was markedly different from my pre-book world. My telephone was constantly ringing, whether I answered it or not. So, I just stopped answering it altogether. People in the street would stop me and bombard me with stupid questions, all kinds of them. While the questions varied from person to person, the main theme remained; how to use this "Balancing Formula" for maximum effect. While waiting for answers that would never come, some would just smile hopefully; others would really prepare for words of pure truth, with a pen and paper in their hands. At work, a few of my colleagues approached me with very concerned looks on their faces. A few of them managed to catch me at the right time and the right place for what they thought was the right question.

"Are you all right, Al? Maybe you work too much." When I would answer that I was perfectly fine, every one of them would give me another question;

"Are you sure?"

I really never read Greg's book. I originally thought I did not have to; now I knew I had to. Two artificial sick days gave me forty-eight hours to rest and catch up on my reading. It gave me ample opportunity to learn, what people thought I wrote in this book. Now I knew why I was asked by my psychiatric colleagues whether I felt ill. I would have asked the same question to anybody that somebody proclaimed himself as the world's savior. If this "Einstein" would announce to the whole world that he has discovered a formula with unbelievable practical implications. This formula would promise the unfortunates of this earth that by using it, their lives would be improved ninety percent.

The next few days, I spent wrestling the shame that I was growing accustomed to, after learning what I was actually selling to those success seekers... air packaged, attractively wrapped up boxes. The air that they were inhaling free of charge, twenty suckers per minute, twenty four hours of day. My colleagues could see through the baloney.

But what we thought was selling air; Greg had a vision of selling them hope. And hopeless people thirsted for this hope. They ignored the professional nay-sayers, because each word offered them salvation.

All the unfortunates; rejected and dejected, dumped and fired, trapped and jailed, aged and widowed, shelled out for this crazy book from a crazy author and raised the book from oblivion. And they were not finished. It was not a one-time thing. They continued to raise it, exault it. There were so many of them pushing with such strength, that pretty soon, the book catapulted to the top of The New York Times Bestsellers list.

As the success became apparent and I was beginning to be treated as a wonder boy, another discovery awaited me. The discovery that comes with enormous success. Everything bad is forgotten; everything nasty is forgiven. I was the man among men. I was only human. This kind of discovery could not go unnoticed and unmonitored by me. A few weeks of being noticed, praised, raved produced a second person in me. This one ignored what made him famous. He just assumed, he deserved to be famous. He started to believe, he was born to be famous.

So, of course he started to love the fame.

Chapter 16

A mountain climber got up from the table. It was time for him to go. There was a dream to fulfill. After several unsuccessful attempts, he learned his lesson. The mountain he wanted to conquer required more serious preparation and more importantly, a deep respect. Neither one had he given to this relatively small but menacing mountain.

This time, he thought he was ready. He trained long and hard. He also developed an almost professional admiration to this mute opponent, the kind that you read about in books about two mortal enemies who have been fighting throughout time, that genuinely understand one another.

The climber looked around and one by one closely observed the people from the party that he was ready to leave behind. Among those, there was one face he had a problem confronting. His departure anxiety did not improve, when he spotted her with tears coming from both her eyes and occupying both sides of her face.

With a heavy and aching heart, he went to her, tried to dry her tears with his lips.

"Are you sure about this? You don't have to go." She pleaded.

"If I don't do this, I can never respect myself and that would mean, you would have a very unhappy person beside you. So you have to be happy I'm doing this," he answered.

"I guess, you're right. I know you're right. It's just hard to digest an idea, that you might never come back."

"It's getting late." A man with a surprisingly cheerful face, interrupted. He could not hide the pleasure he was getting from getting rid of the competition.

So the climber left to rise above the mountain, leaving the surrounding people behind on the ground... he left all of them, those he loved and those he did not.

For twelve long days, he struggled with nature, with downpours and a glaring sun that beat down heavily upon his exhausted body. Not the snow nor the wind could contain his will power. All this time he remained alone with his few tools in his bag and a big dream in his mind.

At the end of the twelfth day, after he made it to the summit on the cold dark and snowy day, he stood there alone. His pride was satisfied, his dream was euphoric and his head was light. He screamed at the top of his lungs, expressing his satisfaction.

After a few minutes of not being himself, it was time to realize that it was lonely up there, without sharing the moment with the people he loved. Somehow his mind was conversing with him, that he was much more fulfilled, when he was pursuing success than now when he achieved it. Then, he had a dream and he lived with it. Now, the dream was gone. Only a few minutes of celebration and then nothing. Just like a drug addict, longing badly for his fix, but after the rush of the peak, he would be in the dumps, searching for another fix.

As an intelligent man, he quickly realized that there had to be another dream for him, as soon as possible. This was the only way for him to keep himself going. Therefore, he had to come up with another mountain to conquer.

Then, the time came to descend. He could not stay on the top alone. He even missed the people he hated. For practicality sake, he put down on paper the amount of miles he had to cover, before he could return to earth. The amount of miles down was the same as the way up.

He could not stay there. Even being the only person on the summit, that would qualify him as the king of the place at this particular time.

THE BALANCING GAME

He had to follow a very natural curve. He had to descend the same route as he climbed up. He could not help but hum a tune, a theme song he heard when he was a kid.

And he began his descent from the summit without complaint because he knew even gods fall to earth. So, who was he to complain?

Though it took him seven days to return, he still had to endure all the hardships in similar quantities as when he rose.

When he rung the bell at her place, he did not really look temporal. Maybe that is why she could not recognize him when he opened the door.

"It's me. I'm back. I made it." Tired and happy, he prepared himself to enter this familiar place.

When the door opened, she did not move. Shocked, she could not believe her eyes.

"I see," she said with mixture of relief, sadness, and a great deal of anger. "So I see."

"Can I come in?" He asked her, thinking foolishly that she was so overwhelmed from the mere sight of him. She stood there by the door and was shaking her head with haggardly unkempt hair and a pale face without make up. She looked different without make up. She also sounded very different without make up.

"No," she said firmly. "I'm not ready for you."

"She is right, you heard her, and she is not ready for you." The climber had another shock to endure. A man was standing next to his girlfriend, and the man who stayed with her as he departed continued to comfort her as he returned.

"Does this tell you something?"

"Of course it does," managed the tired, hungry, and distraught mountain climber.

"You go after your dreams. You create them with remarkable ease and keep them alive. You go up and go down. It's a selfish pursuit. Don't you think you have to pay for this hobby, you enjoy so much?"

She had her say and she expressed herself eloquently. Before she was finished, she had one question to ask.

"What do you expect us grounded people to do?"

He was not invited in. He was not offered help in any way. He was not asked if he needed water, bread, warmth or even a hug. Nevertheless, it did not matter to him now. He knew that he would not accept anything from these earthly people. He made a decision. He would rather be alone with his dreams, than try to share those dreams with people who had no interest nurturing his passions.

The climber was having yet another dream. He believed there were people somewhere, like him, walking around with similar dreams.

He believed in a balance. By his theory, there had to be believers to oppose the nonbelievers. Quality against quantity, less but better.

With these thoughts in mind, a smile occupied his weary face, while he started to wander in the streets of this big city, with a lot of loneliness.

Chapter 17

1

One Sunday morning, a telephone rang and woke me up. Still half asleep, I recognized Mr. Friedman's high-pitched voice. He started apologizing. I stopped him right away and asked him if he knew what time it was, and if something was wrong.

"Nothing to get excited about," he said. However, he did want to talk to me and was afraid if he would not catch me on this early Sunday, then he would not be able to talk to me for another long week.

He was right. I avoided him intentionally. I did not enjoy talking to this money-grubber. His material motivations were obvious with his every move, so my mere association with him lowered my self-respect. But I've dealt with much worse than Mr. Friedman, at least he was not accused of killing anybody or molesting a neighbor's child and I did have those kinds of patients. From time to time, I found something in common with him. Even though I masterfully avoided him on many occasions, he successfully located me on others. He had his ways and one way was to call my unlisted number on Sunday seven o'clock a.m.

"What time is it Mr. Friedman?" I asked him even though I already knew the answer.

"Al," he started.

"By the way Mr. Friedman, you didn't answer me what time it is," I wanted him to tell me the time.

He did not answer me. Instead, he tried to explain to me, the thing he was about to discuss was actually for my benefit. I did not really take the statement seriously but I chose to let him talk.

"Al, I understand that I don't really have your respect, because you think, whatever I do or say is tainted with financial motivation. And you are very right. I don't believe in favors. I believe in financial security. Whatever I'm going to say is a step to enhance my financial stability. You are a logical man, Doctor. Things that I might actually benefit from, don't always hurt you. My proposition today, we might find mutually beneficial."

"I'm listening Mr. Friedman. I know what you're doing." I said with an unhappy smile on my face. "You are making sure I'm fully awake before you make your case."

"I told you. You are a logical person. Now, here is what I think you should do. Your book is becoming controversial. This is good, very good. But too much controversy opens up too many doors and invites too many different interpretations. This is not good for your peace of mind."

I knew what he meant. The book was a "how to" guide, with many confusing messages in it. It was obvious why it was causing so much controversy. Now I was listening to Mr. Friedman and what he had to say. Now I felt like I was ready for good advice. He was quite a salesman.

"Mr. Friedman, what do you think I should do?" I asked, causing surprise on the other side of line.

"Now you're finally making sense. I sincerely think, you should come out strong and state, what exactly you meant when you offered certain promises to those millions of readers. It would also be smart, if you take some questions from them and give them clarifying answers."

Mr. Friedman was right. I could not afford to hide any longer. I was very much in the middle of this controversy. It was time for me to come out, stand up, and like Greg said, "bring it to my territory." I remembered Greg's other words too, "you shouldn't be ashamed of something you are so big a part of. Your name is on that book. Go out and fight for it."

THE BALANCING GAME

Mr. Friedman sensed a change in my standing about the book's promotion and was quick to suggest, that it was best to begin on a very popular radio personality's show. I personally listened to the program a few times, while driving home at night. Robert was known as a very intelligent talk show host. He also was different from his colleagues, most of whom were obnoxious, loud and inconsiderate pigs. He certainly did not strike me as one of those big mouthed characters, who would spend his time, talents, and resources to achieve embarrassing extremes.

Mr. Friedman sounded ecstatic when I told him I would consider an interview with Robert Sander. He also warned me to be ready for extremely tough questions, with some of them being insulting.

"You have to watch out about that balancing formula thing Doctor Al. I think this is where they would be hitting you the hardest."

2

There were ten minutes remaining before going on air. I got a few instructional pieces of advice from Robert. He looked very simple; dressed in jeans, a T-shirt, and worn out sneakers. However, this seeming skimpiness from outside, could not mask the extreme intelligence he possessed. We chatted about many little things, but the book itself was not even mentioned once. He probably wanted the interview to be spontaneous. Ten minutes of small talk with this simple, down to earth person calmed me down.

The minute we were introduced on air, Robert turned to me and asked the question that gave me an indication that this would be a long and tough night.

"Dr. Al, why would a person like you, busy and successful as you are, put aside your whole life, take years of hard work and patience to write a book like this?"

I thought I was ready for any type of question, but when this uncomplicated first question came, I hesitated with my answer. Robert thought I needed a little help and maybe I did.

"Is there something in you, that compelled you to do this?" He rephrased the question.

"There is no one particular thing that provoked the sleeping writing giant," I tried to kid. "When I was a kid, I dreamed that one day I would write something that the whole world would read. But that was so many years ago. This dream, like many other childhood dreams, I managed to put aside very easily. I cannot really explain it. Maybe that dream haunted me. Or maybe because I really genuinely think, I have some ideas, that could be shared with people and maybe some people would benefit from what I had to say."

Now, I was relaxed. Other than Greg, there was no greater expert on The Balancing Game than me. So with Greg in virtual hiding, I was untouchable with my interpretations and my word was gospel.

Before the show actually started, I was warned by Robert, that there would be provoking confrontational questions and I shouldn't be engaging in a foul mouthed shouting match with anybody. If that would take place, then the show would be cut off so listeners wouldn't hear the swear words. Soon, questions started to come in and I was there to answer. Robert picked up a caller. He was a man named Burt from a small town in North Carolina. He had a funny accent but not funny question.

"Dr. Al, this question is for you. Are you a psychiatrist?"

"Yes, I'm a psychiatrist." I answered. I felt there was another question coming, set up by the first one, and this one could be nasty.

"Doctor, is it true that there is a high percentage of mental illness among psychiatrists?" Now, I knew what Robert was driving at earlier. I looked at Robert and found him encouraging me with his looks to answer the question. I knew I had to do my part. This character did not sound stupid.

"You are absolutely right," I answered.

THE BALANCING GAME

"Then do I have a reason to suspect you are a mentally sick psychiatrist, after you proclaimed that you discovered that crazy balancing formula?" The guy had logic, while he was delivering a blow under the belt. In reality, it was just a tough question.

Now I had to react and I did. I was not trained extensively in human behavior, to take low blows and let assailants get away with it.

"Out of curiosity, Tom, are you a lawyer?" I asked.

"Yes, I am a criminal lawyer and I can smell something fishy." He was getting excited.

"I'm a psychiatrist and probably a very good one." I knew an antidote against agitation and over-thinking. This antidote is calmness, and that enables me to preserve the maximum amount of thought power.

"Tom, you have to give me credit. I guessed your line of work. Now I want to take another guess. I know many psychiatrists. They are very close friends of mine, and you are no psychiatrist to me, making this diagnosis. I'm going to be on this show for another fifty minutes. Observe me and listen to me. Maybe at the end of this show you will change your original diagnosis. I won't say, "I'm not crazy". I'll let you to be the judge of that, by the end of the show."

"And one more thing, you are lucky you are not a psychiatrist. With your diagnostic abilities, you would be spending a lot of time in courts defending yourself."

Robert showed me his thumb up, for a job well done. The next calls turned out to be much less hostile. One of them, Rachel with an unconvincing voice, called me a genius, for creating the balancing formula, which as she stated, if properly applied, could help a lot of people to better their lives.

Then there was this man, Mitch from somewhere in the Midwest. He mentioned a few instances, in which he applied the balancing formula and he claimed, it worked every time. The simplest one was when he recently got separated from his wife. He still loved her very much and was quite frustrated. He was also in a very bad mood, knowing that his wife did not want to hear anything about them getting back together.

She would not even talk to him or answer his phone calls. Then he heard about this balancing book from his friends. After carefully reading the book, he decided to use the balancing formula.

First, he sat down and did his homework. He wrote down everything about his wife, however good or bad. The homework convinced him that getting his wife back was his priority. Then he intelligently organized things that would make her happy. He went a few years back, and remembered everything good that they did together. Then, he had inside information on her. After analyzing intelligently, he was able to assess, what changed in their lives and more importantly what could be changed back. Finally, the time came to perform efficiently. He ran out and got thirty six red roses nicely packed and wrote something like, "for old time's sakes, would you take a chance on me?" The letter referenced their wedding song. Roses were her favorite flower, but he chose 3 dozen roses for each decade they spent together.

The next day he got a telephone call from his wife, calling him to give him a second chance. All the letters of the balancing formula were complete. He followed H+O+P+E just like the book instructed.

"Mitch," Robert interjected. "I still don't understand how this book helped you to get your wife back."

"You see, after like I said, I did my extensive homework and organized things in my head; I determined that my wife was on my priority list, that meant for me, that I should devote myself to getting her back. That cleared up two things for me. Goal and motivation, just like the formula says. Without those two, like Dr. Letne suggests no success can be achieved. The homework made me think this way. There is a lady, I spent thirty years with her and frankly I didn't think those years were all that bad. She was angry and confused. Somebody offered her something different and she started to consider it. She could make a mistake very easy. I sent her roses, something I knew she loved and reminded her of all the good times we had together. My wife had a choice to make and Dr. Letne's guidance helped me get my act together, so that she chose me. I don't know about you, but I'm very much convinced that this man helped me to get my wife back. And I thank you for this. God bless you Doctor."

There were many calls that night. Some nasty like the first call. Others appreciative like the second call. I answered all those calls, and I noticed I had no problem doing so.

"How about money, you are making a lot of money, aren't you?" Robert wanted to know.

"Of course I'm making money on this. The book has been on the New York Times bestseller list for weeks now. The American people seem to be interested in what's inside. Every time you attract people's attention and they are ready to pay for it, you should make money in a capitalist country. It's very simple. You have a product. You have a market and you have demand. I don't think it's wrong legally or ethically, to make money by having some talent and by working hard. One thing I should stress though, and you might not believe this, but the truth is, financial motivation was the last thing on my mind when I was writing this book. Money and fame were not my motivational factors."

"Did you ever think that the book would make it this big?"

"Frankly, I didn't. There is another statement I should make. This book was something in my head a long, long time. I felt like I had to unload this heavy burden that I carried in my head. But once I wrote the book, I felt relieved. My philosophy is to try everything your heart feels like doing. So when my time comes, I'll have no regrets. I believe firmly in a few things in life and one of those is, to go after all your realistic dreams, and not necessarily for success. After all, not every attempt will end up with a good outcome. Statistically, people don't tend to regret things they have done and mistakes they have made. There are far more regrets for the things people didn't do and mistakes they didn't make."

"Doctor, I read this book a few times, and every time I read it, I would feel, that the writer of this book would be, not unhappy, but rather an angry man. Maybe that's why I think you succeeded to empathize with so many people. After all, at any given time, there are a multitudes of angry, frustrated people out there. Maybe this translates into your astronomical success, don't you agree?"

"I don't know how angry I look through this book. What I know is that I have no reason to be angry. I'm a young doctor, with a successful career and a satisfying personal life. When I was writing this book, I was very serious and focused. And when you are serious and focused, you may seem kind of angry."

"Then, what you are saying is, you are a happy person?"

"I'm an achiever. I see so many things to be achieved and not yet achieved, that sometimes I feel like a failure. To answer your question, I should be a happy person but I'm probably not. There are very few people who are truly happy, and thank god, I am not the one of those happy ones."

"We'll take one last caller from Fred in Chicago. Fred, you're on the air."

"Dr. Letne, I read your book and I found it hateful." The voice sounded familiar to Al, but the caller's voice only intensified.

"Doctor, I've talked to my priest about your book and we agreed that your book is against the church and its teachings. What religion are you Dr. Letne? And why are you so angry at God?"

"I'm not angry at God," I said, before I was interrupted.

"Is it true you hate God?"

"No-" I tried again to respond.

"Admit it! You hate God and the message of the message of this book is that the church won't help you! You're an atheist! And a blasphemer! And a heretic! And you're doing the devil's-"

THE BALANCING GAME

"I'm sorry Fred," Robert said, cutting off his call, "and to our listeners, but Fred was getting a little out of control there, so we ended the call. He wasn't letting our guest, Dr. Al answer his question, which I believe is an important one. Where does this book stand on religion?"

"Well," I started to answer before I was hit with a dramatic realization. The voice on the phone... it was Greg's voice. It was mildly distorted, but unmistakable. I froze momentarily. Why would Greg call the show up and rant against the book? That's when I realized that it was part of Greg's plan all along to add the element of religion to the book's reception.

"Well," I started again, "the book is not anti-religion per se." I gathered my thoughts and tried to channel Greg's drunken rants. "It's true that it's a different philosophy on life and the philosophy revolves around the necessity that each individual must help themselves. In that way, it is mildly against the dogma of the various established religions. Praying to those gods will not help you get that promotion or help you get your wife back or make your friends respect you. Only you have the power to achieve those things for yourself. And by following the balancing formula, you can do that. And by playing the Balancing Game, you can change your outlook on the sadness and misery in your life and perhaps even make you appreciate the things you do have. The book is not aimed at attacking religion, but if those positive messages are against the establishment, then so be it."

"Fascinating, Dr. Letne. Thank you for your time. If you want to know more about The Balancing Game, you can buy the book... just about anywhere or visit the website. Thank you again Dr. Al Letne for your time. Up next..." Robert kept going until the commercial break.

The interview was over. I felt drained. I also felt relieved.

3

A few weeks after the book made the bestseller list, things started to get out of control. My identity became very blurry in my eyes. While I continually avoided many of the speaking engagements that Mr. Friedman arranged, I still had to show up to some of them. In those speaking appearances, I had to defend the crazy book, the crazy theories it espoused and the crazy formula that promised a lot of things to a lot of people. The craziest thing was, none of the above belonged to me.

After expressing views from my side, I would get questions, really tough ones from the audience. In one instance, somebody asked me how his friend's drug overdose, could be adequately balanced in that person's life. "By your theory, his tragedy should be accordingly matched with something extraordinarily positive, equal in intensity with the height of the tragedy." The question was so tricky and so sensitive, the smartest thing I could possibly have done, was just shut up and pretend I did not hear the question. Instead, I opened my big mouth and came up with a stupid answer.

"If you are implying that the balancing theory, should be read this way... Since we aren't in position to measure this immeasurable abstract in units, we won't be able to measure the degree of tragedy and the degree of that few minutes of pleasure the person experienced before his death."

This was stupid what I said. I was the first to admit it. Greg's balancing theory sure had its holes. And these holes were not all small.

The above incident was not the only one of this kind. There were more questions equally as difficult. But in all fairness, most questions were softball questions that expressed boundless admiration.

The book was becoming more than a mere financial phenomenon, but rather a cultural movement towards self-actualization. Some people pointed out to me that they purchased black wristbands from some merchandising company. Those wristbands had "Balance" imprinted on them. I was surprised when I first saw it, but when I began seeing it worn by people on the street, I was stunned.

While the balancing formula appealed to the doers, who were often wealthy members of society, most of the readers, supporters and followers were the poor who needed to believe in the balancing game, that they could calculate future happiness from their present sorrow.

One person asked me why wealthy people still die. With all the money they possess, wouldn't they be able to buy life? That is kind of cruel to them. Considering that most of the rich are greedy, it would be probably unbearable for them to know that they not only going to lose their lives, in addition, they would be losing their wealth too. Maybe it does not really pay to be rich after all. The person who asked the question would not envy the rich, understanding that they had to leave all this wealth behind. In fact, it was entirely plausible that this rich person would have to leave money behind to someone that hated his guts or to someone that he mistreated

4

As time passed, I started to catch myself being two persons and having two personalities, with completely different sets of thoughts, two sets of views. This was not easy to handle. Wherever I would go, I would be followed by euphoria and confusion. My thinking processes started to diminish drastically.

But there were still enough senses left in me. I noticed that I was really starting to be affected by the fame, celebrity status, and the attention, that they brought, and money and respect, that all this generated. Being an honest person, at times, this would bother me, but only for a short time.

This could not last long, without causing a high degree of confusion in me. This is inevitable in a person with some degree of integrity and honesty left in him. I was honored, when this confusion knocked on my door, thus reaffirming the fact, that I still possessed some very important virtuous qualities.

On the one hand, there was the profiteering side of me, very much ready to accept and indulge. On the other side, there was the guilty side, aroused and provoked from the actions that were taking place on the other side. At times I felt like, I was stealing something from somebody. Powerful guilt and powerful profiteering got together to see which one would emerge as the dominant trait inside me. They could not go on fighting like this. Common sense was calling for some kind of coexistence.

The time came for me to depart from all this, to the place, where this confusing coexistence would leave less damage to my soul, spirit, body; in short to my whole being.

My departure from New York would mean that at least for awhile, my phone would stop ringing with all those numerous stupid questions. It also could mean that I would not be seeing my annoying and obnoxious agent. Besides, there was a chance to avoid myself in the familiar territory.

Once a conscious decision was made to go away, everything else worked out fairly well. I called up the Psychiatric Association and reinstated myself for the symposium, which was to be held on a beautiful Bahamas Island that was supposed to start in a few days. I agreed to give a small speech about the mind altering drug Prozac. I accepted the responsibility quite reluctantly. However, if that is what was standing between me and getting away from all my chaos, it was a small price to pay.

I canceled my appointments, arranged coverage for my emergency calls with a friend and pretty soon with my tickets for my Bahamas escapade; I was ready for the take off.

Mr. Friedman did not take the information about my unavailability for two weeks, lightly. In fact, he became hysterical and called me a few names, which I skillfully ignored, by removing my ear from the phone for a moment.

"I don't believe this guy," he was still on the other side of the line, fuming, even one minute later, when I returned to the phone. "This is the time when you are supposed to be everywhere, doing promotions, signing autographs, giving interviews, showing up on all kinds of shows. Now, you are telling me you are going away for two weeks. Are you crazy? Maybe you are crazy. No wonder people think psychiatrists are crazy. This is show time. Your book is still hot. Trust me, in a few weeks nobody will recognize you and nobody will need you!"

I hung up on him. I accomplished my task. I let him know, I would not be in the city for awhile. Mr. Friedman had to swallow my schedule. I warned him long before the book started to emerge. I specifically told him that I was very much against promotional activities and he agreed to accept that hindrance. I understand that his agreement at that time was a product of a tremendous amount of pessimism towards my book's future potential, but that was his problem. I had my own problems to handle and I was in no mood to take on his.

There was one more person I had to contact before my departure. This contact I was afraid, could not be made by phone.

Greg saluted me from his usual corner, raising his right hand occupied with a glass full of vodka. I could not see much of him in the familiar darkness. As usual, I looked at the wall with his shadow on it.

I could squeeze out more information about him from the distorted contours of the silhouette, than I could by looking directly at him. His head still with his chin up, his torso also appeared straight, not curved. He seemed happier than usual and he was swinging some sort of stick around in the air with reckless abandon. But both his arms appeared to be shaking, which may have been from excitement.

"Al, you son of a bitch, you did it, you did it. Congratulations. This is to your success." He was in good mood and was not about to hide it.

"Wait a minute, Greg. If anybody should be congratulated, it must be you. I did it? No way. All I did was put my signature on the paper. Let me get a drink, so I can properly give you your dues."

When I equipped myself properly for toasting Greg, I told him the truth. I told him, that I thought and still think that he was crazy. I told him that because of this book, my life changed very much and I was afraid it would continue to change. I told him how I wake up frightened in the middle of night to properly identify myself. I also told him that he was a genius.

"This drink is to you."

He did not say anything, for another twenty seconds. Then he asked.

"So, you think I'm a genius?"

"I think you are one screwed up, emotionally deranged character, but I also happen to think that you are a genius. You have that funny, crazy, unorthodox way of touching people. You sit here, in this dark, cold small room, playing with the minds of millions of people. They read you. They follow what you ask of them. You give them hope. You give them a future. This toast is to you. I would like to wish you good health, but I'm not even sure that's what you want. I would like to wish you success, but I'm not sure that's what you want. I don't want to wish you something you don't want. So whatever makes you run, Greg."

I emptied my glass in no time. Greg followed my example silently. We both remained silent for minutes.

I was relaxed here. I did not have to close my eyes in order to not see anything, and thus I avoided irritating my eyes. I did not have to search for fresh air. Through the widely open window, I was getting plenty of it. I did not have to force myself to avoid heavy thoughts. With the help of the vodka, any thoughts became weightless.

THE BALANCING GAME

"So, how does it feel?" he broke the silence.

"How does what feel?"

"How does it feel, to be a best-selling writer?" Now I knew, he wanted to know how he would feel in my place. He probably always wanted to become a best-selling author and now when he did write a bestseller, he wanted to know what the recognition felt like.

"I don't know Greg. For me, it's a little confusing. I'm not really a firm believer, in what you write about. This is very hard for me to pretend to be you. It's not just awkward. It's also kind of sickening. On the other hand, I can't say I don't like to be asked, recognized, praised, and revered. I also feel weird claiming I did something big like this, when in reality all I did, was signed my name."

"You'll get used to it. I really never thanked you properly, for what you did for me. I understand perfectly the magnitude of inconvenience and discomfort that you experienced."

"It is hard. In fact, it's so hard that I decided to go away. If I don't escape I might go crazy, and we know what being crazy is, don't we?"

"You can't run away from this one. The only right thing to do is to accept the whole thing, convert yourself to a believer. Then you'll be able to face anything with no fear."

"You are not really helping me with your advice. You obviously have no idea how it feels to be somebody you are not."

"Of course I have no idea" Greg's sad comment reminded me of something.

Remembering who I was talking to, I looked around and saw things or rather failed to see things; which made it clear for me. This was not a place for me to complain and this man was not a person to complain to.

We chose to stop talking again. I do not know exactly what he was thinking about. With me, it was not regret that occupied my mind. In fact, it never crossed my mind to regret going along with Greg's crazy ideas. The fear of uncertainty, infiltrated me throughout my body and soul and it horrified me. This uninvited occupation of my personal space by this scary fear could not leave my emotional and physical being untouched.

One thing I was right about... My whole being needed to get away from him, from them, from it.

"Greg, I'll be leaving in few days for Paradise Islands. There is a Psychiatric symposium scheduled. I thought it will do me some good to spend some time away from all this."

Already by the door, I stopped and looked back.

"So long Greg. Take care of yourself. You hear me? You genius son of a bitch. You know what, why don't you write another bestseller for me, while I'm gone."

I wanted to leave this room with a joke. The joke was not funny. That is why I was so surprised when I heard him laugh really hard.

I made him laugh. This made me happy. He was laughing for almost two minutes. Then he reached out his left hand, the one without glass of vodka. I had to go back and shake his hand. I felt his sweaty palm.

There was another place on my body, that felt something wet and burning. This was on my face. It was one big tear drop, that was making its way from my left eye to the left side of my upper lip. In slow motion, it eventually reached the destination point.

Now my lip was burning. The salty sweat irritated everything on my face on its way to my mouth. I could not help but imagine that this tear, while it began its journey from my left eye, actually originated in my heart.

A strange feeling took hold of me every time I left this room and its inhabitant.

Somehow I would think I was seeing him and this place for the last time.

"Hang in there Greg." I would whisper in his direction without him hearing me. "Just hang in there please."

I got home quite late. I consciously avoided reviewing my mail,

THE BALANCING GAME

telephone and email messages. Soon, my body was showered in very cold water. The cold shower cooled more than my body. It also lowered the temperature of my heated thoughts. With the relaxation of my body and my soul, came more perspective. Suddenly things did not appear as gloomy as they looked minutes before.

Now I was promising myself, things would work out fine. The worst thing that could happen was, I might throw up a few times on the plane from motion sickness. But this would not be a major problem. Two weeks of Paradise Island with a lot of water, sand and beautiful women could easily neutralize this minor inconvenience.

I could not complain, at least for now. Pretty soon I was humming some tune. I do not remember the name of the song. But I do remember, that it was not about darkness and cold. It was something about pleasure and a lot of it.

Chapter 18

1

The first day of my Bahamas trip was completely wasted. I spent the whole day sitting in the air-conditioned auditorium listening to various speakers from all around the country. Any other time, I would very much have enjoyed this kind scientific symposium. But this one was different. I had different goals to achieve this time.

When I enrolled for this scientific gathering, I was hoping this conference would be arranged for a more vacation experience, rather than having a heated scientific exchange of opinions. But this unfortunately turned out to be very highly organized. Many big name speakers discussed hot-button topics in psychiatry. Maybe because it was well organized and serious, one day of attending the conference, was more than I could handle. I even saw that The Balancing Game was scheduled for discussion on Day 2.

So, I specifically ignored the psychiatric symposium on the second day and visited the famous Bahamas beaches. I spent a few careless hours, doing no thinking, just relaxing and enjoying the scenery; I loved every minute of it.

While I don't consider myself a beach person, I could not help thinking how relaxing it was, the feeling I was getting from just lying there. I was getting vibes of the difference between indifference here and the passions from the rest of the world. And the apathy was intoxicating.

By ten o'clock in the morning, the temperature must have hit somewhere high in the eighties. The beach was not yet full of people, but it was already full of revelry and ignorance of daily thoughts and problems. By my definition of life, this type of place could easily represent paradise.

My perception of the place did not change when in addition to the blue sky hovering overhead, the beautifully clear water in front of me, and the incredibly clean sand below, I saw shapely half naked female bodies running all around me.

As a mature person, I understood that none of the above hedonistic virtues belonged to me. I was not bothered by this technicality. I felt like a true Olympian, for whom the participation in the event was more important, than winning itself.

A beach attendant already prepared my beach bed with towels on it under a gigantic palm tree and very close to water. I could see the ocean tides reaching my bed. The tide would only touch the leg of my cot, and then it would harmlessly subside. The beach boy did not really leave after he completed his job. His purpose for being there was completely different from mine. He was working there and was sweating for money. For him, this was no paradise. This was his place of business. He looked too human to me. His already tired sweating face expressed a better mood after his service was handsomely rewarded.

Very soon, I looked like a typical capitalist; sitting on the beach bed, with an inoculate tropical drink in my hand, observing the view. Maybe seeing these scenes inspired socialists to dream about human equality.

My enjoyment of the environment did not decrease in intensity, until the powerful sun had increased its heat and reached its peak. By that time my skin was red, sore, and begging me to leave. This decision about leaving was much easier, when my stomach started acting up and demanding attention. It needed immediate refueling.

While I was solving problems of very local importance, suddenly I felt like I was watched. I got that feeling, when I saw a shadow in front of me. I looked around and I saw a woman very colorfully dressed, even for the beach. She was staring at me with amusement.

"Dr. Letne, you look like you are about to make a big decision." She said as she walked towards me while swaying her hips with sexual provocativeness. She stopped just as she passed me. Now, she was standing a little to my right.

"Yes I am," I answered, now with a better opportunity to evaluate this intruder of my privacy. She was almost topless. Her buttocks were completely exposed to the sun or anybody who cared to see them. After grading her indecently exposed parts very highly, I then took a look at her face.

The evaluation was completed and she passed any test I could muster. But I wanted to know, who the hell was this woman that struck up the conversation and knew my name?

My questions were answered without me asking any.

"I noticed you yesterday in the symposium. You looked very bored, just like me. You wore a badge with your name." She was measuring me up shamelessly.

"You're okay, I guess," she concluded.

Amused, I started to walk away. While I liked the material I was seeing, I was very wary of this woman regardless of her looks; why would she come onto me so strongly?

"Wait a minute. Maybe you are lucky today. My name is Mrs. Skulks and I'm bored just like you."

"Listen Mrs. Skulks," I stopped for a second to decline gracefully, whatever she was about to offer, when suddenly I remembered, the name sounded familiar.

"You are not really related to that Dr. Skulks, are you?" I meant this distinguished looking bearded and aged speaker that put everybody to sleep yesterday.

"Yes, I am. He is my husband. Do you think you can handle the situation? Is it too heavy for you?"

"Does your husband know you're doing this?" I asked. But by this point I knew, this situation wasn't heavy for me and I was sure, I could handle it. I abandoned the idea of leaving. My Olympic spirit disappeared as soon as a certain part of my body started to influence my decision making process.

Now I didn't feel like it was enough just to participate. I wanted to conquer her too.

"Yes he does," she responded though I forgot what I asked. "We have a deal. As long as I don't embarrass him publicly, it's fine with him. At least he won't have the pressure of performance tonight. We won't embarrass him, will we Doctor?"

She sounded truthful. I could trust her. Even a woman looking like this, tells the truth sometimes. Maybe because she was dressed like this, I believed her even more.

"I know I am a bad girl, a very bad girl. My husband isn't good at punishing me. Maybe because he is too old. Men mellow with age, become soft. You won't feel sorry for me Dr. Letne?"

I was no saint in life. I had a few relationships, easily qualifying as kinky. This one was shaping up as one of the kinkiest, and I could hardly wait. I wanted to clear up the minor details before proceeding. And I hoped it would be meet my satisfaction.

"Mrs. Skulks, when you are saying punishment you don't mean anything bloody, do you? You know I'm a psychiatrist, not a surgeon."

She laughed. "I can't stand blood. One thing before you give me your room number. Are you good at spanking?"

"No, but I'm a good learner." I gave her my room number.

"Try to stay sober tonight. Remember, you have a lot of work to do. And don't you dare to fall asleep on me."

"Don't worry; I won't," I said and with the eyes of that Olympian on the path to a medal. The material and color of the medal I did not know yet. But I was ready to find out tonight.

2

By exactly eleven o'clock, the knocking began, and that was quickly supplanted by a pounding at the door to attract my attention. I expected the knock to be much softer and sexier. This pattern was nervous and manly. I just had to open the door to find out who actually was producing this inappropriate noise, disturbing my horny mood.

Two people were standing at my doorstep. One that was very much in my plans for tonight, and the other one I would wager was her husband. I was ready for something kinky, that at times a sexually deprived young wife of a very old man could create. But there is a limit to everything and I would rather never cross this barrier.

I probably looked shocked. My open mouth was an apt indication of my surprise. It remained agape for some time.

"Dr. Letne, sorry that I didn't inform you before, that I'll be introducing you to my husband," Mrs. Skulks broke the silence. "As I told you this afternoon, I never hide anything from my husband. I don't intend to start anything new tonight."

While she was talking, the other member of her family was observing me very closely. He finished his observation, turned around, and gave her a kiss on the cheek.

"He looks fine to me. Have a good time honey." I thought that's what I heard as he walked away calmly.

My mouth remained agape. I didn't know what the hell was going on. My common sense was telling me to close the door on Mrs. Skulks and forget about Fantasy Island. But this was very hard to do. She was very sexually provocative at eleven p.m. She asked me if she could come into my room. My mouth defrosted fast enough and said, "yes" in a hurry.

She entered into the room and walked around a little. Then, she noticed me standing by the door watching her walk.

THE BALANCING GAME

"You probably want to know what that was all about," she asked.

"Some explanation would be nice." I said.

"Don't make a big deal out of it. My husband wanted to get a close look at you, before he would approve. And you know what, he liked you. Without his acceptance, we would be doing nothing, and I mean nothing. I'm a very loyal person."

"Of course you are."

I remembered I was a psychiatrist. I have seen and heard enough. This one would not even qualify in the top ten oddest sexual experiences. This understanding put things in prospective. Dr. Skulks was gone. Mrs. Skulks remained... and she looked demonically attractive, sexually. And when her body was beginning to expose itself, I thought of nothing but her, well, not her exactly, but of having sex with her.

She was as bad in bed, as she said she would be. Mrs. Skulks had no shame. She did a lot of grabbing, sucking, kissing, and biting that night. She also did a lot of demanding... like being punished wasn't satisfied with soft spanking. We also had intercourse, multiple times.

When we called it quits, we were both satisfied. Mrs. Skulks delivered what she promised. I delivered what was expected from me. Dr. Skulks had to be a happy man too. Making his wife happy that night would make him a proud husband. People get satisfaction from different things. After all, I did not win any awards for my own qualities as a husband, for that brief marriage to Mary.

I still looked upon that marriage with fondness, because even though we were not well suited for each other, Mary's presence in my life dramatically improved my self-esteem and hopefully, she looked upon our moment of marriage with some appreciation as well. But, Mrs. Skulks and her husband found a way to make their union work, so again, who was I to judge?

3

The next morning I was sitting in a cafeteria, slowly dealing with my breakfast and sipping my coffee carelessly. Even at this late hour, eleven o'clock a.m. The place was bumping. Most of the people probably preferred to stay in bed late, after whatever they were doing last night. I looked around. Nobody looked busy or preoccupied.

Then I noticed when a short man dressed very warmly, quite inappropriately for the island's standards, walked in.

There are many people who are memorable for one reason or another, and the man I saw in the cafeteria was memorable for all of those reasons. He did not walk alone. There was a very impressive looking long legged young lady following him. I had to extend my attention towards this person because of his gorgeous follower.

"Talk about balance," I told myself and went back to my leisure activities. I was slowly finishing up my coffee, and the rest of my food was methodically disappearing from my plate.

I had no plans today. Since it was Sunday, I did not have to attend any scheduled meeting.

The only time I had to keep, was eleven p.m., when Mrs. Skulks and I would go back to do the good deed for me, for her, and for her husband. Last night turned out to be quite a treat. While I did not remember all the details that took place, I would remember enough to look forward to having the same experiences again.

So, having something to look forward to, I could easily kill time by playing in the casino or just lying on the beach.

Plans are just that: plans. You can and should plan, but you should know, statistically they change more often than not. And if that is accurate, when plans change, we ought not to make a big deal of it. It's easy to say, but when your plans change, it's often difficult to handle. A plan change was exactly what was coming. The short man, dressed very inappropriately for this time and place, was about to be the main contributor to the change.

I had to lift my head, in order to look up to the person that approached my table. He said something, which I could not hear well, because I did not devote my attention completely to the question. My guess would be he was asking me, whether he could sit at my table. And before I even opened my mouth to answer him negatively, this character was already occupying a seat right in front of me, across the small, very small table.

I looked around. Somewhere in the corner of the place, the striking girl, that accompanied this short man in, appeared busy reading a magazine. Then I looked at him again with a look that demanded some explanation.

"Dr. Al Letne." He was inspecting my face and looked like he was not sure, if he was talking to the right man.

"Sorry, a case of mistaken identity," I said in the hope, that this would make him go away. Whoever he was, my patient, that he could easily be, or somebody else, he had no business disrupting my vacation.

"Now, why do I think you are lying to me, Dr. Al Letne? How come you look so much like that crazy doctor, who wrote that crazy book?" This short man looked and behaved like, he was on top of world with seven billion people in it.

"Listen mister, I have just told you. I'm not the person you are looking for. You probably took me for somebody else. That happens. Now if you don't mind, I would like to be alone. May I remind you that I'm on my vacation and I would very much like to have some privacy."

This wasn't a case of mistaken identity. I started to realize he would not give up. My plea of leaving me alone was not even considered. Soon I started to think that this man was not my patient. Neither was he an admirer of my book. I was sure he had more important things to discuss with me after tracking me down here on the land of paradise, than to express his feelings about the book, with my name on it as an author.

"Dr. Letne, I forgot to introduce myself to you. My name is Kelly, Peter Kelly" the way he pronounced the name, he intended to impress me and attract my attention.

If that's what he wanted to do, he accomplished both with remarkable speed.

Mr. Kelly, if it was him, was one of the richest men in the country. He was very well known, in part because of his controlling interests of many major companies, dealing with airplanes, TV stations, professional sports teams and so on. His name was often mentioned in the media and his pictures were often displayed in newspapers and TVs for the whole world to see.

"Mr. Kelly? Wait a minute, THE Kelly?" Now I was the one inspecting his face and in no time, I concluded this man was, indeed who he claimed.

"Dr. Letne, I need your help. This is about my wife, actually. We are presently separated."

While he was asking for help, his voice sounded like he was about to issue an order for me.

"My wife..."

"Mr. Kelly. I'm terribly sorry about your wife." I rudely interrupted Mr. Kelly. "But the thing is, I'm having a very rare vacation. I hate to mix my vacation with anything but pleasure. If you need my services you can call up my office and my staff would gladly assist you, with arranging an appointment."

The rich and powerful, I had a great respect for them, but not at the expense of my vacation. That's what I thought. I also thought, that after what I said to Mr. Kelly, he would leave me alone. But Mr. Kelly was made of very different material than most of us. A man like him would not go away just because he is told to do so. They pursue things with a maniacal drive, using everything in their

THE BALANCING GAME

power to achieve things they want. That is a demonstrable trait of success.

He stayed, and finally I succumbed and took my eyes off my food to look in his direction. He looked angry and annoyed. A few seconds later he brought his dissatisfied face closer to mine.

"Dr. Letne. I won't take too much of your valuable leisure time. I have read your stupid book and I personally think it's full of shit. But my wife, who happens to be severely depressed, thinks very highly of it. Then I thought maybe she would agree to become your patient. She won't see any other doctor, but maybe she will see you."

Then there were some papers put in front of me. They looked like a check and airline tickets.

"Dr. Letne, here is a check for a half a million dollars. I'm hiring you to help my wife. I want you to be in your office tomorrow morning by ten o'clock. If she won't show up by that time, then you can do whatever pleases you. Here are tickets for New York and back from New York. And your room would be kept for you. By the way, this money is just a half. The other half you will get if and when my wife improves. I'm a generous man for people doing me favors."

He finished what he had to say. He was standing on his feet very firmly and confidently. I was seeing his back already. That could mean, he did not want to hear my answer. He just assumed it was, "yes".

"Mr. Kelly, wait a minute. Do you think you can just come to me, give me this check for a half a million dollars and expect me to drop everything and run back to New York to my office to wait for your wife to show up?"

He turned his face, looked straight in my eyes and just said;

"Yes, I do, and not necessarily because of the money. You would be stupid to let this case get away from you if you believe in what you write in that book. I really don't care what your reasons are. Just be there tomorrow morning. Your plane leaves in three hours, so you better hurry."

Mr. Kelly walked out of the cafeteria slowly. In a few seconds, I saw that blond girl that came in with him, had disappeared too.

I sat at the table for a while, trying to figure out what to do. On the one hand, there was paradise, with its full package of pleasure and an utter lack of worries. On the other hand, there was this check for a lot of money, airline tickets and the most challenging professional case of my professional career. Mr. Kelly was sure I would take this case mainly because in his opinion, this could be a case designed just for me, the author of that crazy book.

I thought a lot. Logic was telling me to forget I ever saw Mr. Kelly and enjoy the rest of my vacation, which was shaping up to be one of the best in my life. Then there was something very unexplainable in me that was urging me to take the challenge.

I also knew that I would never forgive myself if I consciously avoided the challenge of my life. Professional curiosity also demanded satisfaction. In a matter of minutes, I knew I would be in my office the next morning.

In three hours, I was sitting on the New York bound plane. I had a strong feeling I was about to get involved in a very murky situation, the kind I tried to stay away from all my life.

I knew I was making a mistake. But this mistake was the kind that I felt compelled to commit or I would never feel comfortable with myself. These mistakes make our lives interesting. These are the kinds of mistakes we never regret.

Chapter 19

Life is funny, if just because of how little fun life offers. Childish carefree dreams and fantasies are quickly substituted with serious obligations and responsibilities. Broken and grossly distorted images start to speak your language with a heavy foreign accent. Strangers in the daytime, give familiar smiles in the nighttime.

As a medical student, I was fascinated by the event of birth. But contrary to most other people, it was not the birth of a new life itself that interested me. The way a human is made, his entrance in this world terrified me: arms up, clutched fists, and unhappy faces. There was more to it: urinating on everybody around him to mark his territory and disrespect the people that just helped him arrive in this world.

But there was something balancing about birth. As a medical student, I noticed something distinctly balancing about the whole process. With their a"here I come" attitude, these little creatures with Napoleon complexes, with threatening postures, sounds, and jesters; all would end up the same way.

Having witnessed many deaths, it was not the death itself that impressed me. The way dead people appear beaten, surrendered to fate, with arms crossing their chests, as if acknowledging resignation from life. In so doing, he was effectively securing himself in a very peaceful place.

I noticed these contrasts, but I was never able to understand this balance before.

Chapter 20

I walked in my office with an unpleasant feeling. It probably had something to do with my sudden departure from the sun, sand, peace, and semi-naked women. Knowing that at that particular time, I could be resting peacefully and pleasurably on magnificent beaches was making me very uneasy with myself and my decision.

Instead I would have to sit here; listen, hear, and analyze a very rich and very sick woman's mind; something that I would rather not do. I could not hide my internal unhappiness, at least not from my receptionist; I could tell from her cute brown eyes that looked particularly bright this morning. Maybe it was not my visible anger, which caused this kind of physiological response in her. Her reaction also could be caused from the fact that she did not expect me back from my vacation yet.

"Is everything okay with you Dr. Letne?" She asked in a nervous manner, anticipating and preparing for some bad news, which let her minimal Chinese accent slip.

"Pretty much all right, Ms. Lee. I'm just having a patient coming unexpectedly, very unexpectedly."

Ms. Lee did not look satisfied with my answer. She expected more details and something a good deal more tragic from my evident anxiety.

"This patient must be very important to you Doctor."

"Important?" I didn't know yet. But she was definitely an inconvenient patient. I had to add to my answer to be more honest with myself.

"Maybe she is, maybe she isn't. I'm just doing a personal favor for a friend."

THE BALANCING GAME

"Some favor," Ms. Lee exclaimed.

She had time to kill. I had dreams to save. I instructed her to inform me about Mrs. Kelly's arrival immediately, hoping that the time of her arrival would never arrive.

I sat on the reclining chair with closed eyes and tried to stage yesterday's paradise like a steady picture in my imagination. It was very easy for me to remember the sun, the beach, and people around me. After that, I remembered the conversation and proposition with airline tickets and a half a million-dollar check.

And then I remembered the time... the time Mr. Kelly specifically stated. If Mrs. Kelly did not show up in my office by ten o'clock in the morning, I could forget about the whole thing, accept the check of course- and have my reservation in the hotel intact.

I looked at the wall clock. There was one minute remaining before the scheduled appointment. My heart started to pump faster. There was a chance, in the remaining time Mrs. Kelly would not show up. Because there was a chance, there was also a hope. But in a few seconds both the chance and the hope were mercilessly extinguished by cruel reality.

A simple knock on the door brought me out of my surreal mental state, to reenter the stage in the real world. I did not experience any stage fright, maybe that's why my stomach was not filled with butterflies.

My transition from my imagination to reality was smooth. My professionalism was definitely taking over all those distracting thoughts.

My receptionist informed me that the patient was in the waiting room and was ready to see me. I was ready to see her too. In a moment, Mrs. Kelly showed up.

I looked at her as though she just destroyed my dream house, which maybe in reality she actually did. Thinking about my dreams being destroyed did not make my appearance gracious. I was experiencing thoughts of weakness. This could not go on longer than a few seconds. I was a professional and I had a job to do, for which I was handsomely paid. I had to put aside anything else or anybody else for that matter.

I stood up, managed to issue a professional smile.

"Hello, Mrs. Kelly. I'm glad you decided to see me." And now I was truthful.

"Good morning Dr. Letne. I'm sorry, if I caused you any inconvenience," she sounded sincere.

"That's quite all right Mrs. Kelly." By now I was already in my working mood and I really meant what I was saying.

She sat down across my desk and by doing so, gave me an opportunity to take a very close look at her virtue, which had become the subject of obsession of a very rich, obnoxious, powerful, and inhumane person.

She did not really impress me with her looks. She was fairly average looking, definitely not somebody that would force you to do a double take, as she passed you by on the street. She was a small-framed, average height brunette, with very, very sad eyes. Her eyes made her somewhat unusual. They were deep-seeded and perpetually teary.

She was very simply dressed and her manner of speech and behavior did not reflect her wealth and status. She was looking at me now, but in reality she was merely looking in my direction. I did not think she was seeing me. She was looking at me much the way a blind woman would have been looking at me.

But Mrs. Kelly was not blind at all. I took a look at the questionnaire she filled out. Her handwriting was careful, very neat and I also noticed she wrote using very small letters. The miniature size and care of with which everything on the page was written demonstrated that she was meticulous and she was definitely not blind.

The color of the ink was from a pen she brought herself, rather than the one provided to her, which denoted a desire to control uncontrollable situations.

THE BALANCING GAME

She sat attentive, but indifferent at the same time. Her hands on the table were moving aimlessly and were disclosing her nervousness, which was otherwise difficult to detect.

"Mrs. Kelly, with your permission, I would like to go over the information you provided." I said while looking straight at her, hoping to engage her in some conversation and establish verbal contact. This is a basic tenet for any psychiatrist, opening up a patient.

She said nothing. I assumed she had no objection to my doing this. By now I realized, that she would not be an easy case at all. She was sending me a message that she would not cooperate, would not try to help me to help her, which is the worst scenario in any psychiatric case management.

I had a difficult job to do. But whatever index of difficulty existed, I still had to proceed. I went over the questionnaire very carefully. We psychiatrists heavily depend on information patients may provide through this questionnaire. Sometimes from solely observing a patient and reviewing the information provided, we could receive enough clues to understand which direction to go with the particular patient's problems.

There was nothing unusual from a psychiatrist's point of view about Mrs. Kelly. She was the only child in her family and she lost her father very early in life. Apparently he did not secure his family's financial future before passing. Thus, her family was left very much unprepared for the hard road ahead.

Her mother had to work long hours to maintain a decent quality of life. As a little child, she was sent to a prestigious private school. The whole questionnaire was full of answers dealing with securing her future and education. This was very obvious.

Equally obvious was reluctance on the part of Mrs. Kelly to answer questions, that were so crucial for her treatment. Questions relating to her sexuality were left blank, leaving at least a quarter of the whole survey unfilled.

After very expensive schooling and obtaining a law degree, she came to marry a much older and much richer man. Of course, the man she married was Mr. Kelly. Even without those unanswered important questions, I could not say the review of the information was fruitless. I was forming a picture in my mind of a woman, raised without a father's love and without a mother's presence. Then, an old prince came on a young white horse. But, the stereotypically anticipated problems arose, very characteristic of these situations.

I was not discouraged that Mrs. Kelly did not provide any insight into her sexuality. Those questions were very private, and many people had problems answering them without having established some rapport with the psychiatrist first.

I finished reviewing the answers. So far, so good. Now I lifted my face and looked at her. She still continued to seemingly look towards my eyes, but the look was definitely aimless. She was also motionless. Even her hands were without movement now. I was seriously looking for any kind of movement, but could find none. Finally, I was very relieved to notice her steady and regular breaths.

The time came to communicate verbally.

"Mrs. Kelly, it would be very helpful for both of us, if you kindly tell me in your words, what you think the problem is."

I tried to be authoritative, professional, and friendly, all the same time.

Mrs. Kelly remained silent. I knew she heard me. Her stare intensified while she was formulating the words. She needed a little help and she got it from me. I repeated the question much slower, giving her more time to craft the proper answer.

"This morning I woke up at around five o'clock. I stayed in bed for hours, just thinking about what's the sense of getting up at all. Getting up to do what? Or to see whom? Yesterday was the same. Two days ago was the same."

She finished the last words while she was standing. She got up

THE BALANCING GAME

quickly with a preoccupied expression on her face. You could see turmoil in her mind, a mind that was begging for peace. You could hear the sound of anarchy, anarchy that required some order. She needed help. That was obvious. But in psychiatry, like in any other health specialty, people must realize they have a problem, admit it and ask for help to be ready to be helped. Unless they do this, there is no way you can accept an emotionally unstable person and force treatment on her.

Mrs. Kelly was not ready yet. Maybe that is why in a matter of seconds she managed to disappear behind the door. I was not surprised. She was not the first to do this.

I just felt bad. I sincerely wanted to help her. I felt sorry for her, but there was nothing I could do. I got up, lit up a cigarette, and started to smoke. That is how I knew, I was upset. I went to the terrace to breathe some fresh air, swallowed a few cold breezes, as if I was afraid I would run out of air, and I wanted to secure some for the future.

It was approximately eleven o'clock in the morning and the city looked magical for this period of time, at least from my terrace. Though cars were not allowed to make noise by blowing out their horns and sirens, you could hear them causing a ruckus. There were signs of defiance in the air. People were supposed to be dressed in suits and wear ties in this part of the city. But I could see or even feel an aura of noncompliance.

There was rebellious spirit in the people that day, even in the way people were dressed: in jeans and sporting jackets. There were signs of obvious confrontation between the proper and the improper, between the expected and the unexpected and even between the abstract notions of the earth and the sky. People were caught in the middle of all this day's antagonism.

Among others, Mrs. Kelly was caught in the middle of the opposing ideologies of the day. I noticed her standing by the entrance of the building. She looked torn. That is how I knew she was the lady symbolizing everybody's problem-filled lives.

She stood passively, aimlessly observing life surrounding her, watching inactively mobile and immobile subjects alike. I did not want her to see me. I took a small step back. I continued to watch her carefully. I was genuinely surprised when I saw her disappear inside of the building. With considerable pleasure, I accepted the fact that she was coming back to my office.

I caught myself keeping my fingers crossed on both my hands. I jumped back in my office and in my chair. I did not straighten my fingers. That is how much I wanted to help this woman, both consciously as a professional and subconsciously as a human being. I went back in. Now I wanted her in my office.

Mrs. Kelly showed up without a knock on the door. She did not need to knock. I waited for her, sitting in my chair, so when she walked in, she would not know that I actually watched her and willed her back, while her little escapade was staged.

She looked agitated. I noticed she was holding a book in her hands. I recognized the book. It was my bestseller. She raised it above her head and whispered loudly.

"I need help Dr. Letne. Somehow I believe that this book and the writer of this book can help me. I'm so miserable, and if your theory is right, in the future I should be a very happy woman. That's what your balancing theory is about, isn't it?"

She did not really cry, but the way she sounded, it might as well have been a cry. Help was an understatement. She was very much in need of a rescue.

I looked at her and at the book she was holding. Both were shaping up in my eyes as a problem. She expected to be helped by me. I myself needed help. I could not bother God for assistance. By not following any particular religious traditions, I did not think I had a healthy relationship with him. I had to count only on myself.

THE BALANCING GAME

"We can't change the whole world Mrs. Kelly; we can try to change you, but only with your cooperation." I told her and with an authoritative gesture, I pointed her to a chair across from my desk.

She sat down on the chair that she so abruptly abandoned a few minutes ago.

"You have to forgive me Doctor, I'm your patient now. I'm entitled to some strange actions."

"Yes, you are Mrs. Kelly." I answered calmly. I would not say anything analytical. I did not want her to think she had to watch every word and every move, she made in front of me. She had to know; she could behave and talk freely here, without fear of being judged. We had a great distance to cover. We had to start from the most remote part of her past, to the most recent moments of her present, why she decided to return to the building. So it was of vital importance for both of us, that she would not perceive me as a critic of her troubled life. We had to trust each other, in order to survive the bumpy road to her recovery.

"Mrs. Kelly, you might not know this, but I see people like you almost every day. This is the place they come, talk and confess and by doing so they clear and cleanse themselves. I'm trained to listen, give advice and when necessary give appropriate treatment. So please keep in mind, there is nothing you can say, that I have not heard before."

I noticed she was listening now, with considerable interest. I also noticed the way she put the book in front of her on the desk, and how she maintained contact with the book by using her right hand. It did not take long for me to realize, she treated this book like a bible.

"You don't mind, if I keep the "Balancing Game" in front of me, do you?" She asked me in a way that could not permit a negative response.

"Mrs. Kelly, do you believe in this book?"

"I'm not sure what I believe in. I don't know if this book can help me. What I know is that this book is for losers. And I'm a loser so far. I'm ready to play this balancing game. According to this book, I could be, sometime in the future, the happiest woman on the earth, because I'm the most miserable person today."

"Mrs. Kelly, are you a religious person?"

"What do you mean doctor?" She didn't know what I was trying to accomplish.

She was smart. She knew this was not a routine question. I did want to achieve something with this question. I wanted to separate her from the book that she kept spiritual and physical contact with. I thought the idea of God could be a good substitute to this book.

"Do you believe in God, Mrs. Kelly?"

"I believe in anything and anyone that helps me. You'll be my God, if only you can help me, and if this book helps me, it will be my bible."

For one minute, there was complete silence. I could see that this was the type of silence, which is often followed by a long talk. I could see her lips move, without issuing a voice. I observed her doing this a few times. A plane with a long delayed flight was about to take off. It just needed some more runway. It wasn't easy. But on the other hand, what was? Then the plane took off.

She started to talk. She talked about everything she thought was important for me to hear. Almost everything she went through as a young woman, including her first time menstruating, with the feelings of uncertainty and fear that accompanied it. At that very critical time, she had nobody to share her fears with. She did not hear any comforting and relaxing words from her mother, like many girls in similar situations have.

She did not really complain about her mother being busy and not being with her, when she needed her. She did not have to. It was easy to notice that she was bitter.

Mrs. Kelly talked about many things, but I would disregard some topics and register the ones that were relevant to her presence here today. In this regard, there was a story that looked very important to me.

THE BALANCING GAME

Once, when she was in the seventh grade, she felt sick and had to leave school; so she got home a few hours earlier than usual. It was early for her mother to be home. That is why she was fearfully surprised, when she heard noises coming out of her mother's room. She gently pushed open a door that was already slightly ajar and stepped inside. She saw her mother lying completely naked in bed with some stranger on top of her.

As naive as she was, and as young as she was, the first thing she thought was, her mother was in physical danger. Hearing her mother's moaning and her pleas for her assailant to stop, she really thought her mother was being tortured by this criminal.

Frightened and frozen, she continued to witness her mother's screams, "Please, stop, oh please." She also continued to observe this man making some jerky motions, the ones that in all probability were causing her mother's physical suffering. All this came to an end, when the man and her mother simultaneously issued some inhuman notices.

She stood there, thinking that her mother needed help and was not getting it from her. At some point, especially when she heard her mother climaxing, she thought her mother has being murdered.

Standing by the widely open door and still very much in shock, she soon witnessed a completely different scene. Her mother came around and said something that she did not understand for years after that frightful day. She thanked her pain-inflictor very warmly planting a lot of kisses on his lips and cheeks and expressed a hope, that this would happen more often.

"There I was," she continued with a subdued voice, "witnessing what I thought was possibly the last minutes of my mother's life and feeling heavily guilty, unable to help her. And then I heard her thank her assailant and virtually beg him to do these things more often." She was trembling. Not only could I see her quivering body, I could also hear her voice nearly crack on several occasions.

"What happened next" I asked?

"I managed to leave the room, without them noticing me. But that room and the events that my mind registered that day, and never left me."

As she continued to talk, I realized the day was one of the most important days in her life. Conflicting messages were sent to her and she had a problem explaining these paradoxes of life. And so she lived with unanswered questions for years by herself, drawing conclusions without asking, consulting or discussing. Questions were left unanswered and she continued enduring pain and discomfort, caused by uncertainty in life, brought to a young maturing girl. And she faced all this and her whole life alone.

She finished this part of her story and silenced herself for a few seconds. She needed this time to calm her thoughts, all kinds of them, which came from Pandora's box, once it was opened.

At that time she looked tired already. To go through distance that covered the vast emotional territory, caused Mrs. Kelly considerable emotional turmoil and it took more energy from her than she actually had. As a physician, I could not afford to miss this point. Though I was determined, I had to retrieve all the information I could gather, even though I was afraid not to push her overboard.

At this point, Mrs. Kelly was very much at risk from what we, in the business, call overexposure. She had legitimized her past, only to have these negatively charged tides swallow her and wrap her in a mirage filled and secured by depression.

Making people open up their troubled pasts is an art-form, but, knowing when to stop them, that is a masterpiece.

"Mrs. Kelly, I think you should stop here. You had enough today," but she could not hear me. She was in a different world again. Her motionless behavior when she entered was more a product of avoiding her problematic past, but now her motionlessness was something new. This new other world she entered was one that was too much a part of her and it would not let her go. She had a problem opening the door to that world, and she had the same problem closing that same door.

Mrs. Kelly looked like a person with a guilty past; or a criminal with a crime on her conscience. The criminal was finally coming to terms with her crime, after avoiding her past for too long a time. But eventually she would do the same thing every typical criminal does; she would return to the scene of the crime.

There is only so much distance one person could travel, physically or emotionally. And since we were traveling through time, through her past, we had covered more temporal territory than any person should have to endure in one day. There was definitely a limit of how much Mrs. Kelly could absorb without crossing the edge and collapsing from excess.

"Mrs. Kelly," I said in a manner that demanded attention. I happily noticed she responded to my voice and now she was definitely looking at me. I was starting to feel signs of success, but I was also very much aware of how all these signs could disappear in an instant.

She was clearly dealing with whatever condition she had been dealing with when she walked into the office this morning. But, she had made one solitary step of progress. I realized that her progress was a gradual process, in order to leave behind her past as a survivor.

"Mrs. Kelly," I repeated when it seemed to me that she was in a position to comprehend my thoughts. She planted a meaningful expression on her face. There was even a hardly detectable smile on it. More importantly, her watery eyes had a new hope engraved in them, a hope for a better life.

"I think you had enough for one day Mrs. Kelly. You were great and I'm going to reward you for this. You can take the rest of the day off. You deserve it."

Though she did try to argue about how unreasonable it was to stop the session, I could see she was visibly appreciative to return from the past, which was bringing her nothing but pain and suffering. While on the trip to her past, there were very few moments, when she was not wincing in torment.

"Are you sure we have to stop here. I thought I could remember a few more things. Isn't that what you want me to do?"

"Mrs. Kelly, we have to be very careful. I can't let you spoil today's work by overdoing it; it is a difficult process and we took a substantial step today."

Within a minute she was gone. Her driver had to come upstairs to accompany her to her car, before leading her home.

Chapter 21

The next morning, she sat across my desk once again. She chose to sit there, instead of sitting on the reclining chair where most patients feel more comfortable. As soon as we exchanged greetings, I was able to look in her eyes. They continued to have the same fiery spark, as they had yesterday when she left the office. I interpreted this as a good diagnostic sign and prepared myself for another informative day. When she started to talk, I knew, during her overnight break, she had lost none of her steely resolve to challenge her past all the way.

When in high school, like any attractive girl, she would be asked out on dates. And sometimes she would agree and sometimes not. Her choice was often based on the boy's ability to convince her that he had some manners, but that he also possessed the insatiable appetites and characteristics of a cruel animal. She needed someone that was potentially capable of hurting her physically.

The fear of being hurt physically was most likely caused by that scene she witnessed in her mother's bedroom. While she was horrified from ever imagining the pain she had to endure, she would convince herself, that it was a necessary attribute to relationships between a man and woman. An ordinary date with a clean-cut, nicely and cleanly dressed classmate did not provide her with the thrill she sought, enough to enjoy her dating games.

Her youth brought her a serious lack of satisfaction for a curious young girl, growing virtually without a mother's supervision. Those boring proper dates were filled with an uncomfortable amount of talk and far less physical contact than desired. Her dates were completely the opposite of what she heard her female classmates boasting about.

While she understood there were many lies in those bragging stories, she believed those lies were based on something truthful.

But with her, she thought it was different. She did not even know how to lie about these things she did not understand.

She felt as though she were being left behind. That particular feeling comes very natural, when you are seventeen, growing up, and wanting to grow up faster. This feeling is inseparable from the popular parental fear of peer pressure. These pressures were probably particularly weapons against her. Because of these powerful forces, she overcame whatever fears she had about dating a virile, masculine man and agreed to go out with the most monstrous-looking creature in her neighborhood. This one not only looked scary, he also had a violent reputation. She surprised everybody with this decision, everybody including herself.

This was a decision she did not make easily. In fact she had to spend two worrisome days and two sleepless nights, before she bravely approached this boy with big muscles and an even bigger head, literally and figuratively (even though he was remarkably short.) His hair covered much of his face, which gave him a distinctly animalistic quality. That is what she noticed about him.

She thought she could handle the challenge. It was a challenge that she voluntarily and arbitrarily imposed on herself. She convinced herself she would get rid of her long-standing fear of men, if she would challenge the fear itself. People in trouble, often run in the wrong direction for help. They connect themselves to people, who only increase the degree of their danger. Such was the case with Mrs. Kelly. With nobody around to trust, and having a mother with no impact on her life, she did not receive any trustworthy advice.

So she had no other choice, than trust her naive, immature, and subjective instincts. She miscalculated everything about this experience with this animal, and her errors led her to lose all the remnants of her confidence, and to fester in her own guilty conscience. So, after this experience, she was left utterly untrusting of anyone.

The experience turned out to be more than sexual in nature. It was filled with humiliation, and it was not merely the serious consequences of her physical abuse that would haunt her. That beastly individual on top of her never gave her pleasure, and never even tried to please her.

What she actually received instead was pain, and a lot of it. The pain, accompanied with absolute disgust, permeated every level of this relationship. He would pull her hair to the point where he would rip out clumps of her hair from the root with the sole intention of having her scream. A few times, her head was violently thrust into the edges of her mother's headboard. There was often blood dripping from her mouth and there were evident bite-marks on her upper lips. She was left physically bruised and scarred and the degradation and reached every imaginable place on her.

Despite her lack of sexual experience, she still knew that this was not something to brag about with her peers. The damage done to her could not be measured by counting the square inches of injured body parts. The harms that could not be seen could not be measured. Her mind, her psychology, and her confidence were damaged much worse than limbs painted with blood.

She washed herself as soon she regained possession of her body. Bloody spots on her body, were cleaned more easily than she thought. The body pains and bruises would take a few days to heal completely. But the pain and bruises on her higher self, the parts that no soap could reach were incurable, except with time. And the nature of these wounds, required such enormous quantities of time that even that seemed inhuman.

And all this started, when this character that she chose came to pick her up. She let him in the house, sat him in the living room, while she was fixing herself up. She tried to present herself as delectably as she could for her date. She was standing in front of her mother's mirror, in her mother's bedroom. Then she saw him behind her and a little later she was not able to see him at all. She was just able to sense the pain and humiliation that he was causing to her body and her mind.

This all took place on the same bed; on which she witnessed her mother being "mistreated". To her, this bed was the place that she associated with her most horrifying trauma, which would affect her future enormously. Now she had another experience on this bed, which she had to digest, interpret, and inevitably rationalize.

She did not discourage the carnivore, nor did she resist or put up any fight. And because of her lack of dissent, this violent assault could not be classified as rape.

But it did have all the ramifications of the worst rape any woman could possibly experience.

For two weeks, she stayed home. She refused to talk to anybody, even to her mother. The marks of obvious physical abuse were hard to hide. But she offered no explanation to anyone. So no one but her knew what exactly happened to her, and no one including her, could tell how much the events that caused these outer scars would affect her inner life.

In her head, it was she who "asked for it" and she was ready to accept the responsibilities and consequences of her irresponsible actions. She did not totally withdraw from the real world. She would continue to feed herself. Subconsciously she knew this event had its long-standing consequences, but she also knew; she had to survive. So while she continued to punish her mind, she still continued to treat her body with adequate attention.

Little by little, she reassembled herself, and went back to school. Sparse smiles returned to her face. Her smiles were not without grief though, a grief that would stay with her as a constant reminder of something terrible with no name and no face.

THE BALANCING GAME

After the horrifying incident, her life returned to her own standard of normalcy. Studying hard was easy for her. Getting good grades was gratifying and watching TV was pleasurable. Books were her friends, but she maintained a few friends, with whom she could sparsely converse. Days became weeks. Weeks quickly became months and months snowballed into years; the time was ticking away from her past, the time no longer was present in her life, because she did not want it to be there.

At twenty two, she was a senior in an Ivy League College, with the mind of a middle aged woman, but with childish dreams and the looks of an innocent teenage girl. She kept asking herself questions about her life and life in general, over and over again.

"Life, what do you want from me?"

She stopped there as if snapped out of a trance. Maybe because she wanted this question be answered. But even today, this question remained unanswered.

I did not encourage her to stop her story. In fact I looked at her with a very upset face. Her long pause troubled me. She got the message. So, within two minutes, she continued to cruise through the labyrinths of her distorted life path, that eventually landed her in this office.

In that final year of college, she was invited by her friend, to spend her Christmas at her place. She stayed there for a few days, in a quiet, cozy, family atmosphere. In the evening at the supper table, she would watch how her friend had father-daughter conversations, something she had never experienced. She watched enviously as her friend playfully sat on her father's lap. And her friend talked and talked endlessly about silly things. Her envy blossomed.

A few weeks later, something happened to that friend. She had leukemia and so, people said that she was doomed to die-- that it was just a matter of time and that time came for her. She died in peace, joining her mother, who died a few months earlier from the same sickness.

Mrs. Kelly remembered going to visit her friend's father, to personally express her condolences. She missed her friend's funeral because of her final exams, and she felt terrible about it.

After completing her plans, seeing her friend's father and expressing her feelings about how sorry she was, she prepared to leave the house. She looked at the mourning father and suddenly felt terribly sorry for him. He was sitting at the table and looking at her aimlessly. She did not know what happened next. She just remembered that she was sitting on the lap of this short, older man, absorbing an unbelievable amount of warmth, security, and tenderness from him. Those things were strange to her. And because they were new to her, they were scary too.

Scary or not, it was comforting and very pleasurable, in the adult sense of the word. She continued to sit on the lap of this much older, shorter man and was hoping she would not be pushed or discarded. Then came an even better feeling, a feeling she could not describe. She would remember this feeling, as something really good. She could not recount when her dress was lifted or when her underwear was removed. But, that was because she was in a different world and liked it there very much. Afterwards, she realized that it was not just her soul that was so pleasantly penetrated. Her female sexual door widely open, accepted the long awaited guest from a different world.

The rush arrived with a climactic heat and acclaim, but it was immediately followed by silence. After all this occurred, a train full of self-awareness and self-respect arrived late again.

The old, short man turned out to be very lonely, and in very desperate need for close people to surround him, after losing his wife and only child in a matter of months.

The older man, who could afford any of his wants saw in Mrs. Kelly, a young woman that might be able to take over the duties of his wife and his daughter at the same time. The proposal was made in quite a hurry. She accepted the proposition in just as timely a fashion.

She was happy for a very short while. She soon found out what her predecessor had long known, that her old and short husband loved to spend money on women, on young women. When she confronted him to discuss the problem, he would try to reassure her with his trademark statement. "I like them, but I love only you."

Once again, she snapped out of daze and came back to the present. She traveled a lot today. She needed another well-deserved rest. I could not send her back to her past. It was time for her to depart from the past. It was time to sever the ties with her past.

Chapter 22

By the third visit, Mrs. Kelly was even more tentative and even more talkative. She carefully calculated her words. She talked and I listened. I was extremely careful not to disrupt the peaceful rapport, which was beginning to develop between me as a doctor, and her as a patient.

While I was satisfied with the progress thus far, there was no guarantee that the sessions would lead to a satisfactory result. At any time, Mrs. Kelly could decide that these chats were not helping her and walk out of the office. She had tried this before and in cases like hers, it was not uncommon.

The people with these types of problems; very often follow a common characteristic of unpredictability. While trying to overcome the wall between outsiders and themselves, any little innocent or trivial stimulus, could set them off. Many of these people feel so comfortable hiding behind the wall, that they are reluctant to hurdle it even for a chance at actual happiness.

Behind that wall, people like me may only be allowed to visit. From my perspective, those people look like prisoners, lonely and condemned, guilty and suffering for their possibly illusory crimes. And I, acting as their high priced lawyer, would never even ask them if they were guilty. The only thing that mattered for me was to help them escape from their self-imposed prison. In Mrs. Kelly's case, I wanted to help her because she has done much more time than she deserved. And, I would accomplish this by any means necessary, any means whatsoever.

Chapter 23

The long working day was over. I only realized how long the day was after I physically left the building and came in direct contact with the outside chill, the foggy air, and the slight drizzle that tickled my face. Because of the bad weather conditions, I avoided strolling in the streets. I made an energetic attempt to rush to my car, parked one block away.

I really did not have any particular plans for the evening. I got some assistance with my unplanned evening. Without consulting me, I was included in somebody's plans for the night.

I could not get to my car, because of a very simple physical obstacle. A large man was blocking the driver's side door by standing in front of it, thus preventing me from the rest of my day. I made no attempt to approach from a different angle. The big man with a stony face and a scary look, tried to issue a smile. He did not succeed. But he did have success in delivering the message, he was sent to deliver.

"Dr. Letne," Mr. Intimidation addressed me. I could feel it. That's why I was not able to verbally respond. I did manage to nod my head a few times.

"Mr. Kelly would like to have a word with you Doctor. Would you follow me this way please." He turned around before even finishing his sentence and moved away from my car. He clearly expected me to follow him.

I did follow him obediently. For a short while, I was stunned by the power of intimidation, which this strange, fear-inducing giant was producing. Mr. Kelly's name did not really help to put my mind at ease either. After a short walk that seemed to last forever; we approached a stretch limo, elegantly parked by a hydrant. Before letting me in the car, which is what I figured was his plan, the big man had to make the back seat of the limo suitable for a private conversation. To achieve this end, he had to let a very young, very beautiful, and very blond girl out.

The moisture on my face and hair helped me sober up. Curiosity was my new operative state of mind. With unhidden pleasure, I observed her long legs glide through the door. She threw me an indifferent look and walked away, just to stop in the middle of sidewalk.

The door remained open and I started feeling my body gently shoved towards the car. The giant was doing what he was paid for. Soon, I was in the car, realizing that two people had to remain outside in this weather to make space for Mr. Kelly and myself to talk privately. I looked through the dark tinted glass; I could see them both. The girl was still standing in the same place and the driver remained standing by the door; both open to the moody sky's insults. But I did not have the time nor desire to feel sorry for them. I had a few challenges of my own to handle.

I sat across from Mr. Kelly and looked at him carefully. The man looked aged and tired. But still I was able to recognize his confidence, which he powerfully displayed by just sitting comfortably, leaning back and looking at the ceiling.

But regardless of whatever way he projected himself or behaved; he was no superman. He was still just human and still had to deal with ordinary people like me. The real world was demanding his attention and he had a need to talk to a representative of the earth, in this case me.

He looked at me directly and I thought I saw him lift his eye brows and widen his eyes. By doing so, he was letting me know; he wanted me to talk and that he was ready to listen.

Bubbles burst. Mr. Kelly was not a big man. He did not really occupy much space in the car. With all his money and power, he had a major problem to win one little woman's heart. For whatever reason he needed her back. Even with poise denoting apathy, I could see through him. Mr. Kelly was filled with agony. Seemed to me it was the torment of a person who was losing his most sacred possession.

"Mr. Kelly," I started to talk in a very relaxed manner. "I understand we'll be talking about Mrs. Kelly?" As the words slipped out, I realized the idiocy of the question. What else would I be discussing with him? I did not think I could be of any help in his business dealings. There was an ironic smile returned and he nodded his head a few times. This little unsuccessful entry did not upset my stable and confident state of mind. What I truly understood by this time, that even though I was physically on his territory, the field belonged to me. I knew this, and I was ready to let him know this also.

"Mr. Kelly," I heard myself saying. I liked the way I sounded; collected and confident, exactly how I felt. "Your wife is obviously an emotionally disturbed woman. For whatever reason, she broke down. She is shattered. What triggered this exactly? I do not know yet. While I don't see the reason behind it, I see the result of it. I suspect a few avenues as possible contributors to her problems. But, my information is incomplete and my evaluations are still being decided. What I mean is, at this time, I pretty much know where to go from here with Mrs. Kelly."

Mr. Kelly remained still and I knew I continued to have his complete attention.

"Mrs. Kelly should be brought back to real life from the misery and sorrow she is in now. If we allow these things to continue any further, she might slip in a deeper depression and eventually might self-destruct." There was no response to what I just said. Instead, he continued to be inactively attentive. He looked away and then straight at me again, which I interpreted as great interest from his part.

"Mrs. Kelly is a person with needs," I continued. "She is also a young person. This makes her needs more specific. Besides other human things, her physiological needs should be adequately evaluated, restored first, and then her needs must be met. This is a long, difficult rehabilitation process with several stages. One of those stages would include, dealing with her relationships with men. Also attempts will be made to dissociate her from every person or situation, which would be a root cause for her depression. To be perfectly honest, in many cases we urge our patients to stay away from those situations or persons."

During my monologue, Mr. Kelly did not say anything. He allowed me to be authoritative and instructive. This showed me his surprising respectful side. He had committed a major mistake. He allowed himself to be emotionally involved with a woman with obvious power over him. Of course there was a motivation behind this unhealthy relationship... or maybe it was just plain human weakness. Maybe that is why he started to look like a shrinking man. And I was not quite finished yet.

"Mr. Kelly," I could see him sitting up straight now and listening without even taking a breath. "There is a very strong possibility, that I will suggest to her, to terminate all her old relationships and start new healthy ones."

Mr. Kelly made a sharp jerky motion, probably an involuntary motion. This kind of movement is often triggered on a sub-conscious level, beyond his control. I thought there would be a need to clarify what I just said. He did not indicate any sign of a lack of understanding.

"Are you ready for this?"

He did not answer.

"Mr. Kelly, are you ready for this?" I repeated this difficult question.

"Her well being means so much to me," he mumbled very unclearly after a long pause.

This was not an acceptable answer for me. However unpleasant the question was, I had to repeat it one more time.

"Are you ready Mr. Kelly?"

THE BALANCING GAME

However difficult the question was, he still had to come up with a cogent responsive answer.

"Whatever it takes," he responded and with these words he fell back.

I knew the meeting was over and I had to leave. Honestly though, I really wanted to leave. I did not want to sit next to somebody, who was just given such dramatic news to digest. I did not know how his soul's stomach would take it. I was not sure he could handle it without severe suffering and, possibly in his weakness, he might lash out.

There was one thing I was curious about. About those two people outside, about the people in the fog, cold, and rain.

"Mr. Kelly, about those people outside..."

He jumped. He got angry. He screamed. Something touched him, something that dealt with his power. That made him violent. His turf was invaded.

"What about them?" He asked loudly and with an energetic swing of his upper extremities.

"Before we got in the car, it was very, very uncomfortable outside," I said calmly.

Mr. Kelly regained self-control fairly quickly. Though his voice remained angry, the substance of his answer was logical.

"Those people aren't there doing me favors. They are very generously rewarded for services they provide. They have the freedom of choice, but as you see it they chose to be there, just like you choose to be here."

I was sorry I asked. He was most certainly right about their options. This was true with that girl in the street, showing definite signs of being cold, wet, and in severe discomfort. The same principle applied to the driver with a loyal soldier's tolerance.

And finally the same could be said about me. For whatever reason, I was sitting in this car with this mad billionaire, who liked to play monopoly with our bodies and souls. The funny thing was; I relearned something that day; there is something in every person, a weakness, that a shrewd person could use as a bait.

It was high time for me to leave the car and the man in it. I did it in a hurry. I tried not to look at the faces of the two obedient servants. I could not help but notice how quickly both of them rushed into the car to greet the warmth that their "master" provided. I also knew, that they rushed to the car, not because of the uncomfortable nature of the outdoors, but because they wished to maintain their chosen professions.

"Don't analyze things, unless you have to. The deeper you go, the deeper you'll be stuck," I remembered this from some book I read when I was kid.

I went to my car uneventfully. I sat in the car for some time without moving, carefully recreating the conversation with Mr. Kelly. Great confusion occupied my whole being. Maybe it was time for me to get lost and let myself free, as Mr. Kelly suggested. But I had to give credit to the son of a bitch. He knew that I would not go away. It was becoming obvious that I was recruited today as a third person in Mr. Kelly's army, situated in a very deep muddy unknown village, with a different fog, cold and rain.

I was not standing outside his car, but my spot in his little band was much more difficult to handle. My years of training with special forces of medical school, permitted me access to this dangerous terrain.

There must be a reason Mr. Kelly wanted me in the game, even after I told him that the results of the therapy could result with either no cure or even a cured wife who must separate herself from him. Why, why would he want me in the game? I was not ready to learn the answer to that question, yet.

Chapter 24

A man was about to enter the lobby of his building. Then, with one foot in the building, he was stopped by a young myopic stranger, with a musky, expressionless face. The stranger also possessed a few other things: desperation and a small revolver in his right hand. The last two were especially visible and recognizable.

The assailant stopped the innocent man and demanded an answer to a question; an answer that this victim of mistaken identity was unable to conjure.

"Mr. Berg, why did you do it?" The whole scene, the assailant's face, the gun in this crazy man's hand, was frightening and the innocent man was terrified.

But then the victim released a sigh of relief. His name was not Mr. Berg. It was obvious; this desperate young character mistook him for somebody that the young gunner was probably not fond of. His degree of fear subsided significantly.

But something else was happening here. Having plenty of time and a few opportunities to identify himself and clear up this misunderstanding, he deliberately chose to go on in this deadly charade.

"Why, why did you have to bankrupt my family, burn our house, why? Answer me, why? Answer me." The restless stranger demanded answers, and it appeared his patience was wearing thin. His gun-hand drew closer to the innocent man's body.

"Are you the Mr. Berg?"

No, he was not this monster. Instead he was Mr. Nice Guy, the kind that never had any enemy in his entire life. His past was disgustingly and nauseatingly clean.

He was facing this desperate avenger, who had a clear intention to hurt him, and hurt him bad. And he liked it a lot. For the first time he was experiencing what it felt like to be so important, important enough, that his enemies would hunt him down. An intense rush ran down his whole body, with an orgasmic intensity.

His relaxed demeanor calmed the aggressor, who by now himself was realizing, that he might have made a mistake.

"What's your name, mister? I want to know what's your name. You actually don't look like the guy I'm after."

The man properly known everywhere as Mr. Nice Guy, was not about to let this once in a lifetime opportunity slip away. His desire to be important demanded that he lie. And for a worthy cause this lie came easy.

"My name is Mr. Berg. I'm the one you're looking for. Yes I'm the one who bankrupted your father, burnt your house and disfigured your sister."

His last words emanated from a profusely bleeding man. There was a hole in his gut, his gigantic gut, through which blood was seeping out. He did not hear the shot. He could not feel the pain yet. He just felt important, very important.

"Thank you kid and sorry I had to do this to you. I just had to do it." He was thanking his executioner from the bottom of his heart.

The man would live. He did not really want to die. He just wanted to be normal for once in his life, making people angry, not just appeasing their whims. He was ready to pay any price, any price to feel, what it would like, to have such a dangerous enemy.

"What a thing to miss." He would tell his friend later.

"Are you crazy?" His friend would comment.

"Crazy? Maybe, but not stupid." He would snap back at him.

In the hospital, when he was well enough to meet the detectives, he was asked, if he had any enemies.

"Don't we all?" He retorted, with considerable pride.

Chapter 25

1

After several sessions, I decided it was time for Mrs. Kelly to confront the opposite sex. It was the next logical step towards the completion of her rehabilitation to womanhood. She seemed to have accumulated enough confidence to take on the challenge that men presented. Confidence is a key ingredient for the successful treatment of depression.

While I was concerned about the idea of rushing her treatment, I was also afraid, that further delay would cause her to miss the moment when her readiness to accept this particular challenge would miss its peak. Preparation for a great ordeal must continue to grow to achieve true readiness. At preparation's end, the time comes for that preparation to demonstrate its capability and aptitude for dealing with the obstacle.

My thinking was, that since eventually there had to be a head to head confrontation between her and "him", it would be easier for her to handle, if I were to choose the precise time. I thought she could not yet afford to go back to real life, the life that sent her to me. I decided to arrange a showdown on our terms, with a male specimen chosen by me in a location tailored for the situation that I would select.

I had used surrogate services in the past, in order to help my patients return to a state of relative normalcy. I found, that very carefully selected surrogates were many times more helpful, than carefully worded expensive advice. I considered this approach very valuable in Mrs. Kelly's case.

I made all the necessary preparations, but I still had one task remaining. I had to find a person that was exactly right for her situation... somebody who would fit the image of her childhood fantasy; somebody who resembled very much to her father, if she ever have had one. This person had to be at least ten years older than her. He had to have some grayish hair and protective manners of behavior. In short, I had to find somebody who projected trust and understanding. A brief encounter, and possibly even a romantic tryst, with this type of prescribed man, could give quite a boost to Mrs. Kelly as a woman allow her to overcome deep-seeded fears.

The idea came easily. But to find that perfect knight in shining armor was somewhat more difficult.

2

It's amazing how often things that appear so impossible to achieve, start to seem achievable once we put our minds to work. In this case, a few minutes worth of thinking reminded me of a friend of mine that I knew could help. Dr. Nick Collins was my classmate in medical school. While we were never really close friends, I liked him, and I was pretty sure the feeling was mutual.

He was highly regarded as a bright, young doctor, with a great future and he maintained a strong desire to help the disadvantaged. That is why he shocked many around him, when he did what he did. One sunny day, Nick just dropped medicine. You may ask how he dropped medicine.

Nick did not just depart from the field for a short time. He defected from it and ran as far away as he could afford. And if this was not enough for people to digest, he chose a career in what others would consider escort services. Nick, and other people in the know, would call his business a companionship service, obviously in a conscious effort to soften the image of mostly disreputable industry.

For a certain amount of money, his company would provide a

companion, any kind companion. He was heavily involved in finding anything from partners for businessmen, professional introductions, roommates, and of course, any type of escorts for any type of occasion. Because of his superior psychiatric training in the best medical schools in the country, he was able to draw psychological computerized profiles for every person that used his service. By doing so, he reduced the percentage of mismatched companions. Pretty soon, people realized, that his services were far from sinister, which was the stereotype of these associated escort services.

I did use Nick's services on a few occasions in the past, and I was very impressed with the high degree of professionalism, efficiency and elegance that were displayed each time, while achieving excellent results. Most of the time, I would ask him or his people, to find surrogate companions for my severely depressed patients. Loneliness is the worst enemy for a depressed individual; so, it has to be combated aggressively. Since some of these patients did not have a friendly face to rely on, I would try to find compatible people for them to walk with, talk with, and spend time with. I would give Nick specific traits that potential surrogates would have to have and in a few days, I would receive detailed files of a number of potential surrogates. An uplifting and pleasant date was often a preferable conscious choice over long-term treatment using a potent cocktail of medications, each with potentially dangerous and disastrous side effects.

With confidentiality and discretion guaranteed and professionalism in its highest form, the percentage of successful outcomes was quite high.

It did not take much time for me to find Nick's telephone number. His secretary politely took my name and phone number and warned me, that if it was for an appointment, it would most likely be in two weeks. I informed her that this was a personal matter and that she should mention my name to Dr. Collins.

A few minutes later, Nick called me back himself.

"Is everything okay Al?" I could hear Nick's soft and soothing voice.

"Pretty much, Nick. But, I could use your help."

"If this thing could wait until tomorrow, I could see you first thing tomorrow morning." We said our goodbyes and agreed to meet early the next day in his office.

The next morning, I was being led to Nick's office by Nelly, Nick's secretary, who had a notebook in her hands, eyeglasses on her eyes and a business-suit adorning her body. All of the above gave her a look of sophistication. For whatever reason, sophistication was the appropriate word to describe the atmosphere of the whole place.

Nick greeted me standing with outstretched arms and a big smile.

"Glad to see you Al." He looked like he meant it.

"I'm glad to see you too Nick."

After greeting few minutes of pleasantries, nostalgia and catching up, each of us sat on the chairs on opposite sides of his desk.

"Let me analyze you Nick. Sit still. I'll be drawing your psychological profile."

"Only one minute Al, that's all my patience will allow," he looked amused. Then he tried to take the smile off his face. Now he was ready to be painted.

"You are still five ten. You are thirty-three years old. Your hair is dirty blond and skin white like a cream. Your hair has started receding. Your eyes look tired and sad. That's kind of surprising because, I know you're not tired and you're generally happy. I feel you like what you're doing and you like what you have."

I finished my drawing without using my allotted one-minute. "So how did I do?" I asked.

"Pretty close, really close. I'm impressed Professor Al Letne. By the way, I don't think I saw you since Ms. Vestry's case. I believe she is doing quite well. She started singing again. Remarkable story, isn't it?"

"You did a great job Nick. I'm not sure if I have ever thanked you properly for that one." Nick was referring to a young singer with a beautiful voice, but her confidence was completely shot.

It is one thing to have a great voice... another thing to know it. She came to me as a patient, ready to quit singing. After a few sessions it became clear to me, that besides her slight depression, she desperately needed reassurance in her superb ability from people she regarded as authorities in her field. At my request, she provided ten names of people, whose opinions carried the most value.

I gave Nick a call, though I highly doubted he could come up with an audition for her with any of these people. To my surprise, within a week, two people from her dream list auditioned her. Both of them raved about her ability and talent. A few weeks after the audition, she was offered a singing role with a prestigious opera troupe, which she gladly accepted.

"I still don't understand how the hell you managed to make them to listen to her."

Suddenly Nick got up sharply, raised his right arm and exclaimed almost screaming-- "Wait a minute here. Forget about me. Is there any truth in this? Somebody was telling me the other day that you are a best-seller author. Tell me that's not true. Can you imagine, someone so prestigious in my office?"

"It's no big deal Nick, really." I tried to downplay the book topic. "I'm not here to discuss my book, Nick."

Nick sat back in his chair. His demeanor reflected a new found attentiveness.

"Nick, I'm here because I need your help."

"Al, you aren't in some kind trouble, are you?" Now he looked straight in my eyes. "Al, this help you said, it isn't about you, is it?"

"No. Why? What gave you that idea? No. It concerns me a great deal, but it's not for me. It's for my patient, a very important patient. So I thought I would personally interview your suggested companions myself."

"That important, huh?" He was looking at me with professional curiosity.

"Yes, that important," I replied.

"Al, without going in great detail, I need something to work with; who do you need and for whom?"

"Of course," I said. "If this does not go as well as I hope, this could mean big trouble for me. There is a lady that is emerging from a great depression, after being at the bottom of it for years. She is still a very scared and suspicious woman. Her confidence is completely shattered. She just started talking to people again and just to see her get this far, already cost me many sleepless nights. Now, I want her to go out and have a full life, but I need to minimize the chances of her having more failed relationships. She cannot afford to fail. This failure would be disastrous for her and very unpleasant for me. That's why I want to choose somebody for her, compatible for her psychological profile."

Nick did not interrupt me. He was just nodding his head indicating that he understood my logic. He was still waiting for more information.

"She is twenty-seven years old, with average looks, about five-five, soft spoken, and with very polished manners. I think you should have her photograph," I handed him recent picture of her. "I also think you should know her name," I paused.

"And her name is..." Nick showed impatience.

"Muggy Kelly. Mrs. Peter Kelly."

"Wait a minute Al," exclaimed an open-mouthed Nick. "You don't really mean Mrs. Kelly, Peter Kelly's wife?"

"That's right. Now you understand why I'm here myself."

"Jesus Christ! Are you sure that's what you have to do?"

"Yes, I am. I'm sure."

A few seconds elapsed before he absorbed the magnitude of the situation. Then, his professionalism and practicality returned.

"By the way Al, this is very important, legally. Do you know if they are fully divorced?"

THE BALANCING GAME

"Yes, according to Mrs. Kelly," I said bending the truth.

"Good, so, how does Mr. Right look to you?"

"In his late thirties, five ten, very polished, trustworthy, preferably with grayish hair. If possible, someone professional, in the top of his field, powerful, but not overbearing."

"Al, I have to tell you. I'm gonna have a problem finding someone remotely resembling this character." Then, he looked at me and said something surprising that somehow did not surprise me at all.

"Do you realize... that you pretty much just described yourself in a few years."

Cold shivers shook my body for a second. While I could not explain this resemblance between myself and the person with whom I wanted to match Mrs. Kelly, as a psychiatrist I had to admit, this resemblance could not be coincidental at all. It never occurred to me that the person I was looking to match with Mrs. Kelly was somebody with my physical and emotional characteristics.

"I don't think so," I lied.

Nick did not follow my retort. He had a job to do. He leaned over the desk, pressed the intercom button and asked his assistant to come in. Nelly, the lady dressed in the business suit entered.

"Nelly, could you run this information in the computer. We need somebody with these characteristics. Let's see if we come up with anything. And could you do this right away please?" Then he turned towards me with a big smile and warmth asked me;

"So, Dr. bestseller? I can't believe it. I thought you were smart. I didn't think you were that smart."

I always liked Nick. Though never really close, we established our friendship not solely based on actual time spent together. Short chats in the corridors of the university allowed us to develop mutual respect. After every meeting, we would tell each other, "take care" and genuinely wish each other well.

Nick grew in my eyes, though it was not when he dropped out of his promising medical career, or when he opened his companionship service. The thing that impressed me about Nick was how he striving for inner peace and stopped doing the things in life that disturbed his path towards that satisfaction.

"Al," he told me when I met him immediately after he opened his new business, "psychiatry was not for me. I would come home late, very late, scream at my wife and kids. I was pushing them away."

"I drank strong coffee and tried to fall asleep. Of course, I always had problems sleeping. Then I would remember my patients, with all their complaints. This would irritate me further. I looked at my patients like goddamned enemies. They were trying to steal my peace. It wasn't fair, to me and it wasn't fair to them. Not everybody has the stomach to go on like this. I know I don't. I always wanted to help people. That's why I became a doctor. But, I just never felt like I was helping my patients."

My thoughts returned to the present, as we were interrupted with a knock on the door. Nelly walked in with a bunch of files. She left them on the desk and walked out.

There were four files in front of us. Nick picked up the one on the top and handed it to me. I opened the file. There was a picture on the upper left corner of the first page. A middle-aged man with a trustworthy face looked at me from the picture.

Nick now was standing right next to me. He knew this man.

"Smooth operator, very reliable, a lawyer, but he bills for the whole day, even if he spends only one hour on the job. Comes from a family of farmers and is on his own, since he was twenty. Loves brunettes and hates blonds, because get this, all four of his sisters are blonds."

"And you grade him as?" I asked.

"Excellent. Four times tried, came up with straight A's. He made my Dean's list."

"Put him away Nick. He seems too much like a peasant."

A second man had a sleazy look on his face, maybe because of his slicked-back hair. His file was also put aside, after I heard that he was an unemployed actor.

"I don't trust unemployed actors," I said with an already inpatient voice.

The third one had neglectfully combed hair and strong facial features.

"Listen to this. This guy is a character. He is rich, I mean rich. Comes from a very rich, famous family of wine-makers from the south. A few years ago, he came to me all miserable and broke. I didn't know who he was. I knew he had a great education... Terrific all around guy. Well-mannered. I used him a few times, mostly to comfort elderly people. He is a good talker and an even better listener. You should know about the importance of that talent in your line of work. Then I read in the paper that he took over his family business. I was shocked when I learned about his family and how rich he was. And even after he put his life back together, he still works for me as a companion to these poor souls."

"That's kind of weird, don't you think?"

"I asked him why he still does this."

"And..."

"He said, first he was doing it for money. He refused to get any help from his father. His mother was everything to him. I mean, everything. When his mother killed herself, he blamed his father for her death. Since then, he couldn't face his father. And he wouldn't take any money from him."

"And how about now, that he is so rich- why the hell does he continue doing this? He doesn't have to. How much could you pay him for his services, a million dollars a minute?"

"He thinks he has to. He says he has that need in him to help people. "But, like I said, he doesn't need money," Nick said. "He does it for free."

"You mean, you just call him when you think he can help?" I could not believe what I was hearing.

"Actually I never called him- not since I learned who he was and how rich he was. He is the one who keeps calling me all the time and begging me to give him an assignment."

"By the way, how old is he?" I asked.

"Almost 40, but he actually looks a lot like you."

I was quiet for a few seconds. I knew, Nick expected me to make a choice.

"So, is this the guy you're looking for?" He sounded a little inpatient now.

"I don't know Nick. I really don't know. Sounds *too* good. Too damned suspiciously good."

"Listen. Wouldn't it be stupid, if you turn down things in life, because they look suspiciously perfect?"

"Yes, it would. Okay, this is the one." And the choice was made.

3

Things were moving much faster than I originally anticipated. A few hours after meeting with Nick, I got a message from his office, that Mr. Gilmore, the man I chose to be a surrogate mate for Mrs. Kelly, was in town at the present time and that my meeting was already arranged with him tonight. He was staying in a relatively small, not fancy, but cozy hotel.

That same evening, I was impatiently sitting in the lobby of the hotel, watching the people as they entered and exited the hotel. My eyes darted from one person to the next searching for the man. A few times, I thought I saw him when somebody would pass by with a smile on his face. But, as usual, I was caught unawares when Mr. Gilmore finally did approach me... maybe because I expected him to have a smile on his face. He did not.

THE BALANCING GAME

"Dr. Letne. It must be you. It was easy to recognize you. Of all these people, you are the only one who looks like a doctor." With one hand, he shook my hand and with the other grasped my shoulder.

I could see the polish of his manners, could feel his warmth and could smell aristocracy in him, just as advertised.

"And you must be Mr. Gilmore?" I continued to observe him carefully.

Mr. Gilmore asked me if I was hungry. I said no and suggested that we needed a roughly fifteen minutes talk.

Very soon, we were sitting in the corner of a small cafeteria. Freddy Gilmore looked at me and asked.

"So Dr. Letne, what can I do for you?" I could feel, he was not just asking. He was ready to help.

"First of all, I want to express my gratitude. It's so kind of you to just to come here," I started.

"Doctor, a few years ago, I would grab any job, however decent or indecent. I got a break, but not when Nick offered me job. I got a break when Nick didn't take advantage of my desperation. He easily could have taken advantage, considering the nature of his line of work. When I started helping people, I realized how much I enjoyed the process. I was even ashamed, that in addition to the pleasure I was getting from helping people, I was also handsomely paid."

"That was then. Now, I understand you don't have to do this for money anymore," I said wanting him to continue if just so I could find flaws in his logic and judgment.

"I'm still a mama's boy, Doctor. She always told me to help the needy. You said, I don't have to do this. I would tell you differently. Now that I'm rich again, I can afford to be nice."

I was listening to what he was saying and how he was saying it. I was watching the way he moved and the way he used his arms. His logic was in order, his thoughts clear, his manners impeccable, and his motivation understandable.

"The only thing that bothers me Mr. Gilmore, is that you do this for free. I'm skeptical about things that are offered free. By my theory, for nothing- you get nothing."

"Relax Doctor. I might prove you wrong in this case."

He looked me straight in the eyes. He knew how uneasy I was about trusting him with Mrs. Kelly's mind and body. He knew, in order to put me at ease, he had to come up with some relaxing statement, to tell me just "relax Doctor". His verbal assurance was not enough for me.

Mr. Gilmore nodded his head a few times, as if he was saying he was understanding. And he probably was. That's why he continued.

"Listen Doctor. My mother always taught me, if I do good deeds, I should shut up and not brag about it. Well sorry mother." With these words, he opened up his attaché and pulled some papers from it. Then he chose one sheet from the stack and handed it to me.

"Here, I want you to read this for me." He insisted.

The paper was a letter from U.C.P. (United Cerebral Palsy), and the organization sent the correspondence to acknowledge the receipt of a check for one million dollars, as an act of charity and express gratefulness on behalf of thousands of handicapped people.

"Doctor, do you think you can pay me enough to make money a primary reason for me to help this lady?"

Mr. Gilmore slowly removed the clouds of suspicion from my mind.

"Mr. Gilmore, you are on," I said

Then in a few words, I explained the plan to him. The plan involved a fragile minded woman; who was ready to trust her frail soul and brittle body to Mr. Gilmore. Mr. Gilmore was expected to guide her back to a healthy livelihood and help her to become a woman again, providing her with whatever it took for her to be a confident and satisfied woman.

Chapter 26

1

Mrs. Kelly was not thrilled when I explained in detail what was on my mind. I could swear, I saw two different expressions on her face. On the left side of her face I could see anguish. The other side of her face projected fear. Whatever her face was saying, she knew that however gigantic her next step was, it had to be taken. She did not verbally protest the idea, but the fear and pain on her face along with her trembling voice, informed me of the high degree of difficulty with which she accepted this assignment.

"Dr. Letne I have a lot of confidence in you. I'm not even asking if you are sure I have to go through this. If that's what you think I should do, that's what I'm going to do." She sounded resolute in her statement.

"Mrs. Kelly, I appreciate your attitude. You should know- if there were any other way, I wouldn't put you through this. I strongly believe you shouldn't wait 'til challenging things in life come to you. Instead you should meet them head on, on your own terms. This way we'll balance things in your favor."

"So Doctor Letne, what do you want me to do?" She tried to be brave. Maybe that is why she sounded somewhat sarcastic. "You are fixing me up with somebody, aren't you?"

"Mrs. Kelly, I'm not in the matchmaking business. I'm sorry if I didn't explain myself properly. May I remind you, I'm still your Doctor and every suggestion I make, I would appreciate, if you treat the recommendation as my belief that it's in your best interest. It's not my intention to get you married."

"I'm sorry if I insulted you Dr. Letne. I didn't mean to. Please don't think I don't appreciate everything you've done for me. Without that book or your help, I don't know where I'd be. It's just strange and demeaning to accept your suggestion, which by the way, I will follow blindly."

"Mrs. Kelly, I'm happy, you have noticed my desire to help you. I'm afraid, we can't postpone your next step any further." She was not just ready to listen; she appeared ready to act. Action was more important.

"Who is he, Dr. Letne?" She asked without obvious curiosity.

"He is a very nice and noble man by nature. He is not doing this for money. He just wants to help you, in any way he can." I made sure she understood what I was talking about. I did not have to worry about her understanding though. She seemed to take to the idea much faster than I thought she would. While her reluctance to go along with my plans was obvious, I could not help, but notice a distinct absence of shock. After all, she was asked to visit a complete stranger, with the intention of playing the role of a companion to this man. And yet, the questions she uttered were informational only.

In a few minutes, her questions stopped. She began looking at me strangely. The look was expressing dependence. I only hoped it was a reflection of dependence on me as a doctor and not as a man.

"Does this person in any way look like you?" This was a question, I did not accept with excitement.

"What do you mean Mrs. Kelly?" I asked for clarification. I did not receive any.

"Forget it Dr. Letne, just forget it." She forcefully shook her head a few times, as if trying to dislodge a few very uncomfortable thoughts. I did not know if she succeeded in removing those thoughts. Shortly after that, she indicated a readiness to proceed.

"So, what you want me to do?"

"His name is Fred Gilmore. He is a businessman from Chicago.

THE BALANCING GAME

He is kind, charitable, charming and intelligent and just shy of 40 years old. He will be waiting for you tonight at eight o'clock in his room. The room number is 555, easy to remember, isn't it?"

She did not say anything. She just got up, thanked me again and left the room in a hurry. This did not strike me as a positive sign for a successful outcome to the plan I so carefully orchestrated. She left without me telling her the name of the hotel. I deliberately chose not to tell her the name of the hotel first. I wanted her to have chance to ask questions.

But a minute later, the door forcefully swung open with a loud bang and Mrs. Kelly was asking;

"Dr. Letne, did you forget to tell me something?"

"Like what?" I tried to pretend I did not know what she meant.

"Like the name of that hotel?"

"Silly me. It's the Hotel Royal. I'm sure you can find it easily. I know you will, right Mrs. Kelly?"

"If you are that sure, then I better find it easily." She gave an intriguing smile and disappeared behind the door.

2

'It's eight o'clock already,' I thought to myself. It was time for Mrs. Kelly to show up for the date of her life. I could not hide my nervousness. As calmly as I could, I sat at the bar slowly sipping my shots of vodka. I could not hide my inner tension from the outside world. Even the busy bartender had time to notice the trouble in my world. Twice in twenty minutes, he managed to find time to ask me if I was alright. I barely paid any attention to his bracelet with the word, "BALANCE", which he seemed to touch whenever the customers really annoyed him.

Instead of using the bartender's questions as a segue to ask him more about his attachment to the bracelet, I simply responded that I was great. Both times I lied. I was not fine at all. "Never trust strangers," was the theme running through my head. My preoccupation with this stranger Fred Gilmore was almost obsessive. I made decisions of great importance many times in the course of my professional career, but never before had I felt so uncomfortable with a decision as when I chose Fred Gilmore as Mrs. Kelly's surrogate date.

I tried to recall every word from his file and I mentally restaged every little scene of our brief encounter. And still I could not detect anything suspicious enough to magnify a foible into a potential hazard.

He looked very much fit for the task. Then I started to pick on the mission itself. I had much less trouble with the plan. In a matter of minutes, I satisfied my inquisitiveness and soon, I went back through the same limited information... again.

Mr. Gilmore was too noble, too intelligent, too smooth, too good-hearted, too rich, too understanding, too good at everything. Only angels have these qualities and he was clearly no angel.

The laundry list of his positive qualities only made me more nervous. Over and over, I went through his long list of positive characteristics, trying to find something I did not like. Being so picky on Mr. Gilmore and not being able to pick up anything on him yet, made me increasingly suspicious of him. I was becoming more nervous, more drunk and more frustrated.

People around me in the bar would periodically cheer after a Knicks basket, but I was not paying much attention to the basketball game. But when they would cheer, I would try to gather their positive energy and cheer along with them. I would shake my head and comfort myself; "Relax, everything is going to be all right," and seconds after that I would go back to screening Fred Gilmore.

By nine o'clock, I felt more relaxed. By that time, the amount of alcohol I accumulated in my blood vessels was sufficient to calm my nerves even as my thoughts became more organized. My chaotic thoughts transformed into organized raw thoughts, with my memory providing me with all the information I could handle.

I clearly remembered that during our twenty-minute conversation, Mr. Gilmore mentioned his mother at least twice. Once, he said he was still a mama's boy and another time, he said something about his mother teaching him not to advertise his good deeds. Twice in under twenty minutes. A forty year old man, mentioned his mother twice unprompted in a twenty-minute conversation.

Maybe as a psychiatrist, I was too suspicious about the mother-son relationship, but I had to be. I was a professional for long enough to pay attention to this powerful life-long bond, which so often manufactures and manifests in varying degrees of emotional disturbance.

Now that I found the thing that I was enthusiastically searching for, I still did not relax. This new-found realization called for more investigative analysis. I called on my memory for more help. My ability to retain trivial information was diminishing, but still functioning competently.

And it did work. Suddenly, I was remembering something else, something that originally did not seem important. But it was stored and my memory provided me with this vital piece of information.

I remembered the run down on Mr. Gilmore, given to me by Nick. I even restored the whole statement, in which Mr. Gilmore's mother was briefly mentioned. But that brief interjection was very important tonight.

I remembered Nick clearly telling me that many years ago his mother jumped out of a window. Since then, he did not really get along with his father because he was blaming his father for the death of the person he loved so much.

That was it. Even as I was vigilantly searching, I was hoping that my search to find a major flaw would be fruitless. The man, who I so highly recommended as a surrogate to Mrs. Kelly, to this fragile lady with a marginally stabilized ability to deal with real world, was drastically flawed. Yet, he still talked to his mother, even in our discussion. Mrs. Kelly was currently in a hotel room with a person who talked to his dead mother, as if she was supervising his every move.

But, it was worse than that. He idealized his mother, who herself, obviously had severe emotional issues that led to her suicide. Unresolved anger towards his father, a disturbing emotional attachment to his clinically disturbed and now long-deceased mother and pristine mannerisms; definitely had to have What did this all mean? It meant that I made a mistake, a massive mistake.

My philosophical musings needed to give way to bold actions. Whatever, I chose to do, had to happen quickly. I got up and went straight to the phone booth. I dialed information and soon I had a telephone number for room # 555 in Hotel Royal. I was not in control of my own hands. My nerves were in control. With a trembling right hand, I managed to dial and ask to be connected with the room.

There was no answer, or more correctly the hotel's operator told me that room # 555 was not answering. My concern for the safety of Mrs. Kelly grew to a degree, that I was not able to control myself, and I lost my reason in total panic Not even imagining anything in particular. I was just positive that something bad was taking place in that room.

With the terrified words "oh, no!" I bolted from the bar dramatically. I could see many blurry faces talking to me. I do not remember paying for the numerous drinks I had consumed at the bar. But this was not my primary concern now. Mrs. Kelly was.

In a matter of minutes, I was in Hotel Royal territory. It was very hard for me to manage a calm veneer in the building, but I probably did. I passed the desk with a few watchful eyes standing behind a desk and I booked it straight for the elevator. Soon, I was on the fifth floor and by the door of room # 555.

I tried to calm myself, as I was standing in front of the room, where in all probability Mrs. Kelly was at this minute, hopefully successfully handling Mr. Gilmore, emotionally as unstable as Mrs. Kelly herself. It was so peaceful and quiet; my feeling that something would go wrong grew stronger. I put my right ear to the door, in an attempt to sense anything suspicious. I did hear something behind the closed doors, something which succeeded in totally unraveling me.

I heard a woman's voice resembling that of Mrs. Kelly screaming for help. I started to bang on the door forcefully and repeatedly. A few seconds and few bangs later, the door remained close and Mrs. Kelly's voice was still yelling for help. I looked around in the hope that I could find a housekeeper with keys for the room.

In a rare moment of good fortune, I did find her down the corridor. My very primitive and simple lie about me forgetting my keys from the room fooled this woman with a limited understanding of English. In another ten seconds the door of # 555 was closed again, after I entered and slammed it shut.

Once inside, I walked slowly through the narrow hallway, as if I had a few minutes to kill before my favorite TV show. My slowness could be easily explained by my fear that I was anticipating the worst possible scenario. It seemed like I subconsciously tried to at least postpone the bad news that awaited me. But the corridor was short, and even with my slow walking, I covered the distance quickly. There was a man's screaming voice coming from the living room of the one-bedroom suite.

"I should have listened to my mother. I should have listened to my mother at least once."

In a few seconds, I was witnessing a very surreal scene. Very badly beaten, bruised, and with her clothes torn, Mrs. Kelly was lying in a bed and Mr. Gilmore was in his underwear, looking angry and insane, circling around her and continuing to scream at the terrified Mrs. Kelly.

"I should have listened to my mother!"

While the scene was scary, it also brought relief. While Mrs. Kelly's clothes were torn in many pieces, she herself was in one piece, at least physically. This was not the worst thing that could have taken place in this room and I was thankful for that.

When Mrs. Kelly saw me, she jumped out of bed and rushed to me. She hugged me and kept me close for what seemed like a long time. I could feel her body trembling. She would not say much. She just mumbled, "thank you, thank you" and "thank God."

Mr. Gilmore was taking his time putting his clothes on. He did not otherwise acknowledge my arrival. He did not look at me, or talk to me. He just kept saying again and again the same thing about him not listening to his mother.

Eventually, Mr. Gilmore got dressed and slowly walked to the door. Right before leaving the room, he turned to me and said something apologetic, without really apologizing.

"Dr. Letne, I warned her. I told her how my mother likes things. She just wouldn't listen." He proceeded to walk out of the room.

Mrs. Kelly continued to hug me. She stopped thanking me. Now I looked at her. Her eyes were welling up with tears that were begging for comfort and I felt like I owed her that comfort. I was the one who put her in this situation, with this wacko. I was the one who, being a supposedly great psychiatrist, missed diagnosing the paranoia and psychoses of this scumbag. I was the one who urged her to follow my plans, and now she was paying dearly for my mistakes.

I started to hug her tighter, begging her to forgive me. I wanted her to know, it was not her fault. She did not fail at all. It was me who was at fault by setting her up with this degenerate.

I sat down at the edge of the king-size bed, with my arms still wrapped around her. I continued to issue very unclear mumbling, none of which really made any sense- especially since these words were directed at a very scared, confused and emotionally unstable woman. She slinked down to her knees, to survey the damage to her tattered clothes. I could not see her face- because she had her face buried somewhere between my legs.

She was quiet and motionless. I was shaking and numb. And then it happened. The evil took charge of the room # 555. If you ask me now whether I would do anything differently, I would resoundingly tell you that I could not do anything differently. It all just happened and I do not know how it happened. What I recall is, my usually well-controlled penis ended up in Mrs. Kelly's mouth. I suppose she assisted in the process, by putting lying her head on it and starting to rub her face against it. I also suspect she was the one, who actually unzipped my pants and released the monster. I did not know what was taking place, but, at the same time I damn well knew, what took place.

Then it came. With the discharge came a heavy dose of reality. This reality was ushered to me and in me with an unreal female scream. I could swear the scream accompanied a woman's orgasm. She pushed me down. I was flatly pinned to the bed. She lay motionless on the floor.

I did not lose consciousness. But for a while I did not hear, feel or smell anything. When my stupor started to fade, I opened my eyes, and began to evaluate the actual damage. It would be very convenient for me to pretend all this did not happen- That whatever took place in room # 555 was a bad dream. But that would only be wishful thinking. A few powerful exhibits, like pieces of a torn woman's dress, my unzipped pants, and the smell of a carnal sin amounted to indisputable evidence that I could not ignore.

In everyone's life, I assume there comes a time when one stops being in charge of him or herself. I suppose this often happens, when one loses a loved one. For a short while, he or she is directed, advised and guided by grief, because of his or her inability to function properly. I have experienced this absentia, when I had to deal with the loss of my father. The only thing I remembered; was that I remembered nothing.

This time, I did not know exactly what I lost. But I did feel the same aura. I felt as if someone very close departed. I could not exactly pinpoint, who or what I lost, but I knew that whatever it was, I already missed it.

I did not have to get up to learn; I was alone in room # 555. It took two to tango. Clearly one dancer was missing.

As my thoughts crystallized, I was hoping, while I plummeted as a professional, at least my dance partner overcame that dreadful fear of manhood and soured as a woman.

I stopped existing for twenty-four hours. I remembered nothing that did or did not happen during this time.

Then came a phone-call from Mrs. Kelly.

"Thank you Dr. Letne. I feel great. I will take care of myself from now on. Doctor, you saved my life."

Silence interrupted her appreciation speech. This kind of silence is usually produced by a caller, who has finished all she had to say and has terminated the call in a planned manner.

This five second call brought me from being in a stupor, almost all the way back to my normal self.

The earthquake that threatened the building I was in, faded away. The inhabitants of the building remained seemingly unharmed. In fact as a professional, I now felt extremely proud. The Mrs. Kelly project appeared to be a success story.

Chapter 27

1

I was summoned to Mr. Kelly's place, two days after the hotel event. Knowing Mr. Kelly by now, I thought he expected some debriefing about the progress made in his wife's case. He, as a tough businessman, treated this matter very much like any other business matter. As far as he was concerned, he was the one who financed the venture of Mrs. Kelly's rehabilitation and therefore, he was the one in charge. He thus expected to be briefed regularly. That way, at least he still felt like he had some control. Control was important to him as a corporate executive. This was also a way to secure that the money he invested in the project would not be wasted.

The place to which I was ushered in did not impress me. Maybe I expected too much. I thought that such a rich egomaniac would live in a much fancier and more spacious locale. Instead, I saw a three-bedroom co-op on Central Park West, in a five story pre-war building. It was not that the place did not look lush, it just did not look that lush. The place in no way resembled one of those mansions or penthouses that are depicted in movies.

I sat in the living room and observed a familiar long legged, blond-woman, who opened the door for me and now did very little to entertain me in the absence of Mr. Kelly. Much to my amazement, she too had a bracelet with the inscription, Balance.

"Mr. Kelly will see you little later," she said with a sincere smile. She evidently knew me as author of the book she revered.

"You aren't Mrs. Kelly, are you?" I asked.

"No, I'm not and Doctor you know it," she answered with a smile that refused to leave her face.

"I don't know your name," I insisted.

"You don't need my name. Just call me Miss. That will be just fine," she said coyly.

I looked at my watch. Mr. Kelly was ten minutes late already.

"So Miss, are you sure Mr. Kelly knows I'm here?"

"I'm pretty sure he does. That's why he is Mr. Kelly. He knows everything."

"Thank you Suzy. I'll take it from here. This won't be long," said Mr. Kelly as he entered the room and kissed her on the cheek. Suzy disappeared, but not without giving me that familiar smile again.

Mr. Kelly looked serious. He ignored my outstretched arm, ready to be shaken.

"So, Doctor, is there something I should know?" He asked with authority.

"Yes, there is something you should know."

"I want to hear it." I sensed there was a lack of desire on his part to hear what exactly I would tell him about his wife.

"Mr. Kelly, you should know, Mrs. Kelly's emotional status became much more stable now. She passed the release stage and stepped into a new stage of her treatment. This involves her active interaction with reality."

"What makes you think she is doing better?"

"Mrs. Kelly can do things that she couldn't or wouldn't before. She gets up in the morning every day, takes a shower, and has breakfast. She is getting ready to deal with daily life. I take it as a very good sign. She also pays attention to how she dresses and with whom she is associated. I believe she is doing remarkably well, considering the severe depression she was in."

I did not observe anything in Mr. Kelly's poker face; nothing indicated any degree of satisfaction with his wife's treatment.

THE BALANCING GAME

"Anything else I should know?" He wanted to hear more. I thought that the information I provided would be sufficient for him to be happy for his wife.

"Well, I really did not want to bring this up, but I guess you are entitled to know that Mrs. Kelly had an opportunity to interact with a man. As you recall, we discussed the need for her to interact with a man other than you Mr. Kelly. As I remember, you said at that time; "My wife's well-being is so important to me," and added something like "whatever it takes."

His expressionless face remained stoic.

"So, what did it take?" Mr. Kelly wanted to know.

"In order for Mrs. Kelly to get her confidence back as a woman, she had to interact with a man. She did just that. I have reason to believe, that after this interaction, she came up as a clear winner."

"You told me what it took. You didn't tell me, whom exactly it took." Now I was starting to get it. Mr. Kelly wanted more details than I was prepared to share.

"I'm not sure you need to know this. What's the difference if his name was Jack, or Paul? The deal was that Mrs. Kelly would improve. And I know she did improve."

He sat across the table and tried to look me directly in the eyes. By his look, I knew he was about to make a statement that would affect me unfavorably, in fact, very unfavorably. I had to summon wells of courage to deal with whatever scolding or tongue-lashing Mr. Kelly would produce.

Then the statement came.

"I know it wasn't Jack. I know it wasn't Paul. I know it was Dr. Letne."

I did not think Mrs. Kelly told him the details of the events in room # 555. And still I was not surprised that Mr. Kelly was very well informed.

"Dr Letne, I want you to leave. But before you go, I want you to know this. It's true. You helped my wife. And I'll keep my promise. You'll get the other half of the money you were promised. I have to be frank with you. I have in my possession a video tape of everything that took place in that hotel room. I'm considering how to use it. One thing I guarantee you. Nobody screws my wife and gets away with it. And by that I mean, you will suffer."

That is what he said and that is what I heard. This man was threatening. He was also a businessman. I was sure he would pay me because… well, Mrs. Kelly was improved enough to be able to go out and mate. I also knew he would keep his other promise. Perhaps, he would gut me, or go public, but I knew that when he was done, I would be done too.

2

Days of confusion and disgust displaced me from reality to fiction, from the truth to illusion. With time and perspective lost, I was greatly impaired. I would not know where I was. And somehow I felt like I could snap out of all this, any time I desired. But the scary part was, I did not want to snap out of my situation. I liked my untethered position. I also liked the idea how disconnected I felt from all other people, distanced enough that all of their faces became entirely unrecognizable.

If there was rain pouring on my head, I would not know. My skin did not possess that sensation. If the blazing sun were corroding my vision, I would not notice it. My eyes were temporarily blinded . If there were people surrounding me, screaming at me, beating and stoning me, I would not know. All of my senses were now effectively shot.

It is just amazing, how we are treated by fate. Even with the worst imaginable events, some internal instinct for survival is automatically activated. The instincts we hardly knew were in our possession.

THE BALANCING GAME

And there was the other thing. It is hard not to notice something about the balance and its power. The higher the index of life's horrors we experience, the higher the degree of the efficacy of our subsequent awakening.

My drunken father, not known for his religious zeal, used to say, "God gives us life and God gives us a means to survive." I don't know about God. He never exercised his noble, just, and fair power with me. He never stood on visible mountains, so I could recognize his presence. However, I do believe in the power of fate.

Who is not aware of the mighty fate? Who is not touched by her majesty on a daily basis? And I still want to meet a living person, who can honestly claim, he can run and hide from her fearsome claws."

But wait a minute. Who decided we should hide from fate. What is the sense of trying to avoid something so immense, something so... inevitable?

And then, perhaps even when fate delivers its harshest of blows, fate plays a role in our survival instincts that arise. This balancing game trains the less fortunate with an even greater ability to survive the giant blows. The magnitude of this game theory still expands.

3

What do you do when you fall down and each of your extremities are at their lowest? When you are knocked down, the rest of your limbs crash to the floor to protect your head. Much is saved, but much is lost as well.

The face is saved. But, at what expense? At what price? There is a price for everything, isn't there? Your face looks fine. There is not even a single scratch on it. But now you look like a four-legged animal, with all four legs on the ground. Your knees are exposed to outside air, through torn pants. They appear bloody from superficial bruises and scratches. Burning pains distract you from the similar wounds on the palms of your hands.

This is the way you look from the outside. This is the way you are seen by the people standing above. Human curiosity and animal instinct allow them to smell blood and attract more people to the scene. They want to see how you look, how you bleed, what you say. They elbow each other violently to position themselves for better spots, so they can better grasp your humiliation and torment.

Everyone defeated falls the same way. Alcoholics drink themselves to the point of unconsciousness. They go down to forget what happened. Drug addicts lose their shame and under-appreciate their human value and then from that point on, lie passively with open glassy eyes, which can no longer see. The invisible scars that stem from life's beatings, easily lead to a disassociation from logic and the inability to stand on one's own two feet.

Those who are wronged by life, go down as drug addicts do. Some now claim alcohol is a drug too. Maybe we can safely state, anybody who falls to addiction, to drugs, alcohol, mistakes, love, anger, hate and so on… They all fall hard.

I remembered Greg. I remembered his warning. "Never fall down on your hands." But it was too late to heed his wise warning. I was already four legged. I had to remember the other part, of once I was already on the ground.

"When on the ground, you'll look, think, and behave just like an animal. I have a few pieces of advice for you Al. First, never look up at the people, who gathered around to look down at you. That would be a big mistake. Those people look at you like you are an animal. Their human nature would not allow them to recognize you as a fellow human in distress. Their wretched faces would frustrate you further. You should avoid further frustration during this earthly crisis."

"My second piece of advice is, don't you dare think like a human. Don't forget that being human was what actually brought you down there in the first place. If you look like an animal, you should think and behave like one. Without looking at the people surrounding you, use them as ladders to climb. Grab them anywhere you can. Bite them, or crawl on them if you have to. Forget yourself; forget your name. Become Machiavellian. Remember every extra moment down, increases your anger and frustration and makes it more difficult to rise and return to your humanity."

"Get up Al, for God's sake, get up at any price. Once you're back up, people will pardon you; and your disgusting behavior will be easily forgotten. Because they know as a fellow human being; you had to reclaim your humanity. People will forgive and forget, but only if they see you on your feet. Remember, only a standing person's hand can be shaken with respect."

I remembered Greg's monologue. I did not have a problem recollecting the whole speech. Now all I had to do was, to apply his advice to my situation.

Chapter 28

1

I felt like I had to see Greg right away. At this trying time, my body and soul, were filled with confusion and I knew I needed help. I could not handle this alone. I was afraid, I would fall to temptation to lie down and do nothing. This could lead to more aggravation and to a very expensive prescription for a very expensive depression.

The terrifying facts would not go away, just because you change your position from horizontal to horizontal. Only vertically standing people, looking ahead can hope to survive.

I always thought looking up was not healthy for your mind. When you look up, you see something or somebody stronger, smarter or better looking than you are. It is translated into admiration, adoration and respect, and you may think you are merely requesting the respect, but in actuality you are begging for it. You just lie there expecting mercy.

But the cruel statistics do not lie. They tell you the truth and because it is the truth, it hurts. Nobody likes pain; nobody wants the truth. People, who lie down and do nothing, remain motionless and die. Only people standing on their feet, facing front, stand a chance to survive. And a chance to survive is what an entire life is about.

I did not lie down for long, though I wanted to. My brain was analyzing my situation, no matter how gloomy it appeared. There was a lady, a psychiatric patient, whom I was hired to help. Then something happened in that hotel room. Something heavy and sexual happened. Then, there was Mr. Kelly, Mr. Moneybags, apparently the husband of the lady, who mentioned something about videotapes, recording every moment of that heaviness, of that sexuality.

Then, I remembered faces. A female face was grateful and happy. A male face was angry and mean. The first one promised never to forget what I did for her. The second one promised never to forget what I did to her. Two faces, with the same last name, interpreted the same action in totally different ways.

Then there was the person, whose psychological well being was now consuming me. I was now obsessing over my own lack of peace.

2

For one whole day and one whole night, I could not collect one minute's sleep. I could easily see the big round black bags under my eyes. My appetite disappeared. I did not bother to shave. I felt weak and depressed. The last time this happened to me was five years ago, when for four days I ran a fever over one hundred and two. So it was not just my mental exhaustion. It was complicated with a physical debilitation as well.

In search of relief, I rode in a cab, with a driver in more of a hurry than I was. He used every possible short cut and passed almost every red light on his way. Thanks to this crazy cab driver, I was soon standing by the door to Greg's room.

The fact that it was my birthday did not elude me either, nor did alleviate my tension. A big surprise was waiting me, once I found myself in the room. Warmth, an abundance of light and a closed window; all of which made the room easily observable and cozily warm. I never saw this room so normal before. The table was neatly cleaned and it did not serve as a station for alcoholic drinks, which usually occupied most of the room.

After my initial surprise dissipated, I started to look for the person who I believed lived here. I noticed a wheelchair; the one Greg would sit on. Usually located in the corner, now it was positioned in the middle of the room. But I did not come here to observe wheelchair. It did not take much time to figure out that Greg was not in the room.

The bathroom door was closed and I assumed it was Greg who closed it from the inside. Now I started to realize that the balancing man was doing things off of his wheelchair. The fight he had to put up, just to get to bathroom, was probably gigantic. I was so thickly wrapped up in my own problems, that Greg's daily struggles did not keep my mind active.

I came closer to the bathroom and knocked on the door few times. Nobody answered. A few more knocks were delivered with greater force and more concern.

"Greg, are you there? Are you all right?"

"Of course I'm here, where the hell do you expect me to be. I'll be out in few minutes." Suddenly, I found myself sitting on the wheelchair. Strange things started to happen. The room became bigger. The light from a minute ago was losing a battle to the night's darkness, which was unbearably strong and started to irritate and blind my eyes. The temperature in the room rose way above room temperature. And I started to sweat really badly. I also felt like I was sober, stone cold sober.

My perception of everything; light, heat, darkness, calmness, was magnified. And I started to think, as I remained in the wheelchair. I sat there for a few minutes. During this period, I had an opportunity to reevaluate my whole situation. After carefully recalling all of my problems, I came to a conclusion; I was not in bad shape at all. All these sleepless nights and torturous thoughts now appeared like a minor storm in a small glass of water. Those monstrous tides that were about to swallow everything in their way, appeared laughably powerless and innocently tapped the walls of the glass.

Things sure looked a little different from this wheelchair. No wonder the balancing man sitting on this wheelchair came up with the formula and theory. Now I was getting it. The whole picture of the anatomy of the creation of Balance was becoming clear to me. The combination of his brilliant mind, crippled body and unlimited time along with the alcohol; made this small room a place where something big and significant, something extraordinary and superior had to be born. As a result, a very important message would be sent to the entire earth and transform it. And this message was sent by a messenger, seemingly helpless sitting on this wheelchair in this tiny room.

I felt like I was in a historic place, with the aura of a museum. I imagined that every little thing in this room was of great scientific value.

Then, there was this wheelchair- the one Greg used as his horse, while riding in the labyrinths of madness. Sitting on the saddle of this lifeless horse, he rode miles of roads of insanity and chaos. He covered territories unchartered anywhere on this earth. And at the end of this voyage, he arrived at the highest peak in this world. From this summit, he could see anything and everything. This strategically important position, allowed him to penetrate, observe, watch, read, and attack. In addition he could plan and plot. He could also use me.

This wheelchair was now occupied by me. Its true owner had a few human things to take care of in the bathroom; like eliminating wasted material from his body. So, he was human after all. He still had to come down to earth and like the rest of us expel urine and feces. It was hard to imagine though, that he had the same physiological needs as any other human being.

At some point, I made a conscious effort to get up. Soon after that I would experience something, that I would remember as long as my heart would pump blood and my lungs would inhale air.

Some invisible power was dragging me back towards the wheelchair. Mr. curiosity? Or something bigger than mere curiosity was urging me to sit on the horse, with a reputation for being wild and tireless. I resisted, trying to fight off that strange invisible power. But my resistance was futile; it was not forceful enough. In a few seconds, my voyage would begin.

As soon as I sat back on the wheelchair, my eyes demanded to be shut. And I obeyed the request. Then a noise came, a disturbingly strange one, resembling nothing I had heard before. A few seconds of careful listening identified a characteristic feature of the noise. It was regular and monotonous. Though I never heard this loud sound before, I definitely felt this monotonous and regular beat in past. I was right. Of course, they were heart beats. What else could it be? I had to check my heart. The beats were rapid and noisy, but not quite as rapid and as noisy as the noise I was hearing. Then I realized, the beats of the outside world were trying to get in this room. But the tightly shut window successfully resisted the intervention.

Then, there was light. An unbearable light, that penetrated my closed eyelids, was causing sharp pains in my brain. With the noise that would not go away, and the light that would not fade away, I had to make a move that would improve my degree of comfort. And I did move. I stood up and the first thing I did was open the window. Then I rushed to switch off the light. To complete my struggle, I opened the shelf where I thought the vodka was situated, like soldiers in reserve. I called for the mobilization of the army.

Soon sitting back on the wheelchair, with vodka in my hand, an open window in front of me and complete darkness around me. The noises disappeared, right after I allowed them in. The light ceased lighting the room; right as it was switched off.

Now I was occupying Greg's place; physically and mentally. I did not mean to replace Greg. But I did want to know how it felt to sit in his place. Confusing emotions rushed through me. In the first twenty seconds of sitting in Greg's wheelchair, I started to lose sensation in my legs. That scared me a lot. Below the waste, my nerves ceased all sensation, and my fear continued to grow. I had to pinch my legs forcefully, very forcefully. In any other circumstances, this powerful painful stimulator would produce significant pain... but not now.

I heard people talking... all kinds of people: men, women, boys, girls. Then I saw them... all kinds of them: men, women, boys, girls. With people talking and walking, the rainbow of colors ushered itself in the room.

It was then that I knew. While my feelings were lost below the waste, my perception above the waste was increased many-fold... everywhere above the waste: in the skin, eyes, ears, and brain.

In minutes, my transformation from being myself to being Greg was complete. My fear reached its peak. My curiosity was very much satisfied. I had enough. I did not ask for this, me becoming Greg. I tried to get up. I couldn't. Then I tried to summon all my being together. I started to investigate, what faculties remained in my possession. I wanted to make sure; I had my head on my shoulders. Taking my time, I checked my nose, lips, eyes and hair. It comforted me to find out that not everything was lost. Then, I proceeded to touch all my limbs, so I could convince myself, I was not missing any.

I still had to deal with my mind. That's where all these newfound troubles originated. I could not measure the degree of my mind's irritability. I just could not. I had a gross idea of why this was happening. The place in my brain dealing with and governing perception of the outside world was damaged momentarily. This explained my hyper-perception. With no obvious source of heat, it was extremely hot in the room, and even the few drinks in my body already, did not alter my state of sobriety.

I do not remember exactly when the super exaggeration of my senses stopped. But when it did, it left in the same rapid manner, as when it came. I was free. Finding myself without the super-natural spell was as frightening as being ensnared by the spell itself.

As soon as I could look around, I moved my head to every direction within the room. With my eyes wide open now, I wanted to see all the activities in the room. Then I saw something on the floor crawling towards me; something dark and long. First I thought it was a mouse. But it wasn't. It was much bigger than mouse. Then I thought it was a ghost, but it was no ghost. It was much darker than a ghost. It did not look like Greg. It was too long, longer than I imagined Greg would be. But it was him. What else or who else could it be?

Now he was grabbing both my feet.

"Al, this is not your seat." He sounded angry. I never heard him angry before- sarcastic, pompous, confident, depressed, and so on, but never angry. He made it clear he did not appreciate me taking his seat.

"Sorry Greg, I didn't mean to take your place."

"But you did, Al. You did."

I could not see his face. It was too dark. But I imagined tears on his face, streaming from his eyes.

I stood up from the wheelchair and moved away from it and Greg. I let him try to get on the wheelchair. He failed. Then he tried again. He failed again. After a few unsuccessful attempts, he just stopped trying. I did not dare help him. I was afraid to insult him. Then I saw him lying helplessly on the floor and looking in my direction. By that time I realized, he stopped trying to conquer the wheelchair. I realized he did want me to help him. I was no giant, but he was so light, it was very easy for me to pick him up and put him on his wheelchair. He did not resist at all. This surprised me a lot.

"You are so good at putting me in the wheelchair, aren't you?" He asked.

I could not say anything. I probably was. Life proved that I was good at this, just like Greg said. But I was also good at making him comfortable. I did not waste much time. I pushed the wheelchair, with Greg's helpless body on it to the corner of the room, next to the open window. Then I dragged the small table closer to him. To complete the rearrangement of the room as I remembered it, I had to do one more thing. I produced a few bottles of the alcohol from the shelves and put them on the table, at a very reachable distance from Greg. Pretty soon, Greg had his favorite corner in the room, his loyal soldiers of Russian origin in front of him, and was sitting on the saddle of his favorite horse ready to fight.

"So, why are you here?" he asked.

After hearing all my problems, Greg needed a few minutes to say something. During these few minutes, I observed, Greg consumed at least four glasses of vodka.

"Is today your birthday?" He asked finally.

"Al, I want you to do me a favor." Then a pause followed; the extended pause gave me some degree of reassurance, rather it was actually more of a false hope.

"I know today is your birthday. That means you wouldn't have a problem with doing me a favor. Am I right, Al?"

A moment passed... a moment that lasted a lifetime.

"I want you to kill somebody for me."

"Yes, I would," was the answer. The voice of the person who answered, sounded very much like mine. Actually it was mine.

Chapter 29

1

Seven days later, I received an envelope with no name or address of the sender on it. When I opened it one single pill rolled out of it... a small white pill. There was a note, which I knew was from Greg. The note was a plan- the plan. It detailed how Mr. Kelly was going to die. Kelly was currently hospitalized for chest pains, mainly for observation. The plan was a step by step script: how to enter Mr. Kelly's floor unnoticed, how to access the cart with Kelly's medication tray . Then, I was to switch the Capri antibiotic, which Mr. Kelly was taking for his mild bronchitis, with equally innocent penicillin antibiotic pills. The caveat is that these new pills were dangerous to Mr. Kelly, in fact, four years earlier- the man had nearly died from a severe allergic reaction to penicillin. Greg planned for penicillin to finish the job.

Greg had chosen both the murderer and the murder weapon. But, this murder was not to be bloody, and it did not require eye contact or even any contact between the victim and the perpetrator. All I had to do was to play with some little round pills. Those pills would cure my problem. Or, as Greg understood it, those pills would cure our problem.

2

My REM sleep, or my deepest sleep, was rudely interrupted by an alarm clock. It took a while for me before I regained all my functioning senses. Pretty soon, I was back in the real world, where real problems had to be solved by real people.

THE BALANCING GAME

It was only six a.m. when, dressed in my finest clothes, I was ready to leave for the most significant assignment of my life. I paused by the mirror and my mirror image stopped me.

"Looking good. Dressed to kill?"

"Does it show?"

"Yes, it does," answered my reflection. The man in the mirror looked important. Then he asked me a very weird question.

"Al, would you say today is the most important day of your life?"

"How so?" I asked with great curiosity.

"Okay. Why don't you give me the list of the most important days of your life?"

I knew I had to answer. And that answer had to be curt, yet frank, if I wanted to leave the place in a timely fashion.

I closed my eyes. The question was simple. The answer had to be even simpler... or at least that is what I thought. But the answer turned out to be extremely complicated. In actuality, the answer required the complete mobilization of my thought power and utter focus. I had never given this question a single serious thought before.

"How about the day I was born, or the day I got married, or maybe having a baby?"

"You never had a baby," the image shot back. "But, how about today?" He continued, "Do you think today is an ordinary day?" My mirror image felt like a distinctly separate individual as it asked the question.

His curiosity was not out of line. My state of mind was. I was standing in front of the mirror, looking cool and dressed to kill. And I had just that intention, to kill. There was nothing in my behavior to give even a hint of my internal struggle with my conscience; at least not this early morning.

The night was not sleepless. This surprised me. I did not have any dreams either. This amused me. The actual hours of sleep I collected, was approximately average. In fact, it was one hour above my average. This disturbed me.

I could easily recall in my selective memory, how my sleep pattern would deviate from my normal sleeping curve when seemingly insignificant events were anticipated the next day. I would suffer bouts of insomnia whenever I was pestered by the increase of dread on the eve of some historic moment.

I remember a sleepless night, clearly associated with an anticipation of a coming Super Bowl. My favorite football team with a fairly good chance to win it all, kept me up all night. My body, exhausted from shifting positions all night, would be a burden on my preoccupied mind.

There was another night when my body and mind rebelliously refused to resign and retire for the night. I spent that night anticipating a meeting with a hot girl and a loose reputation. The thought of her alone, kept me from my slumber... for the whole night. How many times in my life I had awoken prepared to kill another human being? My whole life, I was trained to be the utmost professional, to be the most human, to be a healer. Years of training, to acquire medical education to save lives, prepared me not to be a violent life taker, but to be a life giver and preserver. But, despite all my training, I remained human, which meant I had not only compassion, but also distinctly sinister intentions.

And suddenly, after conversing with my own image, I felt different, very different, and very powerful. I could sense the power rush through me. It was the power of a god with both the ability to give lives and take life away.

A strange feeling was trying to possess me. Although the sensation was intriguing, it felt like an empty temptation. While a woman was capable of being the main character throughout a person's life, I could become hateful, but still the most influential character in that same person's death. Whether or not the afterlife exists, I could be a person's death parent.

Chapter 30

1

I had no problem getting past hospital security. After all, security had seen me many times before and my presence even at this early morning hour was not suspicious at all. Their training did not equip them to recognize a killer in a healer's body. One of them even made an extra effort, to hold an elevator for me. By doing so, he unwittingly became an accomplice in my sordid task.

The thirteenth floor of St. Judah's Hospital appeared peaceful and quiet... and even noticeably clean, perhaps because of the time of the day. It was before seven o'clock a.m., and whoever had to die, had already departed from this hospital's departure floor. Most of the hospital deaths occur peacefully during the night. The survivor standby-ticket-holders for the flight to the other life, continued to enjoy the remaining moments of their lives.

I always thought of the hospital as an airport, with departure and arrival areas. I called the thirteenth floor the departure floor.

The arrival floor was situated lower, one flight lower to be exact. Flights from unknown locations systematically brought arriving passengers to this floor. This was an obstetrics department and lives were literally arriving at a remarkable rate.

The ominous silence of the departure floor reminded me of my years of residency in medicine. It was exactly this kind of silence, which would scare us of the most. It was this kind of silence that would invariably usher in some kind of storm. Such a lethal storm in the hospital would inevitably mean somebody's death. This morning's silence was no exception. Yet, there I was, acting according to the plan, and if I continued as planned, the storm was about to arrive.

I passed the nursing station, without any of the ten nurses even looking in my direction. The night shift nursing team was endorsing sick patients to the a.m. nursing team. Patients' security was not included in their endorsements. Mr. Kelly's security was already arranged and I could see a big man, with a familiar bald head, standing by the door of his ward, located at the far end of the corridor.

It is so easy to plan to kill a person. All you need is a few ideas and a spattering of details. As I ogled Mr. Kelly's security, I considered the different types of murder: shooting, stabbing, throwing someone off of a building. It all seemed so personal. Even bombing a person from afar seemed personal. But not this. This seemed professional. This was clinical.

Just as the plan indicated, the cart was situated behind the open door of the medication storage room. This location made it easy for me, to remain unnoticed as I approached the cart. Momentarily, I was standing by the cart and staring blankly at the small medication cup, with Peter Kelly's name on it and Capri tablet in it. Changing tablets did not necessarily bring death… not any tablet would do. But the tablet I had in mind, would send Mr. Kelly to his final destination.

Somebody with a brilliant and vicious mind committed himself to eliminate Mr. Kelly.

The Homework (H) was done and the necessary information was obtained. All the goals and information were Organized (O). It was determined that Mr. Kelly had a history of having anaphylactic shock in the past from penicillin substance antibiotics. And he was warned by doctors that his body would not be able to handle another such shock in the future. Now, the (P) performing part was arriving. It was my job to perform.

The (P) performance had to be very (E) efficient; without wasting any extra time, without being noticed.

THE BALANCING GAME

The plan if carried out precisely, had a great chance to succeed. Just like Greg's balancing formula promised;

$$H+O+P+E=S$$

The above formula was only good, if every part of it was properly followed. If there was any deviation at any level, the final result would not be achieved. In that sense, this formula was just like any other chemical formula. Any break in the chain of chemical reactions at any level would prevent the anticipated result.

So there I stood, by the cart with a medication tray on it. Mr. Kelly's tablet was very much within reachable distance. The time and plan called for the (P) performance part of the plan. The Pen. tablet had to come out from my inside pocket and replace the Capri one. And then I could just walk away. Just like that. And the man I so detested so much would never bother me again. And best of all, I did not have to even look in his face as he died.

I was so close to success.

But the (S) success never came, because the formula was not completed as designed. The (P) part did not take place, that made the (E) part inapplicable.

Something hit me, while I was standing there, so close to successfully carrying out the plan. While that something had no shape, no color, and no smell, it was heavy and it shook me to my core. It was not fear, love, or hate. It was something different... something to do with fairness. "Is this fair, to take Peter Kelly's life?"

He never even threatened to physically hurt me. The only thing he did was play dirty in this real-life poker game. You don't kill a card player for playing dirty. That is not fair. The dirty players don't deserve the death penalty.

The dirty play and death penalty do not balance each other. "Measure for Measure", as Shakespeare said.

Then, a big smile came across my face. It was a smile of relief and satisfaction.

On the way back to the elevator, one of the nurses found time to look at me and ask;

"Are you looking for somebody, Doctor?"

"No, I'm not," was my answer.

Chapter 31

I wonder if anybody ever faced guilt in person and described how it looks. What color hair does it have? How many eyes does it possess? Does it look like a man or woman? What is it about guilt, that being so potentially powerful, it barely draws respect from its surroundings? Maybe because guilt is always associated with the conscience, something that many people wield maybe in short supply, but still in significant quantity.

So, can we safely assume that in order to feel guilty in your mind, you should carry a conscience in your head? Perhaps we do not see guilt because it is faceless and bodiless. It has no heart and no legs, no eyes and no arms; just like love and hate. No wonder you cannot see it. Just like love and hate, guilt is a feeling. You feel it, only if you are able to feel. They say, love is a sickness. Being in love, however beautiful, could still feel like losing your mind. A person without a functional brain is not a healthy person at all. He or she loses the ability to reason. The same happens with hate. People who hate usually are blinded by the power of rage. Again blind people cannot see things as they truly are. So, are love, hate, and guilt sicknesses? And if they are, where do their similarities end and differences begin? Who would have a problem recalling the numerous occasions crimes committed- all kinds of them- in the name of these sicknesses? Who can deny, that hate is a powerful vehicle capable of destroying human life?

Is guilt capable of killing? Is it like love and hate equipped with lethal energy eager to demolish anything and anybody that peaks its interest. Would you comfortably put guilt in this regard next to love and hate?

What is it that makes love, hate, and guilt different, to kill or not to kill?

May I suggest one word that makes a world of difference?

The conscience is the difference between killing and not killing. People in love do not summon it when acting without heads. People who hate do not see it when acting blindly.

People with guilt think, take time and talk to themselves, but while talking they listen too. Too much thinking, too much talking and too much listening lead to the harshest bouts of guilt. Too much of everything makes you hear what your conscience has to say. Can you kill while you are talking to your conscience?

Chapter 32

1

I drove aimlessly for hours. I never felt so light in my life. Today I saved somebody's life- a bad man's life, a very bad man's life. But because this man was so bad, saving his life brought me even more pride. It's easy to reach out and help a good man. It is much harder to help a rotten man.

Being a doctor, I have saved many people, but this memory of saving Peter Kelly from me would last my lifetime. Today, by the power vested in me, by some greater authority, I chose not to kill, but instead to pardon somebody's life.

The suburbs were quiet. They did not interfere with either my driving, or my thinking. There were no disrupting noises; there were not many people on the crossroads; there were few cars on the roads. Silence and the beauty of nature soothed me. And I genuinely relished this relaxation. There was a report to be made to Greg. This report was not pleasant. I had to report to him, for the first time about how I had unsuccessfully carried out his plan and how I failed to do him his favor.

2

After spending the whole day driving, at about six o' clock p.m., I was ready for the troublesome report. I decided to make my report on the phone.

"Yes Al," Greg answered the phone.

"Greg, it was a great plan."

"I know," Greg said.

"It was so easy to do."

"I know."

"All I had to do was to switch the tablets."

"I know."

Then I paused a moment before I made my next statement.

"I didn't do it Greg."

"I know." There was no pause from Greg's end.

I needed another long pause to collect myself, after being shattered by Greg's understanding.

"Do you mean, you asked me for a favor and you knew I wouldn't go through it?" I managed to ask.

"Of course I knew. What do you think? I expected you to kill somebody, because of some petty blackmail?"

"But, what about the power of guilt?" I asked. "It's been driving me for years."

"The degree of guilt didn't warrant the degree of the punishment. "Measure for Measure" like Shakespeare said."

"Greg did you say Measure for Measure?"

"Yes I did, why?"

"That's funny. I thought exactly that, before I decided to pardon Mr. Kelly."

"I see nothing funny about it Al. By now, I thought you should understand our... unique connection."

Another great pause seized the moment. The pause exuded a thoughtless, relaxed absentia, rather than a complicated chain of overwhelming thoughts. There was not an ounce of surprise in me. I was so desensitized by now, with so many surprises, statements, favors, and theories.

"One more thing Al," Greg said after I wished him a good night and was about to depart.

"What is it?"

"If you didn't do it, who the hell did?"

"What do you mean?"

"The news reported it a few hours ago. Right after having his breakfast and his antibiotic medication, his face suddenly became swollen, hives appeared over his entire body, he started to wheeze and whistle, his respiration became rapid, his blood pressure went down, and he became unconscious."

Again, there was no element of surprise in me, even after hearing news of this magnitude. Only, my curiosity insisted on knowing exactly what happened.

"What are you are telling me Greg?"

"Mr. Kelly is dead Al, dead. He is gone. From the description that was given, it seems highly likely that he died of anaphylactic shock."

"Greg, I didn't do it. I swear I didn't do it."

"You don't have to swear. I know you didn't do it."

"Then, who you think did it?"

"Mr. Kelly was a very powerful and rich man. Power and money bring a lot of enemies. But frankly if I were the police, I would start to look for somebody, with the most to gain by his death."

"And that would be?" I asked

"You know these people better than I do, how do you not know the answer already?

Look for the other woman."

He hung up the phone. He was tired. So was I.

Chapter 33

Greg had evidently figured out who the killer was, but that was because of his laser focus. As I sat down in my bar stool to organize my own mental homicide investigation, my mind wandered. I started to think about Greg and his role in my life.

In each of us, there is a Greg sitting in a small corner of our minds. You can see his meek shadow on a wheelchair. His right hand may be holding a glass of vodka. He may appear constantly dazed from too much ignorance, hurt and pain. An open window may be his only source of outside contact. But that outside world may be the source of his ice cold demeanor. Each of us has Greg born within us. He stays with us as we grow up. We get along fine at first. Then something goes wrong. We start to ignore him. We hide from him, so we cannot hear or see him. Then, we get fed up with having him around; watching us constantly, correcting us, teaching us, shaming us. So we decide to get rid of him and one dark, cold, chilly night, we trick him, make him lose his senses, sit him in a car in a subconscious attempt to hurt him.

The car goes fast, hits the biggest tree in the neighborhood, crashes and smashes into pieces. Greg is disfigured and his back is broken. The disfigurement leaves him unpresentable and wheelchair laden.

Then, once again, we take him back and grant him rent free space because of our pity and guilt. He continues to occupy the small dark corner of our minds. To decrease his ability to watch us, we anaesthetize him with alcohol, medication or some other numbing device. This way, we assure ourselves, he will constantly be drunk and drowsy. Then we continue to forget and ignore him.

THE BALANCING GAME

From time to time, especially on our birthdays or on New Year's, we visit him and talk to him. He appeals to our guilt and asks us to do him favors. We reluctantly do him these favors. With great amusement to ourselves, we'll realize later, that by doing these favors for him, we are actually doing favors for ourselves; getting good jobs, establishing stable relationships, achieving acclaim and so on and so forth…

He is like a balancing man, who balances our lives. The chaos and anarchy his presence creates within us, turns out to be positively neutralized with the favors we do for him.

At times, when he snaps out of his drunken stupor, hurt and ignorant, he falls out of his wheelchair. That's when we snap too. Left without Greg's supervision, we get lost; we cheat, betray, and do whatever suits our interest, even contemplate the most horrid acts.

But when in trouble, we ask Greg for forgiveness and a second chance, realizing his importance in our lives. We gently pick him up and put him back on the wheelchair. Then he becomes stronger. He resumes watching, advising, and criticizing. We immediately turn the light off, crack the window and resupply him with vodka. Then we leave him again.

Only in times of great need do we go back to him, acknowledging his importance in our lives. We pick up glass our shot, and we salute him.

"It's nice to have you around. Here's to Greg."

As I drank the shot, I wondered whether Greg had become a figment of my own imagination.

Chapter 34

1

About one month after Mr. Kelly's death, I received a call from Mrs. Kelly. She wanted to see me immediately. Mrs. Kelly's tone sounded authoritative.

"Doctor, would you kindly oblige me and meet me in Cafe Morris in forty minutes?"

It was Sunday morning- one of those lazy Sunday mornings. I was still in bed and was not in a hurry to get up any time soon. But, Mrs. Kelly could not have known I was available. I might have had important things to do. It seems that my plans did not matter at all to her.

I felt I had to avoid this meeting, considering what took place only a few weeks ago. It did not sound like a good idea to hang around a woman even remotely related, or connected to Mr. Kelly. She also was the woman with whom I was so disgracefully caught having sex on tape.

"Mrs. Kelly, I would rather not," but I was interrupted before I could explain how I never wanted to see her again. "Doctor, you should do what you're told. I'm not talking to you as your patient now. I want to discuss the fate of the recordings, with the two of us as the main characters. I expect you to be there on time. I have a plane to catch this afternoon for Europe."

"I'll be there," I said. But she could not hear my response. She hung up the phone before I answered affirmatively.

A twenty-minute walk got me to the Morris Cafe. Usually crowded, the coffee shop was sparsely attended on this early Sunday morning. An elderly man with an unshaven face and shaky hands was slowly sipping coffee and at the same time he was trying to peruse the newspaper. His tremors were definitely interfering with both tasks. Coffee spilled on the newspaper. And the elderly man had no intention to do anything about it, nor did he have the wherewithal to do anything about it.

I was amused by his antics and his persistence. Surprisingly this insignificant scene kept me from thinking about the important and potentially disastrous event, which would take place in minutes, with the arrival of Mrs. Kelly.

The old man now looked in my direction. He realized he had been watched. He did not look like he minded. At his age, any attention may make not only his day, but even his week. With my attention, he was motivated. He wanted to prove primarily to himself, and in some degree to me too, that he could still do it; read the paper and drink coffee at the same time.

After a few more failed attempts, he was ready to quit. With a quitter's look in his eyes, he looked at me and shrugged his shoulders. The old man, coffee and newspaper, all of them continued to entertain me. The old age, heart rate increase, stimulating dark coffee, and the news continued to provide him with obstacles. But, he knew he would somehow manage as he had done countless times before. With old age comes time. He understood that in a minute he would try again and again, repeatedly until he would succeed.

I never did get to see him succeed, but I did become confident that he would. After observing the old man's struggle to dominate the newspaper problem, I realized this man had something, I envied. He had a very minor problem and was able to focus all of his energy on this one problem with no pressure on him.

As soon I thought about pressure, Mrs. Kelly showed up. She looked different, very different. She made a splash with her grand entrance. The impact of the splash blinded me for seconds. Once I regained my composure, I recognized Mrs. Kelly looked almost nothing like the woman I remembered.

Two months made a big difference. Two months and her husband's death to be exact. It was not just her new strikingly attractive appearance, or the wealthy manner in which she was dressed. There was something else, which represented Mrs. Kelly. The confidence itself walked with her into this coffee shop.

"Hello Doctor," she was standing next to me now. Somehow I interpreted her distance into determining the appropriate greeting was a handshake. When I stood up and reached out to do just that, I found out, I was wrong. She ignored my handshaking initiative, turned around, sat across the small table and started to stare at me.

"Hello Mrs. Kelly. You look different," I could not help, but commenting.

"I know. Thanks to you, Doctor. But that's not why I'm here. I'm kind of in a hurry. I have an afternoon plane to catch. So let's not waste time."

I moved forward, put my hands on the table and prepared to listen.

"You should know that Mr. Kelly left everything to me. He didn't have any kids after his daughter died, or any other close relatives. What that means is, whatever he owned, I now own." She stopped talking. She expected me to say something.

"I'm listening," I said something.

"Those recordings no longer exist," she said.

"What videos? I know nothing about recordings." I said.

"That's right. There were never any videos." She looked solemn as she stated this matter-of-factly, but she continued.

"One more thing. Here is something that belongs to you." With these words, she took an envelope out of her purse and put it on the table in front of me. My curiosity was easily satisfied with a little effort. I opened the envelope and pulled out a check for five hundred thousand dollars.

"My husband was a businessman. I know a deal was a deal for him.

This is the other half of the money that was promised to you, in case I would... improve. Do I look better to you, Doctor?"

"Yes, you do."

"You have to know how much I appreciate your book, Dr. Al. I do feel much better. I owe it to your book and that crazy balancing formula. And I believe there is more to come. According to the balancing theory, my best days are still to come. A woman like me, going through all the bad experiences that I went through, I should have a lot of big good things coming."

I looked at her very carefully now. The change was not just obvious. It was shocking. This lady knew exactly where she was going. She looked like she was choosing her own destiny. Then, I looked in her eyes. The contrast between her eyes now and when she first showed up in my office was unbelievable. Those deep and mournful eyes, that needed rescuing, were replaced with protruding determined eyes. The owner of these new eyes needed nobody's help. This person looked like she knew her direction and was ready to do anything to arrive at her destination.

Then a thought occurred to me. The thought that came to me after I remembered Greg's statement, which followed my question to him, about who killed Mr. Kelly.

"Look for the other woman," Greg told me then. I didn't pay much attention to what he said then. But, after looking in Mrs. Kelly's eyes, I could not help but invite that strange thought in. The thought was knocking on my mind's door and was asking to be let in.

"Mrs. Kelly," I asked, "did you know, Mr. Kelly had a constant female companion, who literally lived with him. Actually, for the last few years, she spent more time with him as a wife than you did. Is that right?"

"Why do you ask?" Mrs. Kelly looked surprised.

"I'm just wondering. In this relationship, you were "the other woman"?"

She thought for a few seconds, before she answered.

"You can say that, I guess."

"I have another question to you. Mrs. Kelly, did you know Mr. Kelly was allergic to penicillin?"

A smile appeared on Mrs. Kelly's face, a nervous smile.

"What exactly you are trying to ask me, Doctor?"

"You don't have to answer, if you don't want to."

"I know I don't have to, but I will. I am so grateful for your book, there is no way, that I won't satisfy the author's curiosity. No, I didn't know he was allergic to penicillin."

She made a mistake. She had the choice not to answer. She did when she didn't have to. She probably never dealt with lawyers. If she did, she would just not recall their strong advice. 'Do not volunteer information,' was the golden rule that was so often grossly overlooked. In this case, the information was provided to a highly trained psychiatrist, and this psychiatrist knew she lied. He knew her well, really well. Too well not to notice her enormous bluff. Besides, she was with him the last time he had was accidentally dosed with penicillin.

My God, I did commit a crime after all. I transformed a helpless, depressed, inert woman to an independent, energetic, vicious killer. I created a monster.

Mrs. Kelly was on her feet now. She did not know the thoughts running through my mind; I did not want her to know.

"Doctor, Mr. Kelly trusted me a lot. He was smart fellow; he knew what he was doing. No wonder he left everything to me, and I mean everything."

"I know he trusted you Mrs. Kelly."

Then she disappeared. For now, she was on top of world. But only for now. As I know, the earth is round and it spins in circles as it moves- she would return, right where she started. We all live in cycles. And she was no exception.

THE BALANCING GAME

"Yeah," I said to the now absent Mrs. Kelly, who was on her way to her plane, that would take her to her European escapade; "of course he trusted you too much." Maybe in his grave, Mr. Kelly was realizing that although he rarely trusted anyone, when he finally picked one person to entrust completely, he trusted unwisely. He trusted her to death.

As for me, I liked what took place in this Cafe. There were no more compromising videos. I became richer; and not only by the experiences that I acquired. There was a check for half a million dollars in my left jacket pocket. It was situated very close to my heart and touching my heart area while emanating very pleasant warmth through my whole body, from the top of my head to the bottom of my feet.

2

With my newfound understanding and joy, I quickly paid the bill and rushed over to Greg's place. As I opened the door with the key I had been given long ago, I discovered that the apartment was empty. It was not just bereft of a human touch, but was entirely vacant.

Thoughts and fears rushed to my mind. First, I thought something happened to Greg... perhaps even something bad. I ruled that out quickly because I was pretty sure I would have received a call before the whole place was emptied.

Then, I wondered about whether my drunken musings about Greg were right. Perhaps, he was just a hallucinatory manifestation of my conscience. Could that be? It made sense and considering that I did not need my conscience at this particular moment. But, as I walked around the empty apartment searching for traces of my former enemy turned closest confidante, I could not believe it. I refused to believe it.

I entered the bathroom and I found my proof of his existence. There sat Greg's wheelchair. Beside his chair were two sticks that I had vaguely noticed during my last few visits, but had not paid much attention to. It was always so dark in his apartment that I could barely see what I was looking at. As I approached the sticks, I saw that they were crutches.

Greg had apparently been rehabilitating. I thought back on his physical condition over the course of his disability. Initially, Mary had told me that his recovery was hopeless. For that reason, I was reluctant to touch the topic of whether he would walk again. But, maybe that's what he wanted her to think. Or more likely, that is how his situation appeared at the time. Hopeless.

Few years had passed and I had not asked about a potential rehabilitation. In those years, I did not even ask him about whether he was getting back into psychiatry. I never even encouraged him to stop drinking. I just assumed he had accepted his fate as a disabled recluse who would live his life vicariously through me.

I gathered my thoughts, after remembering Greg did not have a cell phone. I called the one other person I knew he was connected to… my ex.

"Hi Mary," I greeted her cheerily to try to avoid the awkwardness of our relationship's slow demise.,"

"Al," she responded cautiously.

"How are you doing?"

"Really well Al. Really well."

There was a long pause as she waited for me to continue and I mapped out the rest of the conversation in my head. But, she was less patient than I was, so she broke the silence.

"I'm not going to ask how you're doing because I already know."

"Really?"

"Greg told me. He also told me to expect your call sometime soon. So, I guess he was right again."

"Why didn't he just tell-" but before I could finish, she interrupted me.

THE BALANCING GAME

"It's Greg. He does everything the way he wants it done. He's always got some reason, but he rarely shares it with me."

Again, I was dumbfounded.

"Do you want to speak to him?" But again, before I can answer, I could hear her yell out Greg's name.

"So, are you two back together?"

"It's really none of your business Al. You and I had a clean break, but yes. We're back together."

"Good. I'm happy for you two," I said sincerely.

"He's walking over here now. Take care of yourself Dr. Al Letne." And with that, she was gone. Moments later, another familiar voice emerged.

"Al."

"Greg. Where are you?"

"You miss me already? We're in the Caribbean."

"What are you-" but before I could finish the sentence, he cut me off, just like his old-new girlfriend.

"I know you have a lot of questions, so organize your thoughts."

I obeyed him and put my thoughts together, but with so many different things going through my head, it was proving difficult.

"Why didn't you tell me you were rehabbing?"

"I couldn't. If I did, it would interfere with my experiments."

"What experiments?"

"Well, the book was one experiment and you were another one."

"Wait. What?"

"Well… technically, our friendship was the larger experiment. I wanted to test my hypotheses on you."

Silent, I waited for him to continue.

"I wanted to know exactly how far I could push you, precisely how much I could control you with guilt."

I was horrified.

"That's so manipulative."

"Well, yes. That's what we do. We play with people's minds to make them better. That's what I did with you too. I medicated you with alcohol and made you susceptible to my own machinations."

"But..." I was frustrated and wanted to protest.

"I know. You wanted to help me. You did. You helped support my theories about manipulating an individual and even started on my way towards proving my theories about mass manipulation."

"You mean the Balancing Game?"

"Exactly."

"You don't even believe in it?"

"It's immaterial whether I believe in it. It's helping people, isn't it? It's helping millions of people around the world who believe in it."

"But, it led Mrs. Kelly to kill her husband. Murder."

"I did tell you to stay away from them. I met them both once before, about four years ago when Peter Kelly came into the hospital and diagnosed both of them as serious dangers. But, as to The Balancing Game, I did anticipate some death. That happens with all religions. People interpret them and misinterpret them. People use them as excuses to do whatever they want to do. But, you can't deny how many people religion helps through charity and through some grander power, whether you call it God or placebo. Religion actually works magic. The Balancing Game has that kind of power."

"Religion? That sounds like delusions of grandeur."

"Look around, Al. It's already started. Even you believe in it now."

"Come on." But, I refocused my thoughts.

"How could you do this to me? I thought we were friends and you were just messing with me the whole time."

"Since our accident, everything I suggested was designed to help you. Can you ask for a better friend than that? I helped you get your dream job, realize that your dream girl was not exactly what you wanted which led you closer towards healthy relationships with women, practically handed you unimaginable wealth and respect and most importantly, I helped you deal with your issues with your father. The only time your progress faltered is the time you did not take my advice when I fully expected you to back off the Caribbean. I helped you Al."

"But it all seems so fake... especially now that I know you were just manipulating me this whole time."

"Al, if you don't accept what you have, it will always seem fake."

I let Greg's final piece of advice sink in. He remained silent to let his words resonate. But, now, I could tell he was doing it for affect, rather than a dearth of other advice. I had enough for one day.

"So," I moved to shift topics, "what's next for the great Greg Entel? What could possibly follow starting a religion anonymously?"

"Well, first I'm going to publish on the efficacies of the various methods of control, I employed on you and the followers of The Balancing Game. But..."

As he paused, I could tell he was actually trying to compose himself to prevent himself from getting too giddy.

"I'm working on something else. You'd like it. It's something good- something decent."

"Well, I'm not a part of it, am I?"

"No, Al. We're just friends now."

"Good to know. So, I'm intrigued. Tell me about this project."

"I will, but not yet. First, I need to find a new subject."

"A new patsy?"

"A new subject. But, this project..."

"Get off the phone!" I heard Mary yell from a distance. "Stop working Greg! Just tell him you're on vacation."

Greg momentarily ignored her pleas and continued.

"It's going to be... bigger. Revolutionary."

"I don't understand."

"You will. But for now, I have to go. I'll talk to you soon... and we will always have an appointment on your birthday, right?"

"Always," I said somberly.

"Goodbye Al."

"Bye Greg."

Greg was gone. I was left in Greg's apartment, thinking about all the things I had just learned- that the last few years of my life had just been part of some grand experiment.

As I walked out of the apartment, the greatest sense of relief I had ever felt washed over me. And it was good.

On my way to future, I noticed, quite a few people were wearing dark balance bracelets. And I knew, soon I would join them. I would wear one on my left wrist. It would replace my watch. Knowing time didn't appear important to me anymore; the balance did.

Long life to BALANCE!

The balancing game was officially over.

Greg won; geniuses always do.

Epilogue

A man dressed like a judge, walked down the corridor to see a strange looking young character with long hair and a heavy beard standing against the wall. The strange person was holding a ruler in his hands, trying to measure something in the air. His "Honor" approached the man and asked:

"Sir, would you mind telling me exactly what you are doing?"

"Watch me," the weirdo commands without interrupting his activities. "I am in the process of measuring the height of my future unhappiness. You see, today I am thirty-three years old, a problem free happy man. I figured, if I manage to measure the height of my happiness today, then I automatically will know the height of my unhappiness tomorrow."

After finishing his statement explaining his strange behavior; the odd fellow straightened his posture, lifted his head, spread his arms towards the ceiling, and screamed shamelessly:

"Everything in life is balanced! Happiness and unhappiness! This is terrifying! Today I am an extremely happy man and I am scared. For I know the amount of sadness that awaits me tomorrow."

The screaming slightly calmed the strange man. In a moment, he sat comfortably on the clean hospital floor and is slowly whispering loudly, "I wish, I wasn't so damned happy today."

The man in a judge's robe had no problem realizing with whom he is dealing.

"Are you really crazy?" He asked the strange person.

"Yes, I am," he replied obediently.

"Are you stupid too?" The judge continued to inquire.

The weirdo's face now appeared insulted, his eyes appeared angry and he raised his voice "Am I? Answer me! Am I stupid?!? Answer me! You are the judge. Am I?"

This time, the judge was ready to answer.

"Stand up and listen to what I'm going to say."

The crazy man got to his feet, straightened his posture, and with a look of impatience, looked at the judge as if his life depended on verdict.

His "Honor" was not in a hurry to deliver his judgment. While his mind was made up whether the crazy man was stupid, he still had some doubts. The judge was notoriously feared for his toughness and with reason. He had a long-standing reputation for hating stupidity. But he was a lawman. And the law demanded justice for this troubled man.

The judge's speech was short. But, however short it was, it liberated the crazy man for his remaining years.

"No, you are not stupid, not at all."

When the crazy man heard this, he let himself go. The movements of his body, landed him on the ground, kneeling down, with his arms raised and spread, looking at the ceiling above.

"Thank you, Father for you didn't punish me for the stupidity, I didn't commit."

Then, came something unexplainable. The judge, known for his reserved and stiff mannerisms, became very human. He bent to reach something on the floor and picked it up. He stood in the middle of the corridor.

At this time, the door at the end of corridor opened and an elderly lady with a trustworthy face in a nurse's uniform showed up. "Medication time," she announced with authority.

The aged psychiatric nurse had seen all kinds of odd things in her many years of working in psychiatric wards. But even she was stunned by what she was witnessing.

The crazy man remained kneeling to thank God with his arms

raised. The judge, holding a ruler in his hands, measured the nothingness in the air.

But what is perceived as nothingness by this elderly nurse was quite something for the judge.

He had a few easily forgettable bad breaks in his life, but he did not want to forget them now. In fact he tried hard, very hard to remember every mischief, however big or little that life so abundantly gave him. He was afraid to forget even a tiny unpleasant event that brought him sadness and sorrow. He was hoping he could measure them with great accuracy.

And when the measurement process concluded, he sat and waited for everything good that life owed him. He did not expect any interest for his pain. But he did expect good things to come in the future in the same degree, intensity, and quantity, as the bad things that came in his past.

Heavily preoccupied with their thoughts, the two men did not notice the elderly nurse approaching them. Being around psychiatric patients for over forty years now, her face should not have expressed signs of surprise.

But this was a unique day. Seeing the judge shocked her. Her face paled and her eyes widened, and her jaw dropped. All the signs of shock were present on the face of this elderly psychiatric nurse.

"Dr. Letne, are you all right?"

My patient had been promised a verdict by a former patient on the level of his intellect. He had not eaten anything in days and demanded his right to a speedy trial. The problem was that the former patient, the "judge" had already been discharged.

So, in the interim, the defendant was slowly melting away. His body weight was steadily decreasing and the degree of his anger was on the rise. Something had to be done. When I learned that the orderlies were about to restrain my patient, I decided to interfere. I put on a judge's uniform that was left behind by the patient who wore it before. I was able to recount the crazy man's conversation from our sessions and repeated it to the best of my ability to give him some closure.

"Dr. Letne, are you sure you're going to be all right?" The nurse asked.

By now, I had things pretty much measured. The six feet of life's insults were accurately accounted. The joy in my life barely reached my ankles.

That could only mean that at least six feet of positive events awaited me in the future.

I took out a candy bar from my pocket and handed it to the haggard looking patient, who grabbed it eagerly. He nodded at me with gratitude as he tore off the wrapper and took his first bite in days with enormous pleasure.

Finally, I looked at the nurse and answered earnestly, "I'm going be just fine."